David R. Bird was born in London during the Second World War. At the age of 18, having completed one year of art studies, he became tired of Britain's climate and impulsively emigrated to the British colony of Southern Rhodesia where he joined the British South Africa Police. This was the beginning of a life of travel which resulted in his living on three continents, in five different countries and visiting well over forty. He has been both a civil servant and an entrepreneur, and his pastimes include art, and a number of sporting activities including rowing, running, cycling and tennis. Now retired, he lives with his wife Bonnie in New Smyrna Beach, Florida.

To my wife, Bonnie, in gratitude for her undying support.

David R. Bird

An Extraordinary Man

A Dick Starling Novel

Austin Macauley Publishers

LONDON * CAMBRIDGE * NEW YORK * SHARJAH

Copyright © David R. Bird 2024

All rights reserved. No part of this publication may be reproduced, distributed, or transmitted in any form or by any means, including photocopying, recording, or other electronic or mechanical methods, without the prior written permission of the publisher, except in the case of brief quotations embodied in critical reviews and certain other non-commercial uses permitted by copyright law. For permission requests, write to the publisher.

Any person who commits any unauthorized act in relation to this publication may be liable to criminal prosecution and civil claims for damages.

This is a work of fiction. Names, characters, businesses, places, events, locales, and incidents are either the products of the author's imagination or used in a fictitious manner. Any resemblance to actual persons, living or dead, or actual events is purely coincidental.

Ordering Information
Quantity sales: Special discounts are available on quantity purchases by corporations, associations, and others. For details, contact the publisher at the address below.

Publisher's Cataloging-in-Publication data
Bird, David R.
An Extraordinary Man

ISBN 9798891557208 (Paperback)
ISBN 9798891557215 (Hardback)
ISBN 9798891557222 (ePub e-book)

Library of Congress Control Number: 2024914111

www.austinmacauley.com/us

First Published 2024
Austin Macauley Publishers LLC
40 Wall Street, 33rd Floor, Suite 3302
New York, NY 10005
USA

mail-usa@austinmacauley.com
+1 (646) 5125767

Once again, I have to thank my editor, Carol Anderson-McLean, for all her help, advice and guidance in helping this book to reach publication.

Foreword

The elderly man sat stroking his chin as he contemplated how to start writing his first novel. His ancient royal 'sit-up-and-beg' typewriter sat on the desk before him, with a new batch of paper beside it. He was ready to start, but how would he begin? What sentence would catch the reader's imagination from the word go?

Sitting back in his comfortable chair, he packed his pipe with Borkum Riff, his favorite tobacco, and sat deep in thought as a number of ideas flashed through his mind.

He had already succeeded in writing his autobiography, which he considered to be a fair and accurate account of his first seventy-five years on earth. It summarized his journey through life and many countries and included several humorous interludes and a host of experiences but left no room for exaggeration, theater, or adventure.

His novel, in contrast, using no real names and no existing country, could explore the activities of a youth, similar to himself, but in the form of a make-believe character—a somewhat callow fellow who, through a series of misadventures, excelled at times and failed miserably at others.

Richard 'Dick' Starling exists only in the writer's imagination. His series of adventures will invariably take several turns for the worse as he blunders through some narrow escapes but often seems to come up smelling of roses. The author pictured in his mind's eye how, if he had taken the left fork in the road rather than the right, this could have been his story to tell.

Rolling his first sheet of paper into the typewriter, he began to type laboriously but with a great enthusiasm with two fingers as he cataloged Dick's first three years as a colonial police officer in the fictitious Central African British colony of Warania. He asks to be excused for utilizing the southern portion of the Democratic Republic of the Congo or Congo-Kinshasa for this liberty.

Chapter One

The eighteen-year-old Londoner was not long out of school and not sure what he wanted to do with the rest of his life. With a mop of unruly black hair, a shade under six feet tall, a slim build, dark brown eyes, and an appealing olive-skinned complexion, especially for a Brit whose English heritage went back many generations, he could easily have been mistaken for an Italian. He looked considerably older than his eighteen years and was often mistaken for a mature twenty- or twenty-one-year-old. His name was Richard Starling.

Richard was working as a salesman in a West London department store. The year was 1962, and standing behind his small counter in the TV and radio section of one of London's many department stores, he was gazing at a very attractive redhead who was supervising the construction of a temporary booth where she would be promoting some type of new household gadget that he was unfamiliar with.

Compared with the staff employed elsewhere on his floor, she was quite an eyeful. She wore a pale green flared skirt with a wide red belt, a white sleeveless blouse, and red high-heeled shoes that matched her belt. Dick couldn't take his eyes off her. Her pear-drop-shaped eyeglasses with scarlet frames matched her lipstick, shoes, and belt but in no way detracted from her beauty. Wherever the Greek singer Nana Mouskouri got the impression that 'boys don't make passes at girls who wear glasses', she definitely got it wrong.

This stylish addition to the store's ground floor staff would certainly set a few tongues wagging. Mrs. Sinclair, who worked at the haberdashery counter, was an overweight and nosy old woman who always brought him home-baked biscuits and cakes that she claimed were the main reason why the now-dead Mr. Sinclair married her. Richard thought that was probably what killed him, for they were awful.

To his right was an enormous display of lamps and lampshades. Some hung from the ceiling, others stood on tables or were standing on the floor, and each shade was illuminated by a forty-, sixty-, or one-hundred-watt light bulb. The ultimate effect was that this whole corner of the floor was permanently and stiflingly hot.

Hovering over this array of glowing magnificence was Mr. Patrick O'Hara, a portly Irishman in his mid-forties, whose Irish brogue was so strong that Richard could hardly understand a word he said. Mr. O'Hara was, however, Richard's immediate superior, so Richard always acknowledged his interminably detailed instructions with a polite nod, often not understanding the jumble of words that came out of his mouth.

Further afield were departments specializing in furniture, bedding, garden tools, domestic appliances, leather goods, and hardware of all descriptions, but in a corner office sat the man overseeing the entire floor, Mr. Reginald Palmer. A man Richard despised above all others. He was always immaculately dressed in a smart suit, white shirt, highly polished shoes, and an old-school tie and spoke with the plummy accent of the British upper class, looking down his nose at everyone he spoke to.

Richard, or Dick, as he was usually called, having attended a boys-only school and with very little experience with girls or women, considered the new arrival on his floor as being fairly old, probably in her mid-thirties, he guessed. But with her striking red hair, slim figure, and a disproportionately large bust, she was certainly a sight for sore eyes.

Old Mrs. Sinclair sidled up to him as he was taking in the sights, saying, "What do you think of Miss La-de-dah over there? I can't see her lasting five minutes if you ask me. Too posh by a long chalk."

At that point, the woman walked over toward them and Mrs. Sinclair shuffled off. The new lady smiled and introduced herself as Miss Annabelle Delaney. He took her pale and slender hand in his, noting the bright crimson nail varnish on her long, well-manicured fingernails, and gave her what he imagined to be a firm and manly handshake.

She explained that she was working for a company called An Early Cuppa and was traveling around London, setting up her Early Cuppa booth in different locations to promote their new product, a combined alarm clock, and tea-maker, that, when prepared the evening before and set on a bedside table, would wake the owner at the pre-ordained time with a freshly made, hot cup of tea.

Miss Delaney told him that the booth would be ready to open in two days' time and that she would be his neighbor for the next three months. "What's a nice-looking young man like you doing working here?" she asked. "Surely, you should be working outside in the fresh air."

Her accent was quite posh although her apparent low opinion of his current employment came as a bit of a surprise. However, once in close proximity to her, he was enraptured by the powerful lavender perfume that she was wearing, and together with her bright and lively personality, gleaming white teeth, and beautiful smile, he was smitten.

"Oh," he mumbled, "I'm just filling in time until I'm nineteen. Then I'm hoping to join the police force."

"Oooh! A policeman. I do so love a man in uniform. When's your birthday?"

"Not until August next year. I turned eighteen last month."

"My, you look older than eighteen. You make me feel quite old. I wish I was eighteen again."

With that, she smiled and walked back to her small kiosk, leaving behind an invisible cloud of aromatic splendor, which Dick inhaled with his eyes closed and his lips curling in a secretive smile.

Afterward, he could have kicked himself. Why did he have to tell her he was just a kid?

He rode his motor scooter home that evening cock-a-hoop with joy, for he would no longer have to sit behind his little counter, bored to death, with no one to talk to save Mrs. Sinclair and the occasional customer.

Three days later, with the Early Cuppa booth complete, Miss Delaney turned up bright and early and began reorganizing the booth more to her liking. Dick noted with approval that she was wearing very stylish black slacks, tight around her delightful bottom, but flared around her ankles. Her colorful floral top, with its plunging neckline, displayed magnificent cleavage, and her high heels raised her to about five feet six inches.

At around ten o'clock, she came over to him, bearing a hot cup of tea. "Compliments of Early Cuppa," she said, smiling as she gently laid the cup and saucer on his counter. He smiled back, feeling rather shy and a little intimidated by the woman's confident, brisk yet friendly demeanor and still entranced by that magnificent perfume that he found so appealing. He didn't know it at the time but the perfume was meant to be sexually provocative, heavy with musk, and much preferred by women wishing to exude an exotic and sensual reaction.

They began chatting about this and that, and during the course of the conversation, she asked him where he lived, did he have a girlfriend, and so on. When he told her that he lived with an old aunt in Shepherd's Bush and that he had no other family and had no current girlfriend, she cocked her head sideways looking very thoughtful and muttered a quiet, "Mmmm."

She encouraged him to tell her more about himself, and as he was enjoying her company and all the attention he was getting from her, he went on to tell her that he had joined the local rowing club, enjoyed joyriding on his motor scooter with his friends and had progressed to a green belt in the sport of judo. At this, her big green eyes glistened, and she said she was a regular judo competitor herself with a black belt.

Wow, thought Dick, *she's definitely out of my league.*

As they continued their chat—for it was a very quiet morning—she went on to tell him that she was single, had never been married, but had two wonderful cats at home. Before returning to her booth, she suggested that he join her at her *dojo*, a judo club, one evening for some free sparring, which she called *randori*. Several days later, after a regular cup of tea together at 10:00 every morning, and at three every afternoon, they agreed to meet at her *dojo*, and he subsequently rode his Vespa scooter to the address in Notting Hill that she had given him and turned up as planned.

Dick was impressed with the gymnasium, which doubled as a dojo. Half the floor was covered with a series of thin mattresses with a large white tarpaulin stretched over them, and there were twenty or more people of both sexes, all teenagers or adults, decked out in the traditional *judogi* consisting of baggy trousers and loose heavy jackets. Dick noted that three of them wore black belts and a number of others with blue, green, or yellow. Only four still had white belts, meaning they were beginners.

After donning their respective judogi, Dick, with his green sash holding his jacket together and Miss Delaney resplendent with her black sash tied securely around her small waist, began the usual warm-up, which consisted of practicing their breakfalls—lying down and beating the *tatami* or mat from side to side with their forearms, followed by hurling themselves in the air and landing on their side or back and using their forearms to break the fall. Dick couldn't help but notice that she looked even younger and prettier without her glasses and with no discernible make-up.

Before beginning their randori, they each gave the dojo the customary bow, and then they began the dance, each holding the opponent's lapel or the neckband of their jacket with the right hand and the other holding the right sleeve, trying to get the measure of their opponent and trying, as they moved backward and forward, to get them slightly off balance. The dojo was big enough for three or four pairs of contestants to practice at the same time and their small Japanese instructor, Mr. Michiku, who, as well as offering advice and guidance to everyone, ensured that each individual had a fair share of the mat and that partners were swopped around on a random basis.

After less than a minute of randori with Miss Delaney, Dick saw his opening. As he was moving cautiously backward, she moved toward him, coming up on the ball of her right foot and taking the weight off her left. He swung to his left and stooped into a low crouch, pushing his right hip into her lower abdomen. Then, assisted by her own momentum, he straightened his legs and pulled her right arm and shoulder over his right shoulder, swinging her high in the air and easing her down onto the mat where he dropped on top of her to commence the second phase of the throw or mat work. While lying on top of her, chest to chest, he succeeded in placing her right arm in an arm lock, and she tapped him on the shoulder, conceding that he had won the point.

Feeling mighty pleased with himself for having done such a splendid job, they continued the randori. Within about five seconds, he was flying through the air as she executed a perfect stomach throw, came down on him like a ton of bricks, and, with her legs wrapped around his neck, forced an immediate concession. Every time thereafter that he was partnered with Miss Delaney, she dominated their sparring although he did have some success with a young man of about his own age who also had a green belt.

Happily riding home on his motor scooter, he reflected on his good fortune. On several occasions, he'd had his face buried between Miss Delaney's magnificent breasts, his hands all over her body, and her hands all over his. All in all, he considered it well worth the beating.

The next day at work, she smiled at him and told him that he had done very well for a beginner although she did comment on his apparent lack of concentration at times. He couldn't imagine why.

Their routine of tea at 10:00 and 3:00 continued, and he learned that Miss Delaney had accomplished many things in her life. She had traveled to many countries, mainly in the tropics, and showed him an earlier photograph taken on a small boat in the Caribbean. She was wearing a tiny two-piece swimsuit that left little to the imagination.

During one conversation, she suggested that he visit her in her flat where he could meet her cats, and she could show him other photographs of her travels around and across the world. He, of course, agreed, and the following week, he visited her in the evening, taking with him a small bouquet of flowers. Despite having no transport other than his Vespa motor scooter, he decided to dress in a smart but casual style and wore an open-necked shirt and V-necked pullover beneath his black leather jacket, a newly purchased pair of cavalry twill trousers and his highly prized pair of black 'winkle picker' shoes. Although very conscientious about his Tony Curtis hairstyle, he had no option but to flatten it down with his crash helmet.

Her small flat was situated in the Royal Borough of Kensington, and she greeted him at the door wearing a very brief black mini-skirt, a white halter-necked top, and her familiar red high-heeled shoes. "Right on time," she said as she smiled at him and gave him a peck on the cheek.

As soon as he entered the living room, he was stunned by the décor. The walls were plain white but were hung with expensive-looking and beautifully framed pieces of modern art; one wall was filled with a huge mirror, making the room appear twice its actual size. The entire floor was covered in a crimson deep-pile carpet, and all the furniture was white with the odd splash of green.

He noticed that once again she wore no glasses but had a light dusting of eye shadow, some black stuff on her eyelashes that he later learned was called mascara and a softer shade of lipstick than she wore at the store. The overall effect was stunning, for she appeared younger and more attractive than ever.

She graciously accepted his pathetic little bunch of chrysanthemums and complimented him on his outfit, saying it made him look older and more mature. After arranging the flowers in a small crystal vase, she insisted that he meet her cats. Both Siamese, one long-haired and one short-haired, were brushing backward and forward against her legs.

Lifting one in each arm, she held them against her breasts, and he could hear them both purring contentedly as they gave baleful looks to the interloper who had just entered their palace.

"The short-haired one is called Christmas. He's a true Siamese and a bit stand-offish," she said. "The other is actually a Balinese, and her name is Easter. She's really friendly." Giving each one an affectionate kiss, she placed them down on the carpet, and turning her attention back to Dick, she asked, "What would you like to drink?"

The only alcohol he had ever tasted was beer, but since she had none, he was at a loss as to what to ask for.

She smiled and said, "Why don't you try vodka and lime juice? It's very popular at the moment and would suit the occasion perfectly." She told him to take a seat on the small white leather couch while she prepared his drink and returned a minute or two later with a clear concoction in a small tumbler, which Dick presumed was his vodka and lime juice. In her other hand was a glass of what she claimed was a Bloody Mary, and although he nodded knowingly, he didn't have a clue what she was drinking.

Seating herself beside him, she took an album from the small table beside her and began flipping through the pages, showing him photos she had collected from the different countries she had visited. Dick was in awe of her experiences, the photos of exotic places, the strange people, and the numerous strange animals that she had seen. But he was even more conscious of the woman beside him, her marvelous perfume, the soft fabric of her skirt and blouse that pressed up against him, and the gentle huskiness of her voice.

When she got up to refill his glass, instead of sitting next to him, she chose a comfortable armchair directly opposite him and again asked if he had a girlfriend. He hadn't and admitted as much, for although he had, in fact, had two girlfriends in the past, they had fallen by the wayside. Neither had allowed him to take much in the way of liberties with them although one had allowed him to fondle her rather small breasts. He was still very much a virgin, but wishing to portray himself as a man of the world, he had no intention of telling Miss Delaney that.

She suggested that since they were becoming quite friendly, he should stop referring to her as Miss Delaney and simply call her Annabelle or, if he preferred, Anna. As she was speaking and Dick was sipping his vodka and lime juice, he couldn't help but notice that her short mini-skirt had ridden up her thighs so high that he could see her panties. *In fact,* he thought, *they were strange panties.* They were the same shade of red as her hair, kind of fuzzy and, dare he think it, curly.

She must have seen him turn his attention from her face to her knees and as she continued to talk, she began to smile and very slowly parted them, revealing that of course, she wasn't wearing any panties at all. Her gaze, on the other hand, was fastened on the front of his trousers, which appeared to be at a bursting point. She stood, took him by the hand, saying, "Come on, I think you've lost interest in my photos," and led him into her bedroom.

He followed nervously, realizing that the time had come when he was going to do 'it' and was not entirely sure what 'it' was all about.

What followed was everything Dick had imagined when doing what all boys do when in the toilet, in the shower, or sometimes under the bedsheets. Whether it was the two vodka and lime juices or whether his blood pressure had dropped, he didn't know. But as he watched, he began to feel distinctly lightheaded as she began taking off her clothes. First her shoes, then her halter top, and finally her skirt, for that was all that she was wearing.

Then she stood before him, completely naked, and with a delightful smile, began undressing him. She cupped her two beautiful breasts in her hands and said, "Don't be afraid, Dick. This is all yours." He hesitantly reached out and touched them, then gently kissed them before pulling her body toward him and thrusting his hips against that fascinating curly bush.

What followed was beyond description. He explored every inch of her body, not even believing that this was happening. Finally, she took control of things, gently played with and massaged his erection, and laughingly said, "We have to give him a name, Dick. What do you call him?" He mumbled something about how he and all his friends referred to their appendages as John Thomas.

To which she replied, "Then let's call him Little Tommy although he's not so little now." She went on to explain and demonstrate how to use Little Tommy in a way that would give the most pleasure to them both and after releasing his building frustration, they rested for perhaps ten minutes, giving him time to reflect on what had just happened. He had only dreamed of such pleasures and delights in the past and thought of all the time and effort he had wasted on those two previous girlfriends. They fell into each other's arms once more to perform what she later told him was referred to as the beast with two backs. Afterward, it was time to go home. What he most definitely considered to be the absolute best evening of his entire life filled his head as he wobbled home on his motor scooter in the pouring rain, dreaming of his next encounter with Anna.

Would she invite him back again? Why did she let him do all that stuff? Was she expecting him to pay her? And then came his biggest fear, the one that everyone dreaded. Would she get pregnant?

His mind was so preoccupied that his grip on the throttle became tighter and tighter; his speed went higher and higher, and before he knew it, the scooter slipped out from under him on the wet road surface. He and his motor scooter parted company as he catapulted off the road and into a water-filled, weed-infested ditch where he immediately lost consciousness.

Chapter Two

When Dick opened his eyes, it was the following morning, and he found himself staring at a white ceiling, and surrounded by pale gray curtains hanging from curtain rods. He felt dazed and confused until it slowly dawned on him that he was in a hospital bed and then it all came back to him. The visit to Anna's, the wonderful sex, the scooter ride home, and the fall. Then, all was blank. Thankfully, a nurse soon arrived at his bedside, smiled at him, and inquired, "Hello, young man. How are you feeling?"

"What happened? Where am I? I mean, I can see I'm in a hospital, but which one? And how did I get here?"

"You had an accident on your motorcycle, a pretty bad one. A passing motorist saw you fall and when she went to assist you, she saw that you were unconscious. She flagged down another car and asked them to find a telephone while she waited for the ambulance to arrive, and they brought you here. This is Hammersmith Hospital, by the way, on Du Cane Road. You were actually very lucky. Are you in any pain?"

"No, just very confused. Am I injured?"

"The doctor will be here shortly. I'll let him explain." She handed him a beaker of water and for the first time, he noticed that his left arm was bandaged. When he tried to move it, he felt a sharp pain, and it wouldn't move. The nurse helped him take a few sips of water, telling him to relax and wait for the doctor, and then left.

A few minutes later, a young doctor in a white coat turned up, smiling cheerfully, and asked how he was feeling. "Confused. I can vaguely remember the accident, but don't remember how I got here and don't know what's wrong with me."

"Okay. Well, you've had a nasty bang on the head, but no fracture, thanks to your crash helmet. Your left arm is broken in three places, and you've got two cracked ribs. But apart from that, you seem to be fine. We'll be keeping you in the hospital again tonight, but all being well, you'll be released tomorrow morning. You have to take it easy for a few days. The ribs will heal up fairly quickly as long as you don't do anything stupid—like riding a motorbike. Your arm will be in a cast for two or three weeks, but you should be fully back to normal in a couple of months."

He then excused himself and went off to deal with his other patients.

Dick lay in his bed, absorbing the implications of this news and when the young nurse reappeared, he asked if he could use a telephone to call his aunt, who must be worried sick.

When she returned a few minutes later, she had a telephone on a small trolley, which she attached to a socket in the wall beside his bed and left. His aunt Nancy, a cheerful Irish woman who was a good friend of his mother's and, although not really his aunt, had offered him board and lodging when his parents had died in a motor car accident shortly after he had finished school. After giving her a brief account of his accident and his injuries, she told him that she would take a bus to the hospital the following morning to collect him. He then telephoned Mr. Palmer at work and told him what had happened and that he wouldn't be at work for a few days, as he had a broken arm. Palmer was quite decent about it, saying that he was entitled to a few days' sick leave anyway and told him to take it easy.

After a week had passed, Dick felt that he was sufficiently recovered to return to work. His rib injury was a lot less painful and his arm, now set in a cumbersome plaster cast, was not painful at all, only useless, but at least he could wiggle the fingers that protruded like four Vienna sausages from the end of his cast.

He learned that his motor scooter was a complete write-off, not that he would be able to use it anyway, so he was confined to traveling to and from work by bus.

On his first day back at work, he received many well-wishers at his small counter, including Mr. Palmer, who surprisingly wrote 'speedy recovery, Richard' on his plaster cast. Many others followed suit, including Mrs. Sinclair, who also presented him with a small tin full of her awful homemade biscuits. Just like clockwork, Anna, whom he addressed as Miss Delaney during business hours, served him tea at ten and didn't mention their earlier adventure at first, merely expressing her relief that he was recovering well from his road accident.

Dick was too embarrassed to bring up the subject of the tryst at her flat but was delighted when, after she had expressed her sympathy regarding his injuries, she lightened the mood by saying that she really enjoyed his company when he last visited her. Completely unabashed, she laughingly said she hoped it wouldn't be too long before he would come over, and they could do it again. She added that she had been thinking about him a lot and handed him a document that she suggested he might be interested in completing and posting to the address given at the foot of the page.

"You need to become more adventurous. Become a man of the world and take advantage of every opportunity to travel and explore some of the wonderful things that the world has to offer. I really believe that London is the center of the universe and provides a wonderful springboard for young men like you to launch themselves into a life of opportunity and adventure."

He saw that the document was headed with an elaborate crest of a lion atop some type of shield along with the words 'Royal Warania Police' and as he studied it, he realized that it was an application to join a British colonial police force in Central Africa with an initial term of service given as three years. "I've known several young men who have joined this police force. Some come home with exciting tales to tell, others have stayed and have never come home," she said.

After a week had passed, Miss Delaney invited Dick to her flat for the evening, and this time when she answered the door, she wore only a brief negligee. Handing him a vodka and lime juice, she asked, "Are you ready for some more sexual enlightenment?"

"I'm more than ready," he said as he settled on her sofa, "but with my left arm in a cast I don't know how to manage it." He further confessed that he was worried about her getting pregnant. Blushing, he asked, "You know I'm new to all this. Aren't you worried about it?"

She smiled as she sat down beside him, placed her arm around his waist, and looked straight into his eyes. "Richard, you have nothing to worry about. I have a small device that I inserted before you even arrived. You won't even know it's there, you didn't last time, but it ensures that no little Richards arrive on the scene."

Then, taking his right hand, she led him into the bedroom where she slowly and carefully undressed him and told him to relax, lie on his back, and let her do all the work. Slipping out of her negligee, she lay down beside him, pressed her body close to his, and whispered in his ear, "Have you sent in that form yet?"

While awkwardly groping for her breasts with his one useful hand, he muttered that he hadn't, and she responded by pulling away from him. "You naughty boy. If you don't do it soon, there'll be no more beast with two backs."

Then she tenderly kissed him with her flaming red lips, opening them wide and pushing her tongue deep into his mouth, where it played softly with his tongue. This was Dick's first experience of French kissing, but after a moment or two, he got the hang of it. Before long, she enfolded him in her arms, slid her hands down his back, over his buttocks, and between his legs, and began fondling him. It was more than Dick could take and before he knew it, he had ejaculated all over her hand and the bedsheets.

"Never mind. We'll just clean it up and start again."

On the bus ride home, Dick realized that he was totally addicted to Anna's charms and when he arrived, he frantically filled out the form, posting it the next morning.

Apparently satisfied, Miss Delaney continued with the daily tea service and the once-a-week tryst at her flat. Dick, who had become as subservient as her two cats, gained considerable experience in the process.

Some weeks later, with his plaster cast removed and his arm returning to normal, an official-looking envelope arrived in the morning post. The letter was an invitation to attend an interview at the Waranian embassy in the heart of London. When he explained to his aunt that he had applied to join the Waranian police force, she didn't appear particularly surprised. After all, he'd made no secret of the fact that he wanted to join the police force. She just hadn't imagined that it would be so far away. At least, she assumed it was far away; she had as much idea as Dick about where it actually was.

He presented himself at the Waranian embassy at the appointed time to be interviewed by a corpulent Colonel Merriweather, who gave him an interesting and flattering description of life as a police officer in Warania and presented him with a booklet describing the many facets of Waranian life. Returning home, Dick studied the booklet he'd been given and was particularly impressed with the numerous photographs depicting police officers decked out in a variety of uniforms, riding both motorcycles and horses, attending classroom lectures, and participating in a wide variety of sports. These photographs certainly showed an adventurous, and even glamorous, picture of life in the tropics with sunshine every day. Dick was sold on the idea of becoming a police officer in the Central African colony of Warania and fervently hoped that he would be accepted.

In due course, he was advised that his application had been successful, provided that he passed a thorough medical examination by one of London's prestigious Harley Street medical practitioners. When he appeared at the appointed hour, he suffered the indignity of standing stark naked before the doctor while a pretty young nurse took notes. The doctor held Dick's testicles, told him to cough, stuck his finger up his backside while he bent over a chair, and was eventually pronounced to be fit and healthy.

He was subsequently accepted at the tender age of eighteen years and three months to serve a three-year term with the RWP. Soon after, airline tickets were delivered to his home address with an enclosed letter informing him that his flight was due to depart from London Airport the following month, November 1962.

By this time, he was completely recovered from his injuries and Miss Delaney invited him to one last evening at her flat before he left, promising him even more exotic delights, all of which, she assured him, he had never experienced before. When that evening came, he was greeted at the door by Anna, who was wearing a diaphanous nightgown that revealed all of her delightful accessories. She proffered the now familiar cocktail but insisted that they sit together and talk for a while before getting down to business.

Her talk was delivered seriously and in the manner of a professor addressing a room full of students. She told him of the wonders that he would experience in Africa—the different cultures, the wildlife, the glorious weather, and the many women he would encounter. She said that she had done her best to enlighten him as to the wonderful world of sex, but to his surprise, she informed him that they had barely scratched the surface. "Tonight, I will teach you a little more." And, with that, she took his hand and led him into her bedroom.

Oh, boy, and did she teach him a little more. Oral sex was on the agenda and other things that he'd never even dreamed about were tested, experienced, and enjoyed. However, disaster struck as someone came knocking at the door. Quickly donning a dressing gown, she ran to the door and opened it a crack. There was a huge bellow, followed by a scream. She came running into the bedroom with a very large, red-faced man following close behind. "So, this is what you get up to when I'm away from town, you little bitch," he yelled. Upon seeing Dick, who had gallantly stepped between them, he swung a roundhouse punch. Dick ducked and the man's fist connected squarely with Anna's jaw instead.

Frightened beyond belief and still weak from Anna's ministrations, Dick grabbed his trousers, took a dive between the man's legs, and headed for the door, but not before, as a parting gesture, he bit the fellow hard enough to draw blood from the back of his ankle and happily heard him roar with pain. Dressed only in a pair of trousers, no shirt, and no shoes, he decided to walk the three or four miles home rather than ride the bus, and shivering from the cold, he couldn't forgive himself for his cowardly behavior in Anna's presence.

The following morning, Miss Delaney was absent from her Early Cuppa booth and Dick missed his ten o'clock cup of tea. Over at the Waranian embassy, suffering from a slightly bruised and swollen jaw, she sat having tea with Colonel Merriweather, the man who, several weeks earlier, had interviewed Dick and who was responsible for recruiting young men suitable for the Waranian police force.

He told her that he was delighted that she had been so successful in finding so many perfect candidates for the Royal Waranian Police Force and was trying to elicit from her how she accounted for her success. She just shrugged her shoulders, took the envelope containing five hundred pounds that he proffered, and beamed. "Oh, it's surprising what you can achieve with a friendly smile." She twinkled her fingers at him and left.

Chapter Three

On a late afternoon in November, Dick said goodbye to a miserable, cold, and rainy London and boarded his aircraft at London Airport, pleased that he had worn his best charcoal suit, conservative blue tie, and fashionable, well-polished shoes since everyone else aboard was smartly dressed, the ladies in attractive dresses and the men sporting jackets and ties. As they flew south, day turned into night, the aircraft's lights were dimmed and Dick nestled comfortably into his seat and fell asleep, wondering what the future would bring. Several hours later, he awoke to daylight and was served a small but welcome hot breakfast. As he gazed out of his window, he saw vast tracts of dry brown land below and a brilliant blue and cloudless sky stretching across the broad horizon.

He had never flown before and was fascinated with the aircraft, especially the young and attractive stewardesses who paid so much attention to their passengers. They were due to land in Nairobi for refueling, and over the public address system, the pilot requested that the passengers fasten their seat belts in preparation for landing. In the distance, he could see the city, its many tall buildings reaching for the sky and shining brightly in the early morning sunshine.

The short stopover at Nairobi's airport gave Dick the chance to stretch his legs, and he took the opportunity to avail himself of a shoeshine for the princely sum of one Kenyan shilling. Then back on board his plane for the final leg of his journey, he was content to enjoy the moment, relax, and contemplate the adventures that lay ahead.

Following a tasty lunch, they flew into the Waranian capital of Chimuka in the early afternoon and Dick was disappointed to see that his smart and well-pressed suit was now a wrinkled mess. He was anxious to see who would welcome him, having been told that he would be met at the airport and conveyed to the police training depot. He collected his suitcase from the pile of luggage that had been deposited on the forecourt by a couple of scruffy-looking baggage handlers, but a casual glance around showed no sign of anyone there to meet him.

Gazing around the small airport, he was fascinated by the variety of outfits that the people were wearing. Some men wore only short trousers and T-shirts or bush jackets, others wore suits and ties, and the women, who were far more versatile, were wearing an assortment of colorful dresses and robes, some baggy and others tight-fitting. Many had elaborate turbans and headscarves, the likes of which he had never seen before. Most of their earrings were not earrings at all but colorful wooden discs, some with a diameter of two inches or more, wedged into their very stretched ear lobes. He was beginning to feel very hot and uncomfortable in his English-made woolen suit and felt perspiration trickling down his face, neck, and back when a light tap on his shoulder caused him to turn. A short, round, and bald African man asked, "Are you perhaps Mr. Starling coming to join Warania's police force?"

The man addressing him was dressed in short trousers, a short-sleeved tunic with a multitude of pockets, long socks, and brown leather shoes. His English was good and Dick acknowledged that yes, he was indeed Mr. Starling.

The fellow then beckoned him to follow, and they exited the airport terminal to where a small, rusty, and very dilapidated Ford Cortina was waiting, its only redeeming feature being two rather flashy chromium-plated wing mirrors that adorned the top of each front mudguard. *Obviously,* thought Dick, *they were a rather pathetic afterthought that had been added by the car's owner.* The driver, another African, sat behind the wheel with the engine running, and beside him sat a third individual, gaunt and unshaven, with a miserable look on his face. Dick immediately thought of him as Misery Guts and noted that his gaudy pink and orange shirt didn't at all match his ugly disposition. Neither man greeted him, which seemed a bit odd.

Dick's suitcase was placed in the boot of the car, and he was ushered into the back seat, followed by his chubby greeter, and they drove off. The car coughed and spluttered as they left the airport, but Dick was too busy gazing through the windows at the brilliant sunshine and beautiful blue and cloudless sky to pay much attention to his welcoming committee or his shabby transport. After all, this was third-world Africa. What did he expect?

After they had been traveling for about fifteen minutes, an ominous feeling crept over Dick. No one had spoken a word since he had climbed into the car and any questions or comments that he had raised were met, with the exception of Misery Guts, with nothing but smiles.

The road from the airport was a fairly wide two-lane highway, but they soon turned off onto a much smaller road, and from that onto nothing more than a dirt track. They were surrounded by thick vegetation and some large trees, but no sign of human habitation. Then the car stopped. All three of his companions climbed out and Little Fatty, as Dick now thought of him, beckoned for him to do the same.

No sooner had he stepped out of the car than Misery Guts, who had been sitting in the front passenger seat, slapped him alongside the head, and Little Fatty said, "Give us your watch and your wallet."

Dick, realizing that he was being mugged, immediately turned and ran back in the direction from which they had come. Misery Guts caught up with him in no time, seized him by the collar, and threw him to the ground.

Dick, now paralyzed with fear, decided to play along and when Little Fatty caught up to them, he asked, "What do you want? Why are you doing this?"

Little Fatty replied, "We want everything. We're sick of you white boys coming over here and treating us Waranians like dirt. Now, give me your watch and your wallet and take off your clothes. All of them."

Dick, frightened out of his wits, did as he was told and handed over his wallet and wristwatch. He removed his jacket and dropped it on the floor, but this didn't satisfy Little Fatty. "All of it. Your shirt, your tie, your shoes and socks, your trousers." Dick again complied until he was standing in only his pink underpants, decorated with little yellow ducks. "Yes, those as well." As Dick slowly stepped out of his underpants, Little Fatty remarked on how small and lily white his penis was, and peering down, Dick had to admit that indeed it had shrunk considerably, most probably from fright.

Standing completely naked, he realized that their next step would be to kill him. Throwing caution to the wind, he leaped into the thick bush beside the dirt track and to his delight saw a lake just fifty feet in front of him. He ran and dived in, swimming like a madman toward the other side. He later learned that very few Waranians could swim and that this frantic attempt to escape their clutches probably saved his life. He heard them laughing and one of them shouted as he dived into the water, "Hey, little white boy, you won't last long."

He heard their car start and drive away but decided to stay put for a couple of hours before attempting to return to town. When he was about to swim back, he observed some strange little lumps protruding above the surface of the water, and it slowly dawned on him that these were the eyes and snouts of crocodiles, the likes of which he had only ever seen on television or at the zoo. Even with his very limited knowledge of African wildlife, he decided that his best route back to the dirt track would be to circumnavigate the lake on foot, albeit unclad. *How he had escaped the crocodile's attention on the swim over was a mystery, or perhaps a miracle,* he thought.

Several hours later, as dusk was falling, he regained the dirt track and trudged wearily to the small road leading him to the highway. He was covered in insect bites and dozens of scratches; his feet were sore and bleeding, and he was already feeling the effects of dehydration. He hadn't gone too far along the road when he heard a car coming up behind him, its headlights casting a long shadow before him. He held his thumb out, thinking what a ridiculous sight he must appear to the driver. With little option, he frantically turned to wave the car down with one hand while trying to cover his genitals with the other.

A middle-aged woman in a Morris Minor pulled up beside him and, winding her window down a fraction, asked, "What on earth are you doing?"

With both hands now appropriately covering his manhood, he explained about the abduction and robbery. Covered in scratches and insect bites, his tale must have had a ring of truth to it, for she allowed him into the back of her car, threw him a blanket, and drove him to the nearby police station.

"What in heaven's name were ye thinking, laddie?" demanded the gravelly voiced Scotsman at the police station. "Did you no' think that we would do a better job of welcoming ye tae the Waranian police force than to send a little fat wog to pick ye up?" He threw some ill-fitting but clean clothes to him, saying that he would be transported to the police training depot shortly.

Some days later, clean-shaven and more or less back to normal, he was kitted out with his Waranian police uniform and joined a squad of new recruits for the commencement of his training. He was beginning to wonder how he had managed, in such a short space of time, to transform himself from a relatively happy-go-lucky TV salesman with a nice warm bed to go home to in the heart of London, not to mention a smashing little Vespa motor scooter, to a penniless, propertyless and homeless expatriate in darkest Africa. It was, of course, all Miss Annabelle Delaney's fault.

The squad of police recruits that was his misfortune to join numbered twenty-one upon his arrival. Some were British and some were African, but all appeared confused. They were standing on a parade ground and their squad instructor, a solidly built, swarthy, and bombastic Liverpudlian named Harris, swore constantly, gesticulating and cursing at their obvious stupidity. They had their belt and brace on backward, their Waranian police badges were upside down, their shoes were dirty, their caps weren't on straight, and so on and so on.

Eventually, Depot Chief Inspector Harris, who, he continually pointed out to them, was the highest-ranking noncommissioned officer in the Royal Warania Police Force, had them sorted out and lined them up in three rows of seven. "How many of you horrible lot have ever ridden a horse?" he demanded. Two men put their hands up, which set him off again. "Put your bloody hands down, you stupid buggers. Do you think you're still in kindergarten? Stand to attention and shout 'sir'."

Having established that his wards were unlikely to turn into the household cavalry, he moved on. "How many of you lot have a driving license?"

The same two slammed to attention, yelling, "Sir."

The next question, "How many can swim?" met with a much better response, as all but five of the recruits acknowledged that they could in fact swim. The five who couldn't swim were all Africans.

They were then led off to the stables, where more than one hundred horses were kept. Depot Chief Inspector Harris, soon to be nicknamed Chunky behind his back, took each recruit to a horse. *With a somewhat apologetic air and rather rudely,* thought Dick, Chunky introduced him to his first horse, a steed named Wyoming. Gripping their horses' well-worn and grubby bridles, the recruits led them in single file to an outdoor area where they were shown how to properly harness and saddle the beasts.

No actual riding was to take place for two weeks, but for two hours every morning, starting before daybreak, each recruit would report to the stables and vigorously groom his horse until its coat and hooves shone in the bright morning sunshine. After two weeks, Dick and his fellow squad mates had two hours of equitation after the grooming session. Dick's experience of horses, in common with most of the recruits, was precisely zero, and the learning process was fraught with difficulties. However, over time, Dick learned Wyoming's little foibles and managed to stay in the saddle until, after six months of training, he was considered a competent rider. The training depot had a canteen that served breakfast, lunch, and dinner seven days a week. The food was good and plentiful although rumors were rampant about some mysterious little blue pills that were added to the tea to subdue any extracurricular sexual activities.

As was typically the case with a British police force, RWP police officers did not carry firearms. Nevertheless, recruits were required, in addition to equitation, to perform arms drill, foot drill, and musketry. They also received lessons in Roman-Dutch Law, first-aid, typing, and local knowledge.

After six months of nonstop harassment by Chunky Harris and four weeks at driving school, each recruit was appointed as an inspector in the Royal Waranian Police Force and let loose on the public at large.

Inspector Richard Starling, having received a regular wage for six months, had been able to purchase some civilian clothes and a cheap new wristwatch and had a few Waranian pounds in his pocket.

Once their training was complete, Dick's squad mates were dispatched in all directions. Dick's posting was to the rural town of Umbedzi some seventy miles north of Chimuka and surrounded either by African tribal lands or white-owned farms, which were cattle ranches or planted with acre upon acre of maize. Dick learned that maize, locally known as corn or mealies, was crushed into cornmeal, mixed with water, then cooked in boiling water and colloquially known as mealy meal or *sadza*, the staple diet of natives throughout central and southern Africa.

Dick was transported to Umbedzi in a Bedford truck driven by a very talkative African constable who described their surroundings as they passed through some farmland and part of the Tribal Trust Land, locally referred to as the TTL, that were scattered throughout the country. He pointed out that while the white-owned farmland was generally green and fertile, the TTLs tended to be sparse and dried up. This, explained the constable, was because the white-owned farmland was better irrigated and totally off-limits to goats, whereas the TTL had little or no irrigation and allowed goats to roam freely, and they ate every edible thing they could find.

Eventually, Dick's driver pulled into the forecourt of what appeared to be a small, thatched cottage with a blue lamp hanging over the front door. He smiled as he said, "This is your new home, sir. Good luck." Dick removed his one cheap suitcase and duffle bag from the vehicle and watched it drive off before entering the unlocked front door.

An African sergeant was standing behind a small counter in what was obviously the police charge office and smilingly welcomed his new member in charge. Dick shook hands and the sergeant identified himself as Zibando, senior sergeant at Umbedzi police station. He explained that it was what's known as a one-man station, meaning that there was only one police inspector present, and therefore, as the senior officer, he was the member in charge.

His complement of staff were three African sergeants and ten African constables. His quarters consisted of a compact two-bedroomed cottage with a small poorly furnished living room, kitchen, and bathroom. A small office with a front counter, a battered desk, and a filing cabinet made up the actual police station or charge office, which was equipped with a telephone, a very limited-range two-way radio, and a gun cabinet. The attached carport contained the ubiquitous police long-wheelbase Land Rover and blue police lamp, which he had already seen hanging over its front door.

In the backyard, he was delighted to find two horses that would need regular grooming and exercise. Dick had enjoyed the daily equitation that had been part of his police training and looked forward to regular outings on either of his two mounts, a pair of chestnuts with apparently congenial dispositions. Their names, Warlord and Wayward, were displayed on the front of their individual stable doors.

The nearest police station to Umbedzi was another one-man station in a similar town called Zumba. It was situated about fifty miles to the east as the crow flies, but about eighty miles by road, as the nearest bridge across the Umfurudzi River could only be reached by a devious and circuitous route.

The river ran, via a series of smaller tributaries, from the vast Congo River, which ran hundreds of miles to the north, toward the southeast, and into Lake Mweru that lay on the border between Warania and Zambia. The Umfurudzi formed the dividing line between the police areas of Zumba and Umbedzi. The town of Umbedzi had a population of about five hundred white households, with a hotel, a bank, half a dozen shops serving both the European and African communities, and a large hardware and cattle-feed store catering to local farmers. Approximately two miles to the south stood the African township of Umdenga, with a population of approximately five thousand.

Dick spent his first day familiarizing himself with his new home and the small charge office and in the early evening, clad in civilian attire, he walked the short distance to the main street that ran through Umbedzi and to the town's small hotel, appropriately named the Umbedzi Hotel, which had a bar, appropriately named the Umbedzi Waterhole.

Unlike the English bars that Dick was used to, this bar lacked the cozy warmth that was a comforting feature of the pubs back home. On the ceiling were two slowly revolving fans, with their broad paddle-like blades barely stirring the warm and clammy air. The walls were festooned with a variety of Africana, some black and white shields made of some indistinguishable game skin, and several really ugly wooden masks. There were also some primitive spears, which he later discovered were called *assegais*, and a collection of drums stood on the floor. The drums of varying sizes appeared to be made of game skin.

There were also some spectacular mounted heads of buffalo, kudu, and even the delicate springbok. The Umbedzi Waterhole was fairly well patronized. As he walked in, the buzz of conversation dropped as everyone turned to stare at him. He nodded pleasantly, walked up to the bar, and asked the chubby but attractive barmaid for a cold beer, any beer. "There is only one beer," she said, "a Waranian classic called Chimbuka." She took one from the fridge below the bar, popped the top off, and handed it to him.

Slowly, the patrons returned to their earlier conversations and Dick told the barmaid that he was the new police inspector in town. Her expression softened, and she said that she was sorry about his predecessor. Not knowing what she was talking about, he asked, "What do you mean?"

With a slow shake of her head, she said, "Didn't they tell you about that? Inspector Solly Farringham was murdered two weeks ago. He was out in the sticks looking for cattle poachers with his constable when they came upon a group of men with some stolen cattle. I don't know the full story, but I believe that when they tried to arrest them, they were murdered. All the men hereabouts were talking about it and our farmers have taken to carrying guns when they're out on their farms."

It was an awful story. The men were apparently both chopped to pieces. The whole incident was witnessed by a young herd boy who ran back to Bert Lillyford's ranch to report what he had seen. "It was three days before Solly and his constable's remains were found and by then the animals and vultures had really made a mess of them." As she related the story, her eyes widened, and she became so wrapped in the telling that he noticed that she was wringing her hands in anxiety.

Dick slowly drank his beer while pondering this alarming news. "No one mentioned this to me when I was posted here," he said. "Perhaps I ought to find out a little more about it, for surely someone is going after these murderous swine."

"I don't know what they can do," she replied. "Cattle theft is pretty common around here. Maybe you can catch them. My name is Melissa, by the way. What's yours?"

"Oh, sorry," said Dick, still deep in thought. "I'm Richard Starling, but most people call me Dick. I just arrived today and don't know anyone and certainly didn't know about Inspector Farringham. That's shocking."

Shortly afterward, he said goodnight to Melissa and returned to his quarters, wondering what he'd gotten himself into. Perhaps he'd see it in a fresh light after a good night's sleep. Climbing into bed with only a thin bedsheet for a cover, he fell into a restless sleep, and in the very early morning, he awoke to the sound of a loud screech outside his window. When he looked out, he discovered a brilliantly colored peacock with his tail feathers fully spread. It turned out that this was to be his early morning wake-up call for many months to come.

A man who turned out to be his houseboy arrived shortly after seven that morning. His name was Shadreck, and he explained in passable English that he lived in servant's quarters at the back of the cottage next to the two cinderblock cells and was there to cook, clean house, wash and iron uniforms, feed and groom the horses, and perform any other functions required of him. Shadreck was a small man wearing the customary house servant uniform of a white shirt, shorts, and tennis shoes. "Hello, Shadreck. Did you work for Inspector Farringham? Yes, of course. You must have done."

"Yessir," and looking morosely at his feet muttered, "agh, that was terrible what happened to the baas and Constable Moses."

"Yes, and I didn't find out about it until I got here. A terrible business."

Dick seated himself at his small kitchen table and Shadreck served him a simple breakfast of fried eggs, bacon, and toast. He reflected on his current situation, thinking, *I have a house servant, a pretty barmaid down the road, beautiful weather, and I'm not quite nineteen. What more could I ask for?*

The day following his arrival, newly trained and still green around the gills, he received a telephone call from a colleague, Inspector Taffy Lloyd-Jones, who ran the police station in Zumba.

"Hello, old chap, welcome to Warania. I believe you're just out of the training depot and have taken over poor old Farringham's station. Well, welcome to the back of beyond. You'll soon find your way around, and I'm sure it won't be too long before we can get together for a few beers. I'm afraid I've got a bit of bad news for you. One of my constables has reported seeing a floater on your side of the Umfurudzi. You'd better get down there and see what it's all about. It's probably someone who staggered into the river while drunk or who was high on dagga."

"What's a floater?" asked Dick.

"Oh, sorry. I forgot you're new to all the usual police jargon. A floater is a dead body floating in the river—in this case, on your side of the river. The sooner you fish it out, the better. It will start to stink pretty soon. Good luck." And with that, he rang off.

Following his brief conversation with Taffy, Dick, who had noted his cultured British accent, pictured Taffy as being one of those tall, aristocratic expatriates that he had encountered quite frequently during his six or seven months in Chimuka. Someone along the lines, Dick imagined, of that well-known film star David Niven.

Dick, together with Constable Machaka, loaded the body box onto the roof of the Land Rover and, guided by his constable, reluctantly set off on a dirt track toward the Umfurudzi. He had yet to see, let alone touch, a dead body and was not looking forward to the experience. Directed by Machaka, their journey took well over an hour due to the rough, bumpy dirt trail that was barely wide enough for their Land Rover, but they eventually arrived at the river and began searching along its banks for the body.

When they reached the Umfurudzi, Dick found the slow and meandering river to be quite narrow, perhaps fifty or sixty feet from one bank to the other, and was completely desolate. Tall grasses and trees lined both its banks, but there were some signs of habitation for Dick saw a small, rickety jetty on the opposite bank with what appeared to be an aluminum, shallow draught and flat-bottomed open boat, tied up alongside. The boat had an ancient and small outboard engine attached to its transom, an engine Dick recognized as being something called a Seagull, a reliable little two-stroke outboard engine seen all over Britain. He guessed that the boat belonged to a local farmer who probably enjoyed an afternoon of fishing from time to time and thought his boat was perfectly safe in the grasses and reeds in that lonely spot.

They saw a constable over on the other side shouting and pointing, and they eventually encountered the body, face down in the water and most definitely dead.

Constable Machaka began chuckling and when Dick asked him what was so funny, Machaka explained that this had happened before. Inspector Lloyd-Jones or one of his men probably found the body on their side of the river and, rather than remove the smelly, soggy corpse, gave it a push until it floated across the river to the opposite bank. Upon hearing this, Dick looked for the longest stick he could find, nudged the soft and bloated corpse from the reeds, and, giving it a good shove, sent it back across the river. Lloyd-Jones' constable, watching from the other side, began screaming and shouting, grabbed a stick of his own and when it reached him, shoved it back again.

This went on for some time until, landing once more on Dick's side of the river, the corpse rolled over. Its face was bloated with bits chewed off by fish or birds and with its eyeballs completely missing. Upon looking more closely, Dick realized that the man was wearing a suit, the very same suit that had been stolen from him upon his arrival at Chimuka airport back in November, and the little fat man wearing it, although barely recognizable, appeared to be none other than Little Fatty.

He realized he was on to something here and began the distasteful job of dragging the corpse ashore. Dick was sickened when taking a grip on the man's wrist the skin slid off. Constable Machaka, who was obviously made of sterner stuff, grabbed hold of Dick's once beautiful suit and dragged the corpse ashore. It was then an easy job to lift the bloated corpse into the body box and after a lot of cursing and swearing, they eventually strapped the body box onto the roof of the Land Rover. They then proceeded to the mortuary in Chimuka, where a postmortem could be conducted.

Chapter Four

Before placing Little Fatty in the mortuary fridge with the obligatory toe tag attached, Dick went through his pockets but didn't find his wallet or wristwatch. He did, however, find clenched in Little Fatty's rigid right hand, a torn scrap of pink and orange cloth that closely resembled the colors of the shirt worn by his pal Misery Guts on the day of his abduction.

Putting two and two together, Dick surmised that there had been a falling out between the trio that had kidnapped and robbed him, and he decided that, as a fully trained member of the constabulary, he would endeavor to track them down himself. *He may as well,* he thought, for Detective Inspector Wally Smith, who was supposed to be investigating the case, didn't seem to be having much success.

Two days later, he received a telephone call from the government medical examiner, who had conducted the postmortem on Little Fatty. The doctor had concluded that Little Fatty died not from drowning, but from a lethal stab wound through the heart, which reinforced Dick's theory that Little Fatty and Misery Guts had fallen out. Dick immediately telephoned Detective Inspector Wally Smith at the main police station in Chimuka and told him that one of the culprits was in the Chimuka mortuary and asked how the CID investigation was progressing. "Oh well," said Smith, "there isn't much to go on, and I've not made much progress."

This was what Dick had expected, but he passed on what the coroner had told him and said that he would search for some leads at his end, thinking about a scrap of torn material he had removed from Little Fatty's clenched fist and decided to keep this snippet of information to himself.

Later that day, Dick made a social telephone call to his colleague Taffy over in Zumba and suggested that he come over to Umbedzi at the weekend where they could meet and enjoy a few beers at the local tavern. Taffy agreed to meet him in the Umbedzi Hotel's Waterhole that Saturday at noon.

When Saturday arrived, Dick walked into the bar promptly at noon and saw only one person sitting there, but he couldn't possibly be Taffy. He appeared to be at least forty years of age and was fat, with fairly long blonde curly hair and a ruddy red-nosed face that had obviously not been shaved for a day or two. Dressed in a civilian khaki safari suit, long woolen socks, and shabby leather shoes, he was as far from a David Niven look-alike as Dick could imagine.

The barmaid Melissa, who had been talking with him when Dick arrived, waved him over and introduced him, saying, "Hello, Dick, I've been chatting with your colleague here from over in Zumba. Quite an interesting fellow."

Dick discovered that although Taffy was a Welshman born in Cardiff, he had attended a public boarding school in England, where he had obviously acquired his posh accent. It was customary for Welshmen to be called Taffy, just as Scotsmen were called Jock and Irishmen Paddy, but apart from his double-barrelled Welsh name, Lloyd-Jones was very different from any Welshman Dick had ever met. He told Dick that he had served in the Royal Waranian Police Force for seventeen years and seemed quite proud of the fact that he had been promoted and demoted twice.

The promotions, he claimed, were due to thorough and excellent police work and the demotions due to some undisclosed misdemeanors, the details of which Taffy did not wish to discuss. His passion, however, was big game hunting and during the course of their lengthy conversation, he suggested to Dick that he join him on one of his frequent game-hunting jaunts. As their conversation progressed, it became obvious to Dick that the two of them had very little in common. For one thing, while Dick had yet to turn nineteen, Taffy was much older. As they chatted and the beer kept flowing, one thing led to another until Dick raised the topic of Little Fatty and his recent demise, probably at the hands of his two compatriots.

"Oh, thanks for that call last week. It turned out that the corpse was one of the buggers who mugged me when I first arrived in the country." And Dick went into some detail of the incident describing Little Fatty's two accomplices, particularly the one he referred to as Misery Guts, who he described as being quite tall and gaunt with a scruffy stubble or beard, rotten teeth, and a sour look on his face.

Dick told Taffy that the man's one redeeming feature, in total contrast to his miserable personality, was that he was wearing a colorful pink and orange shirt. He went on to tell him that Little Fatty hadn't drowned at all but had been stabbed through the heart, probably by Misery Guts. He then pulled from his pocket a scrap of torn material that he'd found gripped in Little Fatty's hand when he pulled him from the river and told Taffy that it closely resembled the color and pattern of the shirt that Misery Guts was wearing on the day of his abduction.

Taffy nodded and told him, "There's a frequent troublemaker over in the Zumba township, a miserable bugger and thin as a rake but handy with a knife. He's always seen wearing gaudy, flashy shirts. I wonder if that could be the same chap?"

Dick agreed that this sounded like it could be the individual that he was looking for and asked Taffy to have the man locked up on suspicion of murder when next seen. He then went on to discuss the subject of Inspector Farringham's murder and the murder of his constable when attempting to arrest some cattle thieves.

"Can you believe that the CID still haven't caught the sods? They seem to have brushed the whole business off as though it was of no consequence."

Taffy shook his head. "Well, the CID are a bunch of loafers, more interested in themselves than in other people's problems. Why don't you try following it up yourself? You might get lucky."

They went on complaining in the fashion that most policemen do before making a tentative plan for Dick to go hunting with Taffy when they could both arrange some time off together. Taffy then decided to leave for he had to drive eighty-odd miles back to Zumba, and they agreed that on their next encounter, Dick would make the journey over to Zumba where they would meet at Taffy's favorite watering hole—a pub with the odd name of the Fiddler's Elbow.

After Taffy left, instead of returning to his house-come-police station, Dick looked for the barmaid and, finding her unoccupied, offered to buy her a drink. She was quite a pretty lass, he decided, especially after he had consumed half a dozen beers. She was definitely older than he was but considerably younger than Annabelle Delaney. Although a bit on the plump side, she was nicely dressed and always had a cheerful smile.

She took him up on the offer of a drink, pouring herself a shandy before saying, "I like you and your friend. You make a nice change from the rednecks that usually come in here."

Noticing the wedding ring on her left hand, Dick asked, "Doesn't your husband mind that you work in a bar with all these men around?"

"Oh no, we're way past that," and he couldn't help noticing how she kept smiling and fluttering her eyelids at him in a very comely fashion. She became quite talkative as the afternoon and evening wore on and told him that her husband Arthur was a pilot and traveled all over the area spraying crops for many of the farmers. He was sometimes away for several nights at a time, which left her feeling pretty lonely.

"In fact, I think our marriage is pretty much on the rocks. We have no kids and don't mess around with each other anymore like we used to." With that, she let out a huge sigh.

It wasn't only Dick's ears that popped up at this apparent call for help. Shifting uncomfortably on his bar stool, he suggested that if one lonely night she felt like having company, he would be happy to join her. He, too, felt quite lonely being stuck in his little thatch cottage night after night. The die was cast, he bid her goodnight and with a wink, left the bar.

Being somewhat the worse for wear, he decided to make an early night of it, and arriving home, he undressed and went off to bed, covered in only a thin bedsheet since the night was hot and muggy. He had just nodded off and was having a confusing dream about being shut in a coffin and knocking on the inside of the wooden lid, shouting to be let out. As he awoke, he could still hear the knocking and after a few seconds realized that someone was knocking softly on his front door.

He reluctantly climbed out of bed, put on some shorts, and went to open the door. When he did so, there stood Melissa. He looked at the wall clock and saw that it was after ten. The hotel bar had just closed, so she must have walked straight over.

"Come in, come in," he said, looking through his small charge office into his unsavory living room, which was his nightly abode. She walked in, closed the door, threw her arms around him, and began sobbing and whimpering.

"I'm so lonely and unhappy," she mumbled. "I hope you don't mind me visiting you like this, but I couldn't bear to go back to that lonely house. Arthur is hardly ever at home, and I know he has another woman somewhere. I hate him. Do you think he hates me because I'm so fat?"

Dick stood back a pace, carefully composed his words, and said gently, "I think you're just lovely."

Well, she positively lunged at him, took his face between her pretty hands, and planted a soft kiss on his lips with the hint of a tongue. They stood there kissing and hugging for about five minutes before Dick slowly lowered his hands from her back to her substantial bottom. He then suggested that they sit down on his small and ratty old sofa and with little or no further conversation, they began to explore each other's bodies more attentively.

He was easy game as he was only wearing a flimsy pair of shorts. Melisa, not so much, as she was wearing tight jeans, a buttoned short-sleeved shirt, a complicated bra that fastened at the front, and a flimsy pair of panties, but eventually Dick managed to get them all off and repairing to his bedroom, they commenced performing the beast with two backs.

Oh, what a relief, he thought, *to be back in the saddle again*. While lying on his back enjoying a post-coital sense of satisfaction he hadn't experienced since parting with Miss Delaney, he was gazing wistfully at Melissa, who appeared to have fallen asleep. *She's not at all bad*, he thought, gazing at her naked profile. *She's soft and gentle, even if on the heavy side compared with Annabelle. She is rather warm and comforting. He placed his arm around her and snuggled closer thinking how lucky he was.* "Not bad. Not bad at all."

While happily thus engaged, Melissa turned on her side and opened her eyes before stroking him with her soft and gentle fingertips until he was once more aroused, and they went at it again. Then Melisa dressed, bade him farewell, and disappeared into the night.

The following morning, Dick was up bright and early. He enjoyed a hearty breakfast of sausage, eggs, and bacon and was planning the day ahead of him. Firstly, he would saddle up one of the horses and explore some of his territory.

Donning his police issue cavalry twill breeches, boots and leggings, safari tunic, and pith helmet, he saddled Warlord and set out at a steady trot, wending his way along the dirt road that passed outside his house, intent on exploring further west toward a range of distant, gently rolling hills. As he progressed along the road, he found that it petered out to a narrow game trail, and he slowed Warlord to a walk, admiring the broad savannah that lay before him with the occasional msasa tree breaking the outline of the otherwise flat and scrubby bush. The msasa trees, with their broad flat tops, provided large shady areas for the game to rest during the heat of the day.

They had been gone for about an hour when suddenly Warlord stopped and began whinnying and shaking his head, then shying sideways. Dick, who had become a decent horseman, stroked Warlord's neck and spoke softly to him, trying to calm him down and looking for the snake that had perhaps frightened him. Then, out of the long grass beside them, came a great roar and a huge lioness leaped onto Warlord's hindquarters. The horse bucked to shake the lioness loose with little result, except that Dick went flying over the horse's head, landing on the stony ground.

In a blind panic, Dick ran to the nearest tree and shinned up so fast he was fifteen feet off the ground in time to see Warlord galloping hell for leather back to the house with his stirrups flapping frantically in all directions. The lioness, however, had been joined by two others and all three were below the tree, taking turns reaching up and tearing off chunks of bark with their huge claws, growling, roaring, and baring their teeth as they attempted to reach him.

Dick was petrified, thinking this was the end. In fact, he peed himself as he tried to climb higher, but to his dismay, he found that he was at the uppermost extremity of the msasa tree that he had selected and the branches all around him looked too flimsy and weak to support his weight.

He wedged himself tightly in the tree and watched the three lionesses prowling down below before they lay down and gazed upwards, obviously with the expectation that he would eventually come down, and they could have lunch. Their dreadful smell alone terrified him and no doubt that was what alerted his horse in the first place.

Looking at his wristwatch, he saw that it was shortly after noon. He had no means of contacting anyone, his horse had bolted, and he considered himself up the proverbial creek without a paddle.

As time wore on, the lionesses became restless, began circling the tree, and attempted once again to climb it. *Obviously,* he thought, *lions were not very good at climbing trees.* He had by this time stopped shaking, but dusk was falling and to the west, he saw the sky turn a deep crimson as the sun slowly dipped below the horizon. Then darkness fell, and he began to shiver for, even in darkest Africa, the nights could get surprisingly cold.

He dared not fall asleep; his perch had become awfully uncomfortable; and he could still hear the lions below grunting and growling. No doubt he wasn't the only one who was getting hungry.

His thoughts turned to simple things. His life back in England, his misadventures with Annabelle Delaney, his kidnapping, the murder of Solly Farringham, and now, returning to the present, being stuck up a tree with three lions waiting to eat him.

The long night passed slowly and after what seemed an eternity, he saw the beginnings of the sunrise. As the light grew stronger, he imagined hearing the faint noise of an engine and within minutes a police Land Rover crested the rise, ominously with a body box on the roof, following the game trail that he had taken the previous day. He waved and shouted and looking down saw that the lions had departed. Eventually, the Land Rover stopped right below his perch and who should step out but Taffy.

"What are you doing up there, you silly bugger?" he shouted. Dick quickly scrambled down the tree and leaped into the Land Rover, slamming the door behind him before collapsing like a jibbering idiot and bursting into tears. Taffy leisurely climbed back into the driver's seat, shaking his head as he waited for Dick to stop blubbering. When he eventually pulled himself together, he told Taffy of his narrow escape.

"Where was your rifle?"

When Dick told Taffy he hadn't taken one, his only comment was "Did you think you were out for a ride on Rotten Row?" which is, of course, the famous horse-riding pathway on the south side of London's Hyde Park.

"When going out in the bush, always take your rifle, whether you're on horseback or in a vehicle, and keep it close by. There's wild game everywhere."

"But how did you find me?" asked Dick, quietly thanking God that he did. Taffy explained that when Warlord turned up at Umbedzi police station the previous afternoon, all torn up and without his rider, one of Dick's sergeants guessed what had happened and telephoned Taffy. By the time Taffy got over there and took one look at Warlord, he decided that as it was getting dark and guessing that Dick was done for anyway, he wouldn't head out to look for his remains until daybreak. The game trail was apparently easy to follow, as there were horse droppings along the way, together with splashes of blood from Warlord's injuries as he desperately bolted for home.

On the drive back to the station, Dick thought about the strange-looking leather thing that hung on the coat rack behind the door and learned, when describing it to Taffy, that it was, in fact, a rifle scabbard or holster specially designed for attaching to a saddle. Dick gave himself a good talking to when they arrived back at the station and made a point of immediately attaching the scabbard to his military saddle.

Next on his agenda was to visit Warlord, who was back in his stable, munching on some fodder provided by the houseboy Shadreck. The horse looked its usual docile self but had several huge lacerations on its hind quarters caused by the great claws of the lioness. He telephoned the veterinarian in Chimuka, who agreed to come out that afternoon.

Thanking Taffy profusely for coming to his rescue, Dick assured him that he would come over to Zumba the following weekend and buy him a few Chimbukas.

That evening, he was sitting in his living quarters enjoying a beer and thanking his lucky stars for his truly miraculous escape when the telephone rang. "Hello. Umbedzi police," he said when a frantic voice he recognized as being Melissa's began whispering to him, "oh, Dick, what am I going to do. I've been trying to reach you all day."

"Arthur came home on Saturday night while I was at your place and when I reached the house, he demanded that I tell him where I had been. He knew that the bar closed at ten o'clock, and I didn't get home until almost two the next morning. I didn't know what to tell him, and I was frightened, so I told him I had been at the police station reporting that I had been assaulted and raped."

Her voice became louder and more hysterical as she recounted the pack of lies that she had dreamed up and Dick realized that he was to be her alibi if Arthur came calling. He told Melisa to calm down, that he would make a false entry in the crime register, and that if Arthur decided to check on her story, he would be able to corroborate it. Unfortunately, he didn't question her thoroughly enough and consequently, the false docket that he prepared was not detailed enough to deal with subsequent events when a large young man came into his small charge office the following morning. Dressed in the customary safari suit, long woolen socks, *veldskoens*, and a broad-brimmed bush hat, he had a tanned and rugged look about him. Dick guessed immediately who he was, swallowed, put on what he hoped was a benign expression, and wished him a good day. The man nodded in acknowledgment and identified himself as Arthur Van Tonder, husband of Melissa Van

Tonder, who worked the bar at the Umbedzi Hotel and had been raped two nights ago.

"What are the cops doing about it?" he asked. "Melissa's gone all to pieces and isn't making any sense. She keeps changing her story but says she was attacked by a *kaffir* as she was walking home from the pub, dragged into the bushes, and had her clothes torn off her. She screamed and struggled. He beat her until she submitted and allowed him to have his way with her. Is that what she told you?"

Dick quickly agreed that it was exactly what his wife reported and that they were making every effort to trace the culprit. But with so little to go on, it was almost impossible to guarantee a successful outcome.

To Dick's horror, Arthur reached over the counter with his left hand, grabbed Dick by the tunic collar, and dragged him to within an inch of his face. "You lying little pommie shit. She arrived home without a scratch on her, with her clothing intact, and told me it was an Indian bloke who had attacked her."

"I've heard from the blokes at the pub that you've been chatting her up and now I know for certain that you've been screwing her. This is what you'll get for your troubles."

With a roundhouse punch, he hit Dick right on the point of his nose hard enough that Dick heard the crunch of cartilage as his nose broke to the right, and he dropped to the floor. Sometime later, Dick dragged himself to his feet. Van Tonder had thankfully disappeared, and he staggered to the bathroom where he studied himself in the mirror. His previously somewhat aristocratic and aquiline nose was now swollen and definitely bent, with blood pouring from both nostrils over his mouth and chin and dripping onto his smartly pressed and starched police uniform.

With several groans of dismay, Dick retired to his bed for the rest of the day after telling Shadreck that he was not to be disturbed under any circumstances. The next day went by, and he neither slept nor ate. His nose swelled out of all proportion and as he looked gloomily into the mirror, he recalled the lines of a song he had heard his parents sing back in London when he was just a child, a song that began "Two lovely black eyes. Oh! What a surprise," and smiled.

On the second day, he had a visitor. None other than Melissa Van Tonder who—surprise, surprise—also had two black eyes. "Oh, Dick, I'm so sorry.

I've really made a mess of things and Arthur's kicked me out. Can I stay here with you?"

With a groan, Dick realized that the hole he'd dug for himself had now gotten a lot deeper, and taking another look at Melissa, his misery bottomed out. She no longer had a pretty face, which was her sole redeeming feature. She was definitely fat, and she no longer held the appeal that he first felt when meeting her in the bar. But what could he do? She was here, homeless and destitute, and he was at least partly to blame.

"Okay, you'd better come in," he said. Before the words were barely out of his mouth, she struggled through the door with two large suitcases and a scruffy little dog on a pink leash, which immediately began growling and barking at him.

His efforts to settle her in his spare bedroom met with a variety of reactions, none of which were pleasant. Firstly, it was tears, then the screaming accusations that he had led her on, and finally the obstinate refusal to sleep anywhere but in his bed with him right beside her.

He eventually acquiesced and that night, having packed her off to bed about two hours earlier, tried to creep silently beneath the bedsheet, but she stirred instantly. Pulling him closer, she demanded that he make love to her. Little Tommy refused to cooperate, remaining small and flaccid despite Melissa's desperate attempts to get a rise out of him. This led to more tears, but thankfully she eventually climbed sulkily out of bed and went to the other bedroom, leaving him in peace.

The following morning, studying his face in the mirror, he delicately and very carefully shaved three days' worth of stubble and could see that his bruises had turned from blue to yellow and were beginning to fade. His nose, however, was another matter. Although the swelling had slightly subsided, it was still bent.

Entering the kitchen, he was surprised to find Melissa and Shadreck hard at work, preparing omelets, sausages, bacon, and a mound of toast with a jar of thick-cut marmalade sitting on the table.

Things always look better in the morning, thought Dick. Even Melisa was looking a bit better than she had the night before although that was stretching it a bit. When she joined him at the table, her scruffy little dog sat beside her, looking balefully at Dick and giving the odd growl or two.

In an effort to make conversation, Dick asked if she had slept well, to which she replied that she had hardly slept at all. She then tearfully admitted that she didn't know what she was to do. Arthur hated her. Dick wasn't interested in her, and she had no one else to turn to. He tried to cheer her up, telling her that she still had a job and could probably find she could support herself in some cheap lodgings somewhere in town.

That set her off again. First more tears, then a tirade about all men being bastards, and then her dog started barking at him and baring his teeth when he tried to comfort her.

Finally, it was agreed that she could stay at the cottage for a few more days while she sorted things out, and while she did so, he had to go on patrol and wouldn't be back until early next week.

He hastily packed a few things and threw his police tent and cooking paraphernalia into the Land Rover, not forgetting his Lee Enfield .303 rifle and a couple of boxes of ammunition. Accompanied by Constable Silas, Dick set off. Not knowing where he was going, he drove into Umbedzi, picking up some food items from the local grocery store on the way before heading west toward the far-off range of hills that marked the western boundary of his police district and the border with Angola.

Once he reached the foothills about an hour later, he looked for a suitable camping spot and before long found an ideal patch of dry and stony ground with a slowly flowing stream trickling beside it. Here, he set up camp assisted by Constable Silas. They gathered up some stones, built a small fire pit, and then went hunting for firewood, with Dick clutching his loaded .303 as he constantly cast his eyes from left to right, fearful of another encounter with the wild creatures of Africa.

They got busy erecting a ridge tent for them to sleep in. Then, having collected an impressive pile of firewood, they built a fire and watched the African sun slip below the hills, turning the sky a flaming red and casting the skyline into a beautiful and panoramic silhouette. Dick thought how lucky he was to be here in the solitude of Central Africa rather than in the smoky hustle and bustle of the streets of London.

Silas, with the aid of four stout sticks, placed a steel griddle over the open fire and commenced preparing their evening meal, which consisted of a can of bully beef for Dick and some sadza for Silas, who even went to the trouble of boiling a billycan full of water to make tea. Dick decided that although he had never smoked, he would buy a pipe and give it a try, for this provided the perfect setting.

The following morning, they broke camp and Dick decided to turn back to the east on a different dirt road that Silas insisted would link up with the road to Zumba.

Chapter Five

Dick was now into his second day of driving through the wilderness but still within his area of jurisdiction, an area that he would get to know very well in the foreseeable future. They had encountered no wildlife at close quarters although they had seen kudus, zebras, and even elephants way off in the distance. They had called at several small collections of native huts, which Silas had informed him were called *kraals*. Using Silas as his interpreter, he introduced himself to the village headmen.

Every kraal that they visited was enclosed inside tall grass and thorn bush fencing and contained several mud and thatched huts, several women and *piccanins*, and an assortment of chickens and goats, usually some mangy-looking cattle and several half-starved dogs. The elderly headmen explained that most of the family's menfolk were working in the South African gold mines, where they earned good money and sent a good portion of it home to help feed the family. They explained that the goats and cattle were let out of the enclosure during the daytime to graze but were always brought inside well before dark.

As today was Saturday, Dick intended to make an early start and drive to Zumba to visit Taffy Lloyd-Jones and buy those beers that he had promised him. As it was approaching one o'clock in the afternoon, both he and Silas were feeling peckish, and they began looking for a shady spot to pull over and have lunch when a roaming group of guinea fowl began to cross their path. Excitedly, Silas urged Dick to run them down for these round, spotted birds with naked heads and feathered crests are about the same size, and as tasty to the Africans as chickens. Silas was obviously envisaging some relish to add to his sadza and to share with his colleagues that night once they arrived at the Zumba police station. Dick was looking forward to a salami sandwich and tea for lunch and, later that day, a few beers with Taffy while Silas would feast on guinea fowl if Dick's driving skills were up to it.

Dick accelerated into the flock of birds, sending them running in all directions. He heard a few thumps; black and white feathers flew everywhere and when he stopped, Silas alighted and whooped with joy for Dick had bagged three guinea fowl for the pot.

They found a suitable resting place nearby and Silas was meticulously plucking one of the guinea fowl while Dick prepared their sandwiches when a series of short barks and howls erupted all around them. Whereas before they had seen nothing but dry brown pasture, they now saw upwards of a dozen wild and rangy-looking dogs closing in on them. The animals' tri-colored coats, white fluffy tails, and Micky Mouse ears clearly identified them to Dick as Cape hunting dogs, and their bared teeth and saliva-dripping jaws left no doubt in his mind as to their intent.

Dick thought of Taffy's earlier warning: "When going out in the bush always take your rifle whether you're on horseback or in a vehicle and keep it close. There's wild game everywhere." His rifle was in the Land Rover, not close. *I'm an idiot*, he thought, *What should I do?*

Slowly, he edged toward the Land Rover, his knees shaking while Silas brazenly began shouting and waving his arms at the savage pack, a tactic that appeared to be keeping them at bay. Dick reached the vehicle, but as he opened the door, the pack closed in on Silas, with the leader rushing at him and seizing his arm in its powerful jaws.

Dick grabbed his .303, drew the bolt back, chambered a round, and fired. *Click*. No rounds were in the magazine and now two more dogs had set upon Silas. He began screaming as the pack slowly dragged him to the ground, their jaws tearing at him as they began eating him alive. Dick, now safely ensconced inside his Land Rover, began scrabbling around in search of the ammunition boxes. Thankfully, he found them quickly, filled the rifle's magazine with bullets, poked the muzzle of his rifle out of the window, and fired twice in the hope of scaring the dogs off.

This did the trick and, as the dogs backed off, it allowed Silas time to regain his feet and shuffle over to the Land Rover. Once inside, Dick examined Silas' wounds, which were mainly gashes on his arms and legs. "We need to get you to a hospital, chop-chop," said Dick. Abandoning their lunch, they sped off to the small town of Zumba, where he presumed there would be a hospital or at least a clinic where Silas could be patched up.

As this was Dick's first visit to Zumba, he was at a loss to locate assistance for Silas, so he pulled into the only petrol station on the main street and was quickly directed to the local hospital. Once there, he rushed inside and explained what had happened and seconds later two orderlies ran out with a gurney. They put Silas, whose wounds were still pouring blood and his face turning a deathly gray, onto their gurney and whisked him inside.

Once Silas had been admitted and was being injected and stitched up, Dick used his police radio to call the Zumba police station, spoke with Taffy, and agreed to meet with him at Zumba's main pub, the strangely named Fiddler's Elbow. Following Taffy's directions, he soon found Zumba's favorite drinking hole. Much to his surprise, the Fiddler's Elbow was a freestanding pub and not, as Dick expected, simply a bar adjoining the town's small hotel. The pub, although small, was very busy. The walls were hung with the mounted heads of several species of African wildlife along with a selection of Africana, such as knobkerries, game skin drums, and even a Zulu warrior shield and short stabbing spear.

The floor seemed to be simply made of compacted earth; the walls were brick with a concrete foundation and completing the ensemble, a roof that was constructed of raw timbers and what appeared to be insect-ridden thatching.

The Fiddler's Elbow was by no means luxurious. In fact, Dick thought it more resembled a large, dark, and primitive African dwelling, though there were a few framed photographs hanging on the walls together with a large British Union Jack flag and the national flag of Warania. The few mounted game heads included a magnificent eland, which Dick suspected had been donated by Taffy.

The bar was quite busy, mainly with hardy-looking men enjoying a Saturday lunchtime beer, but Dick also saw two women, one of whom was tall, slender, and very pretty, and two large dogs sprawled at their masters' feet.

When Dick walked in, Taffy gazed at Dick's broken nose and black eyes. He shook his head sadly. "Dick, you stupid bastard. What the hell have you done this time?"

Dick just shrugged his shoulders and asked the barman for two Chimbukas. He then related the events of the past few days. Ignoring his friend's pitiful account of his romantic encounter with Melissa, Taffy asked, when referring to the attack by the wild dogs, "Didn't you have any raw meat in the truck? If you had thrown that at them, they would probably have let your poor constable alone." Dick thought of the three guinea fowls that he had run over, two of which were still lying dead in his Land Rover. They might have done the trick although Silas wouldn't have been too happy about losing his dinner.

As the evening wore on, Dick couldn't help being fascinated by the Fiddler's Elbow. It was, in many ways, very crude yet unique at the same time. It had a long bar that extended the full width of the building and an assortment of tables and chairs, taking up the rest of the floor space. He couldn't resist asking Taffy why the pub had such an unusual name and Taffy, smiling, called over to a slim middle-aged man smartly dressed in a safari suit and sporting a red silk cravat at his throat. "Hey, Percy. Have you got a minute?"

Percy joined them and Taffy introduced them to each other. "Percy, this is my compatriot from across the river, Dick Starling. And Dick, this is Percival Thorndike, late of the Royal Philharmonic Orchestra. Percy, why don't you tell Dick how your pub got its name?"

"Well, do you want the short version or the long version?" asked Percy.

"Oh, definitely the long version," replied Dick. "We've got plenty of time."

"Very well, you asked for it. I attended the Royal Academy of Music in London, intent on becoming a first-rate professional violinist. I succeeded and shortly afterward became a member of the Royal Philharmonic Orchestra, a lifetime ambition."

"After a year or so of playing with the Royal Philharmonic, an aunt of mine died and left me five thousand pounds in her will and shortly afterward someone who I believed was a friend told me of a Stradivarius that he knew was for sale. Of course, you're probably aware that a Strad is the most sought-after violin in the world, and I couldn't resist at least looking at it."

"The instrument looked authentic. An old and faded label could be seen through one of the elongated f-holes in the face of the violin and the sound it produced was fantastically mellow. On impulse, I bought it for a little over four thousand pounds, thinking I was making the deal of the century, only to learn much later that it was a fake. Nevertheless, I used it for several years as I played with the Royal Philharmonic, for it was indeed a fine violin."

"Then something strange happened, not to my violin, but to my right elbow. I kept noticing that as I drew my bow across the strings of the violin, my elbow became increasingly painful and on three different occasions, I dropped the bow completely while in concert. Consultations with various doctors concluded that I had a form of tendonitis commonly known as tennis elbow and in spite of a variety of injections and other treatments, I was eventually told that it couldn't be cured."

"I was at a loss as to how to deal with my problem. Music and the violin, in particular, was my life and now it was snatched away from me. Then I had an idea. No one knew my Stradivarius was a fake. I could try to sell it as an original, which would be worth several hundred thousand pounds or more, and if successful, flee to somewhere in the world where no one knew me. And that is what I did. I now live comfortably in Zumba and enjoy running my little pub." Pointing to a large wooden crest hanging above the bar, he said, "I have that to remind me that sometimes a twist of fate is needed to break from the mold."

Dick looked closely at the carved wooden crest hanging over the bar and sure enough, a beautifully carved violin was displayed at a forty-five-degree angle, crossed by a man's bare arm with a prominent and slightly roseate-tinted elbow. On the scroll below were carved the words *Ik Hatum Tendonitis*. Whether this was Latin or simply Percy's sense of humor, Dick didn't know, but it made him laugh.

Dick thanked Percy for telling his strange tale. He couldn't believe how many interesting and unusual characters he had encountered in his short time in Warania compared to the eighteen years he had spent in England. *Perhaps,* he thought, *most of the interesting people born in Britain just emigrated.* Dick and Taffy became more and more intoxicated as the afternoon turned to evening and, having eaten nothing but a few bags of potato crisps, at closing time they staggered out to their respective vehicles for the short drive back to Taffy's digs. Dick did have the forethought of using the pub's telephone to call the local hospital and was told that Silas would be remaining overnight for observation, and all being well, he would be released the following morning.

Upon entering Taffy's house, Dick was almost knocked over by a huge dog. Taffy said his dog was a Rhodesian ridgeback named Bentley, and this was his usual welcome to first-time visitors. Once introductions had been dealt with, Dick was aware of a distinctly musty smell, and it didn't take him long to realize that it was coming from all around him. Adorning every wall, nook, and crevice were the mounted heads of animals ranging from a tiny duiker to one huge Cape Buffalo head with a boss of at least thirty-six inches. The house was considerably larger than Dick's accommodation in Umbedzi and the furnishings were definitely better.

A lion skin, complete with the animal's mounted head, lay in front of an open fireplace; its teeth bared; and its glassy eyes fixed in a staring gaze. Each armchair had its own footstool made from an elephant's foot. Incredibly, on one wall was mounted an elephant's right ear, which was almost exactly the same shape as the continent of Africa. Carefully painted upon it were the locations of several well-known cities, including Johannesburg and Cape Town to the south, Salisbury, Lusaka, and Chimuka in Central Africa and Tangier, Lagos, and Cairo farther to the north. Taffy appeared with a couple of bottles of Chimbuka as a nightcap and said that tomorrow, being Sunday, they would go game hunting.

Pointing at the window, Taffy said, "There's not much game around here anymore, but if we go out by those *kopjes,* the small hills that you can see out on the ridge, we'll probably see some warthog, kudu, and giraffe. Giraffes are not very good for eating, but the kudu makes excellent *biltong*. Did you know that the Yanks have something similar to biltong that they call beef jerky? I've tried it, but it's not nearly as good."

By this time, Dick had fallen asleep in his chair and hadn't heard a word nor had he drunk his beer. Taffy went off to bed, leaving his guest snoring quietly with Bentley curled up at his feet.

Chapter Six

The following morning, someone was up bright and early making coffee when Dick awoke with a nasty headache, wondering where the hell he was. The aroma of coffee must have woken him, and he could hear some noisy clattering in the small kitchen, so he put an appearance at the breakfast table and was surprised to find a large African woman, barefooted and wearing a white overall, standing at the stove cooking up eggs and bacon.

"Mornin', boss," she greeted him, "breakfast and coffee comin' right up." She set before him a huge mug full to the brim with steaming coffee. Taffy strolled in, wished Dick a good morning, and slapped the cook on her very ample backside. "I see you've already met my gorgeous housegirl, Rosemary."

"Aye, aye," she laughed, "you no' slap my bottom when my husband still be in bed just outside."

An hour or so later, having demolished huge breakfasts, they set off in Taffy's Land Rover with Bentley's head wedged between them, tongue hanging out and drooling with anticipation while his tail beat a steady tattoo against the side window. Dick took his standard issue .303 Lee Enfield rifle with a fully loaded magazine, while Taffy took a more sophisticated Ruger Hawkeye .30–06. They had been driving over rough terrain for almost an hour and were now in an area where the elephant grass was thick and higher than the roof of their Land Rover.

Dick couldn't understand how Taffy could drive through the stuff, but they continued to crawl unerringly forward, parting the grass and flattening it below their vehicle. Eventually, the grass thinned out, and they saw in the distance some zebra and two giraffes, and closer, an adult warthog with five or six piglets trotting along behind her. Dick was thoroughly enjoying the experience, imagining himself in a Dr. Livingstone/Stanley-like scenario, exploring darkest Africa, when Taffy spotted two large kudu antelope way off in the distance.

Taffy said, "We'll leave the Land Rover here and approach them carefully on foot. Move slowly and not directly toward them. They're very skittish. And no talking. Fortunately, the wind's blowing in the right direction."

Dick, nervously clutching his .303, followed Taffy's slow and steady movements until they were less than one hundred feet from their quarry. "I'll let you take this one, but remember, aim for the high shoulder for a clean kill."

Dick, while still standing, shouldered his .303 and took aim. He stared over his sight at the beautiful animal, whose huge twisted horns appeared to be almost five feet in length. He continued to look the bull kudu over and was amazed at its height and its coloring with six or seven vertical white stripes on its huge brown and gray body and a white 'V' below its eyes that pointed down toward its nose.

It was looking straight at him as he stood perfectly still with Taffy right behind him, almost breathing down his neck. He had the animal clearly in his sights but couldn't pull the trigger. He knew in a matter of seconds that Taffy would fire and deliberately raised his barrel six inches before firing into the air, startling the two kudus that immediately bounded off into the long grass and were lost from sight in a matter of seconds.

"You bloody fool," roared Taffy. "How could you have missed? He was as good a sitting target as you could ever wish for."

"I didn't miss, and I didn't want you to kill him either, so I fired to scare him away. Furthermore, I don't think I'm cut out for hunting, so let's just go home."

An uncomfortable silence pervaded the Land Rover all the way back to Zumba and when they reached the police station Dick packed his belongings into his own Land Rover and left, collecting a stitched-up and much-recovered Constable Silas from the hospital along the way, feeling disgusted with Taffy and sorry for the glorious wildlife that was slowly being decimated by people of his ilk.

On the long drive home, Dick couldn't help but wonder what he would find when he got there. A chastened Melissa, a Melissa making herself comfortable, or a wild and angry Melissa waiting to pounce as soon as he walked in the door. In fact, he found none of those, for she had departed, taking with her all her belongings and her miserable little dog.

When questioning Shadreck, the only explanation he got was "The missus left yesterday. Don't know where she gone." That suited Dick quite nicely.

As the days passed, Dick's face returned to its normal shape and color, with the exception of his nose, which he thought made him look rather dashing now that the swelling had gone down. Gazing at himself in the mirror, he thought that he would look even more dashing if he grew a mustache and sideburns, the former to make him look a bit older and the latter coming back into fashion. He then went into town to buy a pipe, some tobacco, and provisions.

A few days later, when Dick answered the telephone it was Taffy, calling to tell him that his constables had located the man they had been talking about. "The thin miserable-looking bugger who's handy with a knife, whom you call Misery Guts. He's still wearing flashy shirts, and can you believe he even pulled a knife on my constables? But they quickly sorted him out, and guess what? After handcuffing him, they searched his house and found a colorful tattered pink and orange shirt that matched the description of the shirt you said he was wearing at the time he mugged you. He's locked up in our cells right now and if you want him, you'd better get back to Zumba pronto as I can only keep him for forty-eight hours."

Relieved that Taffy had apparently forgiven him for his ineptitude at game hunting, he climbed into his Land Rover, this time taking Sergeant Zibando along as Constable Silas was restricted to office duties until his wounds healed. The journey took almost two hours but Dick was rewarded at the sight of Misery Guts, unmistakably the man who had robbed, and assaulted him several months previously, sitting in a cell and nursing a fat lip. "He tried to escape and pulled a knife on us," explained Taffy's constable, shaking his wooden truncheon in the direction of his prisoner. "He's one no good skellum."

Taffy seemed pleased to see Dick, despite their earlier dispute, and gave him the torn shirt that had been recovered from Misery Guts' house. It was the same shirt and Dick was delighted.

"How about going over to the Fiddler's Elbow for a couple of Chimbukas before I haul Misery Guts out of your cell and off to Umbedzi?"

Taffy immediately agreed and relieved that they were pals once again, Dick happily paid for their beers before leaving.

Once arriving back at Umbedzi, Dick phoned the main police station in Chimuka and spoke with Detective Inspector Wally Smith. He explained that in addition to Little Fatty's corpse, which he had already told Smith about, he now had Misery Guts in custody, the man who undoubtedly killed Little Fatty, and who was in possession of the shirt that Dick could swear he was wearing at the time of the mugging. The only culprit now still at large was the driver and Dick could not give a decent description of him and doubted that he could find him. Their best chance was to find the dilapidated Ford Cortina that he was driving. After racking his brains, Dick described the vehicle as being a dull gray with lots of rust, a cracked windscreen, bald tires, fancy chromium wing mirrors, and a number plate that began with the letter 'C'.

Detective Smith told Dick to bring his prisoner to the central station in Chimuka where he would be interrogated and Dick could make a further statement describing how the culprit had been arrested. Further statements from Taffy and his constable would be obtained by Smith.

Upon his arrival at Chimuka's large police station, he met with Detective Smith, handed Misery Guts over, and proudly presented the scrap of pink and orange cloth that he had prized from Little Fatty's dead fingers, along with the ripped and torn shirt that was discovered at the time of Misery Guts' arrest. A perfect match.

"Oh, well," said Smith. "It looks like we've got sunshine here on one count of murdering his partner in crime, in addition to all the stuff that he did to you. Well done. You might be interested in knowing that we fingerprinted that fat chappy that you brought into the mortuary and discovered who he was. His name's Isaac Ndebi, and he has a mile-long list of previous convictions but was mainly a con artist, and guess what, his brother Phineas Ndebi worked at Police General Headquarters. It must have been him who found out about your arrival and tipped his brother off. Now we've got him locked up as well, awaiting trial for stealing information from headquarters and being an accomplice to the mugging."

A very satisfied and complacent Dick returned home, carefully avoiding the bar at the Umbedzi Hotel, and got on the phone with Taffy to update him on his conversation with Detective Smith before he began experimenting with his pipe.

Chapter Seven

Fully recovered from his beating by Arthur Van Tonder and admiring the shadows on his face that were the beginnings of a mustache and sideburns, he decided to find out what the CID was doing about the murder of his predecessor, Inspector Solly Farringham, and his constable.

He first called Detective Smith, as he knew no one else in CID, and was told that the murder was being investigated by his superior, Detective Chief Inspector Kevin Soames, and put him through.

"Ah yes," said Soames when Dick explained who he was and why he was calling. "You're the silly bugger who was stripped naked by your reception committee near the airport and picked up by Lilly Mumford. We all had a good laugh over that, but I see that you caught two of the bastards—one dead, the other alive. Well done, by the way."

"Thank you," said Dick, somewhat taken aback by the fact that he had been the laughingstock of the Criminal Investigation Department. Not wanting to get off on the wrong foot with Soames, he chose to ignore the insult and asked how the investigation was going with respect to Inspector Farringham's murder.

"Oh, not very well, I'm afraid. The theft of cattle, or as the Americans like to call it, cattle rustling, is becoming more prevalent, and we've done all the usual stuff. We've put out a nationwide alert to all police stations, giving the descriptions that we got from our only witness and a description of the four cattle that were stolen. They were all branded with Bert Lillyford's cattle ranch logo, a circle with the letter 'L' inside it, but they've probably been re-branded to disguise or cover the brand completely or, even likelier, they will have been eaten by now."

"Would you mind if I do a bit of investigating on my own, sir? Perhaps I could interview the witness again. He might have remembered something since you last spoke with him."

"By all means, old chap. Anything that you can do to help us find these blighters would be more than welcome, but I should warn you that the two men I sent to interview the witness, a herd boy if I remember correctly, couldn't get much information out of him. Hold on, and I'll look for the location where you can find him."

Dick waited patiently on the telephone until Soames came back.

"Okay. His name is Tambo Chiweshe. He's only fourteen or so, doesn't speak any English, and lives with his family in the Ngonko Tribal Trust Land in a kraal close to Lillyford's ranch. Lillyford will tell you how to find him."

Dick thanked him and rang off. Lillyford's ranch was close to the eastern edge of his police area, but he knew where it was. He was well known to the police for although he was a successful and wealthy rancher, he was known to be very harsh with his African staff and had been warned on several occasions of his intolerance and brutality toward them. Consequently, Lillyford was no friend of the police and Dick knew that any discussion he had with him would be, at the very least, awkward.

The following day, he drove over to Lillyford's ranch, a journey of over an hour, taking Sergeant Zibando with him. Driving up the long dirt road to the farmhouse, he was surprised to see how well laid out the property was. The road was lined on both sides with white-washed rocks and bordered by elegant trees whose branches hung in a canopy over the roadway.

As he crested the rise, he could see ahead of him what appeared to be an immaculate Cape Dutch mansion, similar to those he had seen in brochures promoting the wine estates of Stellenbosch and far from the image of the farmhouse that Dick had been expecting.

Parking in the forecourt, Dick marched up the steps to a pair of huge oak doors and pulled on a plaited rope, which presumably activated a doorbell or knocker. Within seconds, a black servant, dressed in a white tunic, trousers, and shoes and wearing a red tasseled fez opened the door.

"Yes, sir. May I help you?"

"I would like to speak with Mr. Lillyford, please."

"Just one moment, sir," the servant replied, disappearing back into the house and closing the door behind him.

A minute or so later, a white man who Dick presumed to be Lillyford opened the door. Dick thought the man to be in his fifties. Deeply tanned, wearing the usual Waranian outfit of shorts and a bush jacket, and with an intimidating scowl, he definitely looked miserable and unfriendly.

"Yes, what do you want?" he snapped.

"Good morning. Mr. Lillyford, I presume?"

"Yes. Get on with it, man."

"Well, I'm investigating the theft of four of your cattle and the subsequent murder of Inspector Farringham and his constable. I need to speak with the herd boy who apparently witnessed the murders. I understand that you can tell me where to find him."

"Yes, I can. The useless little bastard lives in a kraal about three miles from here in the TTL. My houseboy can tell you exactly where."

"Simon," he shouted over his shoulder, "come here and tell this excuse for a police officer where he can find that stupid little bastard Tambo."

"Hey, watch your language," shouted Dick as Simon came running at the double, but Lillyford pushed him roughly out of the door before slamming it in Dick's face.

Shaking his head in disgust, Dick asked Simon to get into the Land Rover and introduced him to Sergeant Zibando.

Simon spoke very good English and between the three of them, Dick and Zibando obtained clear directions as to how to find Tambo's kraal. Simon returned to Lillyford's mansion and Dick hastily departed the Lillyford cattle ranch with no intention of returning if he could possibly avoid it.

Following Simon's directions, from there they drove further east along the paved road, passing an orange grove whose huge trees were laden with fruit, and they were soon in the Ngonko Tribal Trust Land. It was soon apparent to Dick that the irrigation and care given to the soil and vegetation that he had left behind was totally lacking in the TTL, for the area was in deep contrast to the green and lush pastures of Lillyford's property and the orange grove. Now, they were in the midst of an almost barren landscape. The only animal life that Dick could see was several goats scattered across the land, contentedly chewing on any scrap of grass or shrub that they could find.

Before long, Zibando told Dick to turn left off of the paved road onto a dirt track and after traveling for about one mile, he pointed out a small grass and thorn enclosure over which could be seen the thatched roofs of several huts. "That must be the boy's kraal," said Zibando as Dick drew up alongside the open entrance.

Zibando went inside and soon returned with a skinny youth of about fourteen. His head was knotted with small balls of short black and curly peppercorn hair, and he was barefoot, wearing only a ragged shirt and a dirty pair of shorts. His expression was one of trepidation and his eyes were wide open with fright.

Rather than put the boy into his police Land Rover, Dick stepped out and told Zibando to calm the kid down. "Tell him he isn't in any trouble. This is merely a routine inquiry."

After spending a few minutes assuring Tambo that they meant him no harm, Dick approached the subject of Farringham's murder and that of his constable. Dick fished around in his pockets, pulling out a roll of Polo mints and handing them to Tambo. This seemed to cheer the lad up and as he sucked on one of the Polos, he related what he had seen to Zibando, who translated it for Dick. Tambo explained that he had been working as a herd boy for Boss Lillyford, right on the fringes of the man's property. He was watching over a small herd of cattle when he saw that one of them, a young bull, had wandered away from the herd. The property was fenced, so he wasn't too worried, but after the animal had been gone for some time and was out of sight, he decided to take his stick and bring it back.

Slightly over a small rise, Tambo saw the young bull but was concerned to notice that a section of fencing was trampled flat. The bull had obviously escaped through the gap into the TTL. He ran back to Mr. Steenkamp, the overseer, who was his immediate boss and who worked for Boss Lillyford. After he reported what had happened, Steenkamp mounted his horse and rode over to where the broken fence lay. By this time, Tambo's small herd of cattle had reached it and were scattered all over the place.

Steenkamp, addressing Tambo in kitchen kaffir, swore and cursed at him, smacked him across the ear with the flat of his hand, and told him to help round up the cattle and bring them back onto Lillyford's property.

Once all the cattle they could find were herded together, Steenkamp repaired the fence, noting that it had been deliberately cut. When counting the cattle, he found that four were missing. This led to another smack around the ears for Tambo. "Go and bloody well find them and don't come back until you do."

Tambo, now fearful of losing his poorly paid job, studied the ground on the far side of the broken fence and noticed that not only were there cattle hoofprints in the dusty soil but also human shoe prints. He began following the prints until he was certain that he was on the path of the cattle thieves. His intent was to find them and then go to Mr. Lillyford's ranch, hoping that if the cattle were retrieved and the thieves arrested, he might keep his job.

Tambo walked all day, clearly seeing the cattle trail and what appeared to be four different sets of shoeprints. He could now see the direction in which they were headed and guessed that they would be well inside the tribal trust lands by nightfall.

He had some food and water that was intended for his lunch, but there was no time to eat. As dusk was falling, he found a small area of thorn bushes and bracken that would give him some protection from night predators. He ate the food and drank some of the water before curling up on the hard, dry ground to get some rest.

He woke as the sun was appearing on the eastern horizon and set off once more, following the trail of the cattle and the thieves. He had been walking for only about an hour when he heard voices close by. The flat terrain had become stonier, and he could see much larger rocks ahead. He crept closer and as he peered around one enormous rock, he saw four men with the four *mombies* they had stolen.

He was about to turn away and run for help when he heard someone shout in his local tongue, "Stay where you are," as two figures appeared from the other side. One was black, the other white. They were both policemen, and they were shouting not at him but at the four cattle thieves. The thieves jumped to their feet and one of them ran off. The African policeman chased after him and the white officer approached the three who had remained behind, speaking to them in English, but Tambo couldn't understand what he said. It was quite clear that he was arresting the three men, as he was holding a pair of handcuffs and had grabbed one man by the wrist.

Just then, one of the other men picked up a machete, known as a *panga*, and swung it at the police officer, striking him across the face and causing him to recoil and release his grip. The man with the panga struck him again and again until the officer fell screaming and shrieking as he curled up into a ball, trying to protect his head, but he eventually fell silent. The African constable, obviously hearing the commotion, came running back, but by this time the other two men had each retrieved a weapon, one a long-bladed knife and the other a knobkerrie, and were beating the white police officer to a bloody pulp.

Seeing the constable, they set about him with a vengeance, subjecting him to the same devastating treatment as his colleague until their friend returned. All four men began dancing around with glee before some semblance of normality returned, whereupon they rousted the four stolen cattle and continued on their way, leaving the two horribly mutilated police officers lying on the ground surrounded in pools of blood, blood that was slowly sinking into the parched earth.

Relating this horrific story had taken some time since Zibando had to translate everything that Tambo said into English. When he finished, Dick had several questions in mind.

"Sergeant, ask him if he had a good look at these four men. Would he recognize them if he saw them again? Can he describe them and what they were wearing?"

Again, Zibando questioned the boy, nodding encouragingly as Tambo answered most enthusiastically, raising his voice and waving his hands and arms to demonstrate a point.

Eventually, Zibando turned to Dick. "Yes, sir. He had a very good look at these men and seemed to believe that he could recognize all four of them if he were to see them again, especially the one who first struck Inspector Farringham. He describes him as being very tall and thin, a grown man with a short beard wearing a white tee shirt with some red and blue writing on it. He also wore a pair of very worn jeans tied around his waist with some string and was wearing large brown boots."

"Yes, and what about the others?"

"Not so good, sir. He says two of them looked like brothers and both appeared to be quite young. Perhaps seventeen or eighteen. They had no beards. One wore a red baseball cap, which he had on backward and both were wearing old and dirty white tackies."

"The fourth man, the one who ran away, was the youngest of all, perhaps a little older than Tambo himself. He wore a large pink shirt with buttons and a collar, but Tambo says that it was much too big for him. He thinks he must have been wearing shorts but couldn't see as the shirt came down to his knees. He also wore tackies." Dick took that to mean the cheap canvas plimsolls that were a common form of footwear worn by many Africans.

Dick sat digesting all this information and before long reached a decision. The attack on Farringham occurred about two weeks before he arrived at Umbedzi, and he had now been there for almost two months. The trail was cold and nothing could be gained by darting off into the Tribal Trust Land on a wild goose chase. He doubted that the cattle thieves had gone very far and were probably still in the area.

To have traveled beyond it would have drawn too much attention. He, therefore, returned to Umbedzi and prepared for a patrol of at least a week, which would entail loading tents, supplies, and cooking utensils and then a return to Ngonko Tribal Trust Land with Zibando, picking up Tambo and driving to the scene of the murder. He filled in Taffy as to his intentions, telling him that one thing that puzzled him was why, when Tambo was such a good witness, did DCI Soames' two African detectives not follow up more aggressively on these leads?

Chapter Eight

Two days later, Dick was dressed in uniform but wearing a khaki bush shirt instead of his usual safari jacket. Accompanied by Sergeant Zibando, he picked up Tambo from his kraal and handed the boy a new packet of Polo mints that he had remembered to pocket before leaving Umbedzi. They proceeded to the spot where Tambo had last seen the cattle thieves and from where the bodies of Farringham and his constable had been recovered. It was exactly as Tambo had described it. Huge boulders dominated the area and Dick saw the remnants of some animal droppings, cow pats that were undoubtedly those of the stolen bovines.

"Which way were they headed when they left here?" asked Dick. After Zibando put the question to Tambo, he pointed southeast, deeper into the Ngonko TTL.

They climbed back into the Land Rover and, with no track or road available, drove around the huge rocks and boulders and headed across the rugged terrain's parched and open landscape. From time to time, Zibando or Tambo pointed out faint shoeprints or signs of cattle having crossed this way. After driving for about thirty more minutes, the land became more fertile. Small trees and bushes became more prevalent, and when they saw more goats, Zibando said, "There must be a kraal nearby, sir. The villagers would not allow their goats to roam too far afield."

Sure enough, they soon spotted a small field of wilting corn next to the now familiar grass and thorn bush enclosure that contained a group of huts. They stopped and Zibando went to make inquiries, returning with a native woman carrying a young child balanced on her hip.

"This woman says that four men with some cattle were here several weeks ago, sir. She said that the kraal's menfolk were away working in Chimuka and these men, especially the older ones, demanded food and water. She said the cattle looked very healthy but were obviously tired. One of the old men in the kraal told her that she must give them what they wanted or he was sure they would make big trouble."

After questioning the woman further, it appeared that the old man had heard the two younger ones talking together about looking forward to reaching Tikwani's kraal and the woman knew that this kraal was only a one-day walk away. She said it was a busy place and had a market, but she warned that many troublemakers and skellums lived there.

Dick could see that this might be the lead that he needed and after Zibando had received directions, they were off again, driving toward Tikwani's kraal. Approximately thirty minutes later, they saw several trees ahead of them. The ground was becoming even more fertile and Zibando told Dick that there must be a river nearby. Ahead, they could see a collection of mud and grass huts in what appeared to be a small settlement. Some of the enclosures held cattle, and there were many goats roaming freely.

Dick drove into the center of what appeared to be a small village, but which was really no more than a cluster of kraals. When Zibando climbed out to question one of the villagers, he was told that although only one of the enclosures was called Tikwani's kraal, the name had been adopted by the entire community.

Dick was aware that the men that they were after were desperate and dangerous and had brought along both his Lee Enfield rifle and the station's .38 revolver, which was loaded with six rounds of ammunition and secured in a blue, military-style webbing holster on his belt.

Taking Tambo with them, Dick locked the Land Rover leaving his rifle inside and walked through the area, greeting any villagers they passed in an effort to appear nonthreatening, and even friendly, but they were casting glances in all directions, hoping to find some clue as to the cattle thieves or the stolen cattle.

Most of the cattle seen inside the individual kraal enclosures were thin and bony, not at all similar to the healthy cattle seen on Lillyford's ranch. Although taking into consideration their long walk and lack of proper nutrition for the past ten weeks, they would certainly be in a far worse state than when they were stolen.

A call from Zibando startled Dick, and turning toward his sergeant, he saw him standing at the entrance to a small kraal beckoning him to come over. When he did so, Zibando pointed to two cows, one standing and the other lying down. Both had Lillyford's cattle brand, a capital 'L' inside a circle, clearly visible on their haunches.

"Okay, fetch the headman out here and find out where these cattle came from." After disappearing into three separate huts, Zibando eventually reappeared with a white-haired barefooted and wrinkled old man dressed in a pair of khaki shorts and a loose woolen sweater. Zibando spoke with him and then told Dick, "He says that his son brought them to him several weeks ago, explaining that he had bought them from another village elder and was going to use them as *lobola* to purchase his new wife."

"Where is his son now, and what is his name?"

After conversing with the old man, Zibando replied, "His son's name is Wilfred Ngoshi, and he has gone to Tsitsi's kraal on the other side of the river to negotiate the price for his new bride. If successful, he will return here, collect the cattle, and take them to him."

"Very well," replied Dick. "Find out how we can get to Tsitsi's kraal with the Land Rover and then we'll go there and hopefully find our friend Wilfred."

Another long conversation followed before Zibando sighed and reported, "There is no bridge to cross the river, but he says it can be forded about one mile from here at this time of year because there has been no rain."

Tambo, who had been seated in the Land Rover throughout this lengthy conversation, was wide-eyed and nervous, realizing that this could have serious repercussions for him and his family, but the two policemen were paying him little attention, so he sat, working on one of the precious Polo mints that he was carefully sucking, trying to make it last as long as possible. "Okay. Get directions and let's go," said Dick. Fifteen minutes later, they were back in their Land Rover, heading for the ford. Dick could see that it was a regular crossing point and that the river, probably a tributary of the much larger Umfurudzi River, was only about twenty feet wide, the water was clear with a gravel bed, and he could see that it was only ten or eleven inches deep. The Land Rover crossed with no difficulty and, as the old man had directed, Tsitsi's kraal was a two-hour walk from the river, which Dick estimated to be about five miles.

They followed a rugged footpath, the Land Rover bouncing and crashing through the dry undergrowth on either side until they saw a clearing ahead with a sizable kraal nestled among the trees.

Dick sent Zibando in to confirm that this was Tsitsi's kraal and when he reappeared giving Dick the thumbs up, Dick told Tambo to stay in the vehicle and followed Zibando inside. The kraal contained several huts with three young women seated around a calabash, shucking corn from their cobs and nattering while a few chickens pecked at the ground and two tethered goats stood off to one side. Occasionally, one of the women would throw a piece of corn at the chickens, which caused quite a ruckus and made the women laugh.

The laughter died on their lips when they saw Dick, and he left it to Zibando to question them. Turning to Dick and pointing to the prettiest of the three women, Zibando said, "This woman is the one Wilfred wishes to marry. She is not happy and says Wilfred is a cruel man who already has three wives, but her father, Everest Tsitsi, who, like all Africans, considers cattle to be a sign of wealth, has agreed that for the price of two good mombies, he can marry her."

Dick studied the woman, really just a girl of perhaps sixteen. She was still a slender young girl with large, clear eyes, a small nose, and dark lips. She wore a shapeless smock of bright green that hung to her ankles, but even this could not disguise her high breasts with her slim waist flaring out to sizable hips and a fairly large backside, which he knew African men found most desirable.

The other two, perhaps slightly older, were more heavily built and, as was quite customary, wore nothing covering their breasts, but this didn't seem to worry them in the slightest.

Dick had learned that once the lobola was paid to the girl's father, the deal would be made. Wilfred would marry the girl who, becoming wife number four in his household, and therefore, the junior wife would be given all the menial chores to perform. This would make wife number three happy as she would move up in the chain of command, wife number two would be ecstatic and his number one wife would have no work to do at all, just boss the other three around and take life easy.

As unfair as this arrangement may have seemed to Dick, it was the way that things had been in Africa for thousands of years and nothing he could say or do would change that. Getting down to business, he told Zibando to ask where Wilfred was and after another long and drawn-out conversation he said, "Wilfred and his future father-in-law, Everest Tsitsi, had gone over to the next kraal, which is Wilfred's kraal and where his wives and children live. They will not be back until late afternoon."

Dick had by this time decided that Wilfred was probably the tall, thin man with a beard who was the ringleader of the group that had stolen Lillyford's cattle and murdered the two policemen. He told Zibando to put the women's minds at rest by telling them that they had no further inquiries and that they would be returning across the river. When his sergeant had done so, the three men climbed into the Land Rover and drove back toward the river.

After driving for about a mile and well beyond where they could be seen from Tsitsi's kraal, Dick pulled over into a small thicket of trees and bushes and together with Zibando and Tambo, drank some water and ate a cold meal. Dick didn't want to light a fire and make anyone aware of their presence.

Dick said to Zibando, "Let's walk back toward Tsitsi's kraal at mid-afternoon and conceal ourselves sufficiently close to witness Wilfred's and Tsitsi's return. Hopefully, it will still be light enough for Tambo to recognize if Wilfred is the man he saw attack and kill Inspector Farringham. If so, we'll arrest him on suspicion of murder. If not, we can still question him about those two branded cattle that he brought back to Tikwani's kraal."

After trudging through the sparse undergrowth, they found a perfect spot not more than a hundred feet from the kraal's entrance. It was in deep shade beneath a sprawling tree with plenty of bushes to conceal them. They sat patiently as one of the women came outside with a long stick and chased some goats inside. Smoke was rising from inside the fenced area, indicating that preparations were being made for the evening meal. They could hear the three women chattering and laughing and the occasional bleat of goats. Insects were beginning their evening chorus, but there was still no sign of Wilfred or Everest.

Dick had no sooner whispered to Zibando, "Perhaps they've decided to stay over at Wilfred's kraal until the morning," than two figures appeared in the distance walking toward the kraal.

"Watch closely, Tambo," Dick said, and Zibando translated quietly.

As the two men drew closer, Tambo whispered something to Zibando, who said, "He says that's the man, sir."

"Okay, wait until they've entered the kraal. Then we'll go in. Remember, this man is dangerous, but I have my gun and regardless of whether or not he resists arrest, as he probably will, we must restrain and handcuff him immediately."

A minute later, Dick and Zibando moved, telling Tambo to stay in place until they called him.

Entering the small gap in the grass enclosure, Dick saw Wilfred talking with the three women, but there was no sign of Tsitsi.

Approaching Wilfred, Dick grabbed him by the wrist and announced, "Wilfred Ngoshi. You are under arrest for the murder of Inspector Farringham and his African constable and for the theft of four cattle from Lillyford Ranch. Zibando, put the handcuffs on him behind his back."

Dick was expecting the tall and rangy man to put up a struggle but was not prepared for what followed. Everest Tsitsi came charging out of one of the huts, swinging a large panga at shoulder height and narrowly missing Dick's head. Realizing that he was about to become victim number three, he struggled to wrench his revolver free from its clumsy holster as he stumbled backward and tripped over one of the women seated behind him.

As he fell, he managed to withdraw his revolver from its holster, found the trigger, and fired one shot, instantly feeling a red-hot pain in his right foot as the bullet pierced his boot, went through his foot, and into its heavy leather sole. Looking up, he saw Tsitsi about to cleave Zibando in two with his panga and fired a second shot, aiming for Tsitsi's torso but miraculously striking him in the throat instead, sending him coughing and spluttering to the ground. He dropped the panga, clutched at his throat with both hands, and, with his eyes wide in terror, tried to draw breath. With blood gushing through his fingers and across his chest, he convulsed for a few seconds until he lay motionless in the dry, blood-spattered earth.

The three women by this time were huddled together, screaming and crying. Of Wilfred, there was no sign.

"Oh damn, damn, damn," shouted Dick. "We found our man and now he's got away." He hopped over to where Tsitsi lay in a small pool of blood and could see that the man was dead. "Well, I had no choice," he said to Zibando. "It was either you or him."

"Thank you, sir. Thank you. But your foot, sir, your shoe. It is pouring blood. We must take your boot off and bandage it."

With no chance of chasing after Wilfred, and watching an obviously frightened and bewildered young Tambo cowering in a corner of the kraal, Dick allowed Zibando to remove his leather boot and thick woolen sock. This entailed much yelling and cursing from Dick, but his foot was eventually bare and with a hole through top and bottom, Zibando dressed it in the torn-off tail of Dick's sweat-drenched bush shirt with consummate care.

With Tambo on one side and Zibando on the other, Dick was slowly carried and dragged the one mile back to the Land Rover. He had no choice but to leave the body of Tsitsi inside his small kraal to be collected later. Since neither Zibando nor Tambo could drive, Dick sent them out to find a suitable stick, which Zibando, using a piece of string and some inventive knotsmanship, attached to the accelerator pedal.

Using his left foot to operate the clutch and footbrake, his left hand to change gears, and his right hand to operate the accelerator, he was left with no option but to use his knees, preferably the left one, to operate the steering wheel. In this fashion, Dick managed to make the return back to Umbedzi, a journey that had taken them less than two hours to accomplish on the way out, to the local hospital in under four hours, having dropped Tambo off at his kraal on the way.

Lying subdued in a clean hospital bed, his injured foot cleaned, probed, stitched, and dressed, he wondered how long he could string this out for. A very compassionate nurse had suggested that he could probably be released in the morning, but he hoped like hell that she was wrong. It turned out that she was right, however, and the following morning, aided by a pair of crutches, he was unceremoniously evicted.

***

Once more ensconced in his small and cramped single-men's quarters, he telephoned Detective Chief Inspector Kevin Soames at the Chimuka CID headquarters.

"Good morning, sir. This is the silly bastard who was stripped naked by his reception committee near the airport. Inspector Richard Starling."

"Ha-ha. Glad you haven't lost your sense of humor," he said. "What can I do for you?"

"Well, sir, it's actually what I can do for you." And he related what he had been doing for the past few days, omitting the fact that he had shot himself in the foot but telling Soames the name and location of Wilfred Ngoshi, cattle rustler and murderer, and the whereabouts of two of the four stolen cattle and the body of Wilfred's deceased prospective father-in-law.

He couldn't resist adding, "I don't know who the two detectives were who initially questioned Tambo, but they either didn't question him at all or if they did, then they made a rotten job of it. It was really quite a simple matter to track down the cattle and one of the thieves. You might want to look into that."

"By God, that's jolly good work, Starling. I'll have someone on it straight away, and they'll be in touch. Regarding the initial investigation, I'll look into it immediately and get to the bottom of it. This all sounds very suspicious."

That evening Dick sat back in his lumpy armchair, placed his right foot on his footstool, and began packing his pipe with some Borkum Riff pipe tobacco before lighting up with a Swan Vestas match and sipping an inch of Johnnie Walker Black Label from his prized Waterford lead-crystal whisky glass. He called Taffy, suggesting that he come over for the weekend to commiserate and then, with a sip or two of whisky still in the tumbler and his pipe as dead as a doornail, his last thought before nodding off was of Annabelle Delaney and her insatiable appetite for sex.

Chapter Nine

The following morning, Dick awoke to find himself still slumped in his chair, with a sour taste in his mouth and painfully aware of his bandaged right foot. He managed to take a shower without getting the dressing on his foot too wet, had a shave, and was dressed in a clean uniform. Then, casting the crutches aside in favor of a walking stick he found lying around in one of the closets, he hobbled to his desk, where his telephone had been ringing on and off for the past half hour.

"Good morning. Inspector Starling, I presume?" The caller identified himself as Detective Inspector Muzeki and was calling in regard to the murder of Inspector Farringham and his constable. Pleased that DCI Soames had put someone on the case so quickly, Dick told Muzeki what he had discovered and Muzeki agreed to come up to Umbedzi immediately and take over the investigation.

Dick instructed Shadreck to prepare the spare bedroom for Detective Inspector Muzeki and began work on a docket, showing in detail the progress he had made in the case.

Later that day, Muzeki arrived in an unmarked gray Ford Anglia and sat down with Dick to discuss how they were going to proceed. Dick was impressed with the man's take-charge attitude. He was a man of about thirty, tall and well-built with skin the color of ebony, and being a native Waranian wouldn't have to go through the rigmarole of using an interpreter every time he had to question someone.

Muzeki inquired about Dick's injured foot and, embellishing his description of the encounter with Wilfred Ngoshi and Tsitsi, Dick described how he had saved his sergeant's life by shooting Tsitsi. During the process, he described how he had inadvertently shot himself in the foot, thus allowing Wilfred to escape.

After considerable debate, Dick said, "Let's first pick up Tambo at his kraal before visiting Tikwani's place and searching for the four stolen cattle. Then we can make further inquiries with the locals and question them about how the cattle came to be there, who brought them, who owned them, and who was feeding them. Only then will we know how to approach Tsitsi's kraal. Finally, we'll go to Wilfred's kraal, well-armed and ready for trouble."

Muzeki pulled aside his light cotton jacket to reveal a shoulder holster containing a short-barrelled revolver and said "Why don't you remain in Umbedzi since you won't be of much use with an injured foot?" But Dick insisted on accompanying them, if only as an observer.

Muzeki, being a CID officer and therefore more accustomed to the type of clandestine activity that would be necessary, proposed that he enter the kraal with only Sergeant Zibando, both in plain clothes. With that half-arsed plan established, the three of them set off the following morning. Muzeki, without much choice, elected to drive the station Land Rover with Dick beside him and Sergeant Zibando in the seat behind them.

During the drive down to Tambo's kraal in the TTL, Dick again raised the issue of the poor job that the first two detectives had done in failing to question Tambo properly and failing to follow up on the crucial information that he later gave to Sergeant Zibando.

After a minute or two of serious consideration, Muzeki spoke. "I'm embarrassed to tell you that the two detective constables, who were originally sent to investigate, should never have been sent in the first place. The murder of two police officers, an inspector, and a constable, and the subsequent investigation should have been given priority and headed up by, at the very least, DCI Soames himself."

"They were sent because DCI Soames was away on leave and Detective Sergeant Ngoshi was taking his place. Yes, Ngoshi, the brother of the man whom we are now going to arrest. Ngoshi suspected all along that his brother was the culprit, and as the saying goes, blood is thicker than water. He sent a couple of junior incompetents, knowing full well that they would make a hash of things. That's the truth of the matter and when this investigation is completed, you can rest assured that Ngoshi and the two idiots who were sent to investigate will be dealt with."

Dick absorbed this staggering news in silence. Then, nodding his head, he merely said, "I hope you're right and that those bastards, especially Ngoshi, are dealt with harshly."

They first called at the small kraal where Tambo lived. Zibando explained to Tambo who Muzeki was, where they were going, and that they would need him to identify the four culprits if they could find them. Dick produced yet another roll of Polo mints much to Tambo's delight.

They then drove to Tikwani's kraal and went to the kraal where Dick had first seen the two cattle with the Lillyford's brand, but they were no longer there. Leaving Dick and Tambo in the Land Rover, D.I. Muzeki and Sergeant Zibando spoke with the father of Wilfred, the same wizened old headman that Zibando had questioned on his earlier visit, and asked where the cattle were.

The old man was reluctant to reply, but after some prompting, he admitted that Wilfred had taken them, presumably to Tsitsi's kraal to pay for his new bride. When questioned about the other two cattle, the old man, already shaking nervously, wouldn't look Zibando in the eye and denied all knowledge of any other cattle. Watching him cast his eyes in all directions as he spoke, the two seasoned policemen smiled since they were well familiar with this dead giveaway.

Muzeki decided that it was his turn to question the old man and asked him how the two stolen cattle had landed up at his kraal. When he was told that his son Wilfred had brought them, he asked where he got them from. The old man, almost at the point of breaking down in tears, admitted that he suspected that they were stolen, for they were much more robust and healthier than the cattle normally seen in tribal trust lands.

He admitted that he didn't know where the cattle came from but had agreed to feed and look after them for Wilfred, as he was afraid of him. Even though he was his son, he knew he was violent and a thief.

"Very well," said Muzeki, "let's search these other kraals before we question this old man anymore. He looks like he's ready to drop dead from shame and fright, but I still think he's lying."

They returned to the Land Rover and Muzeki told Dick that they were going to search all the kraals in the community generally known as Tikwani's kraal because neither he nor Sergeant Zibando thought the old man was telling the truth when he said Wilfred had taken the cattle to Tsitsi's kraal. They suspected that he had just moved them to another nearby kraal.

Because they were in plain clothes, rather than using the police Land Rover, they went on foot, so they would draw less attention to themselves. Dick watched them wander off, wishing that he'd stayed at home. He had young Tambo sitting in the Land Rover with him, but since neither could speak the other's language, they sat in silence, with Dick listening to Tambo sucking on one Polo mint after another. Taking a look around Tikwani's kraal, Dick thought how much it resembled a small village. There were even three or four small buildings, presumably shops, and a market square where several dozen people were milling about, and hawkers had a variety of fruits and vegetables laid out on newspapers or blankets. One area had several tethered goats and some chickens lying in the dirt with their legs tied together.

As he sat half asleep, the serene and peaceful atmosphere was shattered by two pistol shots, and he saw people running away from the general direction that Zibando and Muzeki had taken barely a few minutes before. Cursing his inability to move at more than a shuffle, he tried to see what was happening. Tambo began jabbering excitedly but Dick didn't know what he was saying. Then Zibando and Muzeki came running toward him, Muzeki with his revolver in his hand and Zibando holding his shoulder, which Dick could see was covered in blood when he came closer.

Muzeki reached the Land Rover first and leaped into the driver's seat. "We've found him. We found Wilfred and all four of Lillyford's cattle. The skellum stabbed Zibando and ran off and by the time I had drawn my gun and fired at him he was too far away, and I missed."

"Which way did he go?" asked Dick, watching a shivering and obviously shocked Zibando climb slowly into the back of the Land Rover. "Agh, he obviously didn't go far. He's hiding in one of the kraals, but it will take hours to find him, and Sergeant Zibando is very badly injured. I think we should go back to Umbedzi, get some reinforcements, and take the sergeant to the hospital. Then we'll come back, collect the cattle, find this skellum Wilfred, and make him tell us where his three friends are."

Utilizing his first-aid box for the umpteenth time, Dick sighed and dressed Zibando's shoulder wound, which after a bit of cleaning didn't appear to be too serious, and they left Tikwani's kraal. They dropped Tambo off at his kraal, telling him that they would be back to pick him up again that afternoon, and then Dick told Muzeki to stop at Lillyford's farmhouse on the way back.

Arriving at the impressive mansion once again, Dick hobbled from the Land Rover to the front door and pulled the plaited rope. Once more, Lillyford's servant Simon opened the door, still dressed immaculately in his clean white uniform with the tasseled red fez.

"Hello, Simon," said Dick. "Please tell Mr. Lillyford that Inspector Starling has some good news for him." Simon disappeared back inside, closing the door behind him, and after a minute or two, Lillyford appeared, still scowling. "Well, what's the good news?"

"We've found your four stolen cattle, and we are pretty confident that we'll soon have the four men who stole them in the stocks. We'll be back after lunch with some more men and suggest you have a truck and trailer ready so that you can come with us to recover your cattle."

"Well, bugger me," Lillyford exclaimed, a smile creasing his sunburned face. "My tax dollars at work for once. I hate to say it, but well done, m'lad, well done. I'll get a cattle wagon organized right now, and it'll be ready when you return."

Dick returned to his Land Rover and, with a satisfied smile, asked Muzeki to head for Umbedzi Hospital and then back to the police station. There was work to be done.

***

Once back at the Umbedzi police station, Dick called one of his other sergeants and told him to muster six of his constables and have them uniformed and ready to leave in an hour. He then telephoned Tommy Crystal, a local businessman with whom he frequently had a drink and knew he owned a Bedford five-ton truck. "Hello, Tom. Dick here. Can you do me a big favor and lend me your truck and a driver for the afternoon? I'll arrange compensation from HQ, of course, but I need it right now."

"Don't worry about compensation. Just buy me a couple of Chimbukas next time I see you. I'll send the truck over right now."

Within an hour, Dick was back on the road with Tommy's Bedford following behind. They called in at Lillyford's ranch, where the man himself was waiting with a cattle truck and driver and the convoy went off again, heading for Tikwani's kraal.

Muzeki drove them first to Tambo's kraal and from there to the kraal where he and Sergeant Zibando had discovered Lillyford's cattle. The beasts were still there and Lillyford, after inspecting them and complaining about their poor condition, instructed his driver to load the animals up using a long ramp, which they dragged out from inside the truck.

While Dick leaned on his cane and watched, Muzeki hauled the men, women, and children out of the huts and began questioning them, sometimes trying to coax some information from them and at other times forcefully demanding the whereabouts of Wilfred. Before long, one of the women, an older woman who obviously saw that if they didn't cooperate, they would all be carted off to prison, told them where they could find Wilfred.

With six constables and an armed Muzeki, Dick felt sufficiently safe to hobble along with them. After only a few minutes, they had surrounded the small, screened kraal in which Wilfred was thought to be hiding.

Dick and Muzeki, with his pistol drawn, entered the enclosure with one of Dick's constables and Dick called out, "Wilfred, we know you're in one of these huts. Come out with your hands up, and you won't get hurt. Otherwise, we'll come in and get you."

Muzeki issued the same warning, but there was no response. "Okay, we'll do it the hard way," said Dick. Muzeki and the constable began forcing doors open, entering and ejecting the inhabitants one hut at a time. Once all six huts had been cleared, Dick examined the group of about twenty individuals that seemed to comprise the occupants of the entire kraal. Two old men, two younger men, perhaps in their late teens or early twenties, a boy of about thirteen or fourteen, and a collection of women and small children of all ages, but no Wilfred.

A shout from outside the kraal's grass enclosure sent Muzeki scurrying outside to return a minute or two later with Wilfred securely handcuffed and being escorted by two constables.

"This skellum was caught trying to crawl beneath the grass and thorn bushes at the back of the kraal," said one of the constables. Holding a long knife out toward them, he continued, "And he had this tied to his waist, but we were on him before he had a chance to use it."

Dick congratulated his two constables on a job well done and then, looking over at the group of twenty or so individuals that he had so roughly evicted from their huts, told one of his constables to fetch Tambo from the Land Rover.

When Tambo arrived, Dick said to Muzeki, "Ask him if he recognizes anyone in this bunch." Tambo excitedly pointed out the two young men and the boy, saying that they were the three that he saw killing the two policemen. The three of them of course immediately took to their heels and fled, but being surrounded on all sides by stout grass and thorn fencing and with six constables in hot pursuit, they were soon arrested, securely handcuffed, and, together with Wilfred, were led back to Tommy Crystal's truck, and taken to Lillyford, who was waiting patiently with his driver and their cattle truck.

Dick limped to Lillyford and asked, "Well, sir, are you satisfied with how this sorry excuse for a police officer handled your case?"

Lillyford smiled slightly before saying, "Okay, Starling. You did a good job. Thank you."

Dick nearly fell over backward. The man was human, after all! Perhaps he should push his luck a bit further. "Young Tambo was really a great help and was very conscientious in following those men in the first place. Without him, I doubt that we could ever have recovered your cattle. Any chance of giving him his job back? It's the only money his family has to live on."

"I'll think on it," was Lillyford's only response. But unbeknownst to Dick, once Lillyford returned to his ranch, he summoned his foreman Frickie Steenkamp and told him to give Tambo his job back plus a fifty-pound reward for a job well done.

Dick and Muzeki stood face to face and, smilingly, shook hands. A mission well accomplished.

Chapter Ten

Dick soon learned that his station's annual inspection was due in the near future. Apparently, according to Taffy, every station in the country was visited once each year by a senior officer of the Royal Warania Police Force, who would inspect the police station building, the vehicles, horses, and equipment belonging thereto, and the individuals stationed there. A thorough examination of all police records would be made and the member in charge, in this case Dick, would parade his African constabulary with a display of foot drill as practiced at the police training school.

The Umbedzi police station had missed last year's inspection due to Inspector Solly Farringham's unfortunate demise, but Superintendent Oliver Billings would be arriving in precisely three weeks to conduct this year's inspection. Dick, now approaching twenty years of age, and with his foot completely healed, took this information in his stride. He would have a haircut, have his men polish the Land Rover, smarten up the charge office, and be well prepared for Superintendent Billing's visit.

When the great man arrived, Dick, appropriately dressed in his smart winter uniform, drove to the Umbedzi Hotel where Billings was staying and took him back to the station. Billings was similarly dressed in winter uniform, which consisted of a barathea jacket and trousers, white shirt, blue tie, and well-polished brown leather Oxford shoes plus a Sam Browne and a small brass crown on both epaulets, indicating him to be a commissioned officer.

He turned out to be a long-serving member of the force, who had worked his way up through the ranks and was an old-school policeman to the core. Dick estimated that Billings was close to retirement age, which in the RWP meant that he was somewhere between forty-five and fifty, and discovered that the man hailed originally from the town of Coventry in the county of Warwickshire, England. The man was rather stout with a red nose, probably acquired through an abundant intake of alcohol, and had a ruddy and wrinkled complexion and a short, bristly mustache.

After formalities had been dealt with, he instructed Dick to have his men on parade at two o'clock that afternoon. Dick summoned a fully recovered Sergeant Zibando and repeated the superintendent's instructions. At precisely two o'clock, they walked out to the forecourt, where ten smartly uniformed police constables and their three sergeants stood on parade and, upon the words 'ten-shun' from Sergeant Zibando, slammed to attention.

Dick and his senior officer walked slowly along the line of policemen. Billings picked out the odd individual for minor offenses, one for having his hair too long and another for not polishing his boots properly, but generally, he found the men to be well turned out. Sergeant Zibando then had his men march to and fro, screaming orders for them to right and left wheel and calling out the time in the age-old tradition of 'left, right, left-right-left' before screaming 'Halt' in a voice loud enough to wake the dead. Dick deemed the parade to be an outstanding success and instructed Sergeant Zibando to allow the men to return to their quarters.

"Now, let's inspect the paperwork," Billings said. "Then we'll go to your quarters for a cup of tea." As he began flipping through the crime register, he caught sight of the rape case that had occurred several months previously. "What's this all about?" he asked. "This looks like something that our Criminal Investigation Department should have handled."

Dick quickly explained that it was, in fact, a false report, no rape had occurred and the woman had withdrawn all charges. "But if it was a false report, why was the woman not charged? Making false reports and wasting police time is an offense."

"No, sir," replied Dick, "the woman was involved in a domestic dispute with her husband and has since left him and left town."

"Hmm," muttered Billings. "Most unsatisfactory, but I guess we'll have to let it go. Now, let's have that cup of tea."

Seated in the quarter's uncomfortable armchair, Billings told Dick that a new era was coming to Warania. For some time, Britain had been granting independence to several of its African colonies, and it was only a matter of time before Warania too would gain its independence. With this in mind, there would be several changes within the RWP that would facilitate the transfer of power when it comes about. One of them would involve recruiting

African women into the police force and distributing them to both urban and rural police stations. "I'm pleased to say that some of these women have already been recruited and trained and one will be stationed at Umbedzi as early as next week."

Dick took some time to comprehend what Billings had told him and absolutely flabbergasted, asked, "Bu-but where will she stay? She can't stay with the African sergeants and constables in their compound, and she certainly can't stay here."

"Why not?" replied Billings. "You have a spare bedroom, and here, she will be safe from problems with her male colleagues. Of course, there would be no question of impropriety for we are all aware of the RWP's attitude toward miscegenation, and I'm sure that a young man like yourself wouldn't even dream of it."

"But she's an African constable. I agree that she should have her own quarters separate from the other constables in the compound, but she should also be separate from me. These single quarters are for inspectors. She can't stay here," he protested stubbornly. Without expressing his thoughts to Billings, Dick wasn't at all sure about his commanding officer's claims of impropriety. Self-satisfaction had its limits, and he was sometimes tempted to deviate from the attitude that Billings was referring to.

"Well, to tell you the truth," Billings said rather awkwardly, "she, along with most of these newly trained women, will shortly become inspectors once they've proved their mettle and had a bit of grounding in practical police work. I think you'll be quite surprised. The one you're getting is very well-educated and articulate."

With that, Billings stood, obviously anxious to drop the subject, and said, "Well, I must be off. Take me back to the hotel, and I'll have a driver pick me up in the morning."

"Oh, have you met that cute little barmaid they have down at the hotel's bar? Quite a feast for sore eyes, that one." And with that, Dick's annual inspection was over.

Needless to say, the following day, once he was sure that Superintendent Billings was safely on his way back to Chimuka, he took a stroll over to the hotel and popped into the bar for a quick look-see. The bar was more crowded than usual, with two men standing at the bar counter chatting with Billings' sight for sore eyes. This was the new barmaid replacing Melissa, who had disappeared some weeks before. She appeared to be in her early twenties, slim, blonde, very pretty, and giving her full attention to her two customers. He turned and departed from the hotel for this was no place for a uniformed police inspector, and he returned home planning his modus operandi for hopefully bedding this delightful wench.

At five o'clock, dressed casually in shorts and a safari jacket, he sauntered into the hotel bar, pleased to see that Billings' sight for sore eyes was still behind the counter, and ordered a bottle of Chimbuka. "Hi," she said to him, smiling. "I haven't seen you in here before, but then I'm pretty new myself. My name's Sandra. What's yours?"

Dick introduced himself, telling her that he was the local police inspector living down the street and that he often popped in for a beer or two after work. Sandra went off to serve some other customers, but he remained seated at the bar and before long she returned. He asked her where she was staying, and she told him that the hotel had provided one of their rooms for her with all meals thrown in as part of the package. She explained that her recent arrival in Umbedzi was due to the fact that she had recently broken off her engagement to a city banker in Chimuka and wanted to get out of town and sample life in the sticks for a while.

After a third beer, Dick told her he must leave, and on the walk home, he repeated an oft-heard saying, which he believed was first coined by Lord Baden-Powell upon his return to Britain from Ghana. When patiently waiting and planning for a benefit of some kind, whether it be an ambush, a stake-out, or capturing the attention of a delightfully attentive barmaid, the sentiment was 'softly, softly, catchee monkey'. He smiled as he sat down to the bangers and mash dinner that Shadreck had prepared for him, considering himself quite the Casanova.

Every evening after work, he began visiting the Umbedzi Hotel's Waterhole for a few beers and a chat with Sandra. On his third or fourth visit, he was delighted when she said, "I really look forward to you coming in here. You're not pushy or fresh, like some of the other blokes. Do you have a girlfriend?"

He smiled as he twirled his mustache, saying that no, he had no girlfriend, mainly because there were no girls to be had.

"The bait has been taken," he thought. She laughed and added, "well, I'm a girl, and I'll be your girlfriend if you like," And, with that, Dick thought romance had entered his life once again.

Dick asked her where she would like to go on their first date, and she told him, "I've heard of a place about an hour's drive away. It's in an orange grove next to a farm owned by someone called Bert Lillyford and apparently every Sunday afternoon they have a group called the Blackjacks performing there."

"Oh, yes. I know Bert Lillyford's place very well. He's made quite a name for himself in these parts as quite a nasty bugger, but I think when you get to know him, he's not so bad. I didn't know about the rock group performing in the orange grove. Can you get off work this Sunday?"

"I'll try and will let you know tomorrow," she said and waved him goodbye as she went to attend to another customer.

On his arrival back home, he went to bed early and did what he'd been doing a lot lately before cleaning up with a tissue and falling asleep.

The following evening Sandra told him that she was free on Sunday, and he arranged to pick her up at the hotel just after one o'clock.

Sunday arrived and Dick carefully groomed his face, admiring his mustache and sideburns, both of which were a little bit curly. Perhaps, he mused, he should wax the tips of his mustache when it gets a bit longer like they used to do in the old days. Freshly showered and donning a newly purchased lavender-colored floral Hawaiian shirt bought off the rack when he last visited Chimuka, he felt extremely elegant even though his khaki shorts, long woolen socks, and veldskoens probably matched the attire of ninety percent of the white male population in the country.

He drove to the hotel in his police Land Rover, and there she was, waiting for him, wearing a flared, polka-dot dress, a bright red belt that emphasized her slim waist, and high-heeled shoes. *She really is pretty,* he thought. Her curly blonde hair was artfully arranged and hung below her shoulders, her face was surprisingly devoid of make-up, a dimple appeared on each cheek as she smiled at him, and her startling blue eyes sparkled.

They set off for the orange grove, a journey of about an hour, and he told her how lovely she was looking. They made small talk, and he would have held her hand except that he had to keep changing gears, and they had a bulky police radio between their two seats.

When they reached Bert Lillyford's farm, Dick slowed down and a mile or two beyond was the huge orange grove that he had passed a few weeks earlier. Sure enough, there was a sign advertising Sunday's weekly performance by the Blackjacks.

Turning off the main road, they followed a dirt track for about half a mile through orchards with trees heavily laden with oranges until they reached a clearing with dozens of cars parked haphazardly. Climbing out of the Land Rover, they could hear music. In fact, it was one of the first of the Beatles songs, *Please Please Me*. They sang along as they walked hand in hand toward a well-laid-out garden full of chairs and tables where a group of four young men, a drummer, two guitarists, and a singer were belting out the number.

They secured a table and Dick went off to buy a couple of cold Chimbukas. They had a wonderful afternoon and each enjoyed a few drinks before Dick, thinking with his little head, suggested they return to his house where he would have Shadreck cook them dinner. Sandra eagerly agreed and off they went back to Umbedzi.

Upon arrival, Dick showed her around his small domain, put his arm around her slim waist, and gently kissed her. She responded eagerly, and with their lips locked together, he slowly began exploring Sandra's body. He felt her stiffen in his arms and when his roving hands began exploring her bottom, she let out a shriek.

"What are you doing?" she asked, breaking away from him. "What do you think I am? This is our first date, and I thought you were a nice man. You're as bad as the rest of them." She snatched up her handbag, swung it at his head with the metal clasp clipping his chin, and marched out of the house.

Chapter Eleven

Inspecting the nasty cut on his chin the following morning as he delicately shaved around it, he frowned at himself in the mirror. Once again, Dick was confused. Perhaps he'd simply got lucky with Miss Delaney and Melissa. Maybe he wasn't the cunning and irresistible Casanova that he thought he was. But even more trouble was just around the corner.

After he completed his ablutions, applied a sticking plaster to his chin, and dressed in his police uniform, a very smartly uniformed, surprisingly attractive, and slim young African policewoman arrived at the station. She spoke perfect English, with no trace of an African accent. In fact, she spoke more like the Waranian Europeans, with a slight rolling of her Rs and long, drawn-out vowels similar in many ways to the Rhodesian or to the English-speaking South African accents. She introduced herself as Woman Constable Allison Majaka, now stationed at the Umbedzi police station.

Dick, of course, had forgotten all about this new turn of events and had given no thought and made no preparation for her arrival. "Majaka, of course. Welcome to Umbedzi." When she held out her right hand, he shook it, surprised at how small, soft, and well-manicured it was. This was obviously one of the new generation of better-educated, sophisticated, and cultured Waranians that he seldom, if ever, encountered.

"I don't know if anyone told you, but it was decided that you should be accommodated here in this building rather than in the African police compound. Apparently, the powers-that-be considered that you would be harassed by the single men down there and would be more comfortable here."

"Yes, I was told that I would be staying in the single-men's quarters but didn't realize that they meant I'd be sharing it with only one white inspector, but I'm okay with that as long as you are."

"Ah, yes. That was a surprise to me also but let me show you to your room, and we'll talk about it later." Muttering to himself, he marched off to his spare bedroom and to his horror saw that it was full of junk. A bicycle, a rusty old barbeque, books, and a few bits of old furniture that should have been thrown out months ago were scattered throughout. "Shadreck," he shouted. And when Shadreck arrived, he said, "Get this room cleaned up, chop-chop. Put clean sheets on the bed and help Constable Majaka here get settled in."

Sitting down at the kitchen table and with his head in his hands, he thought feverishly of all the things he should have thought of beforehand. "We'll have to share the bathroom, the toilet, the dining room table, and the kitchen. And I won't be able to walk around naked. Oh shit."

He could hear Majaka supervising Shadreck as she tried to clean and sort out her bedroom, while he wrestled with the problem of how to come to terms with this disastrous situation.

That evening, after work, he slipped into some civilian clothes and went to the Umbedzi Hotel, where he saw that Sandra was happily serving customers at the bar. When she saw him, she brought over a beer, slammed it onto the bar in front of him, and went back to the men she had been speaking with when he arrived. He was hoping he could wheedle his way back into her good graces and discuss his latest predicament, but he could see that this was going to be a tall proposition. He sat there, blanketed in gloom, wondering how he could have been such a fool. Just looking at her—that sweet smile, those beautiful little dimples on her cheeks—made him sick to his stomach. He'd blown his chance.

As he was sorting through his change to pay for the beer, Sandra came over to him. Cocking her head to one side, she asked, "Have you decided to apologize?"

"Yes, yes. Sandra, I'm so sorry. I was a fool. You're wonderful, and my behavior was atrocious," he said and blathered on in that vein for a minute or so before she raised her hand and looked him in the eye. "Enough. You're sorry and so you should be. Okay, I get it. Now, let's put it behind us and pretend it never happened. You've obviously got another problem. What is it?"

He didn't quite know how to begin, but eventually said quietly, hoping that no one else in the bar could hear him, "I have an African woman staying in the house with me."

Before he could say any more, Sandra placed her elbows on the bar counter, placed her forehead in her hands, and groaned.

"No, no. It's not what you think. I'm merely following orders." She removed one hand from her forehead and peered at him with one eye. "Say that again. Did you say that you're merely following orders?"

"Yes. From headquarters. She's a woman constable, but she can't stay in the African police compound because she's young and pretty. She will be constantly harassed."

Before the words were out of his mouth, he realized he had truly put his foot right in it.

"Well, well, well," responded Sandra. "She will be constantly harassed, so they put her in a house, alone, with you." Her voice had risen sharply and people at the tables began to look their way.

"That poor woman. I think I'd like to come over to your house and meet with her. Tell her to expect me just after 10:00."

Snatching up the change that he had placed on the counter, she marched off, slowly shaking her head.

Dick walked morosely back to his house. Things were going from bad to worse and none of this was his fault. It all came down to Miss Delaney. He decided it was all her fault and began to feel a bit better.

Upon returning to the house, he found Majaka seated in the small living room and reading a copy of the local newspaper, The Umbedzi Gazette. She was wearing a pair of jeans and a light sweater and seemed quite at ease.

"Majaka, I've been down to the hotel for a drink. There's a young woman who works there called Sandra. She said that she would like to come over and meet you when she's finished work, but that won't be until shortly after ten."

"Oh, that's nice. Shadreck has made us dinner. Sadza and relish for me, fish and chips for you. I'll eat in my room." And with that, she tossed the newspaper on the table and stormed off with her porridge.

Perhaps I should have a talk with Shadreck, Dick thought, and he went out to Shadreck's small *kia,* or house, to explain things to him.

"But, baas, she's a *Mfasi*, an African woman. She's one of us. She should not be sleeping in the bwana's house and I, as a man, should not be cleaning and cooking for her. This is not good."

Dick nodded and told Shadreck that he understood, but pointed out that before too long, there would no longer be the same separation between black people and white people that there was today. Independence was coming and with it would come many changes.

He then went on to explain that there was really no alternative but for Majaka to stay in the spare room. She would do her own laundry and cleaning, but Shadreck must give her the same meals that he gave to him. "In return," Dick said, "I will give you an extra twenty pounds each month." *Twenty pounds that Majaka can pay,* thought Dick, as it's her food he'll be cooking. This seemed to mollify Shadreck to some degree and although still visibly unhappy about the arrangement, he agreed to do his best.

Returning to the house, he knocked on Majaka's door and when she appeared, he told her of the conversation he had just had with Shadreck. "So come on back to the living room, and I'll treat you to a beer."

Majaka, looking somewhat embarrassed and uncomfortable, nevertheless joined him in the living room and accepted the beer, and they engaged in a pointless conversation while they waited for dinner to be served.

About forty-five minutes later, Shadreck placed two plates on the table, both containing fish and chips. He spoke not a word and Dick thanked him and told him that he could have the rest of the night off. "You can clean up in the morning."

There was no question but that things had got off to a rocky start though both Dick and Majaka tried to make the best of it. After dinner, Dick picked up a new book that he was in the middle of reading, Wilbur Smith's *When the Lion Feeds*, and Majaka busied herself pottering around in her room.

Shortly after ten, a sharp rap on the front door forewarned Dick that the next chapter in this horrible day was about to begin. He opened the door and Sandra breezed in, asking, "Where is she?"

Majaka came out of her room, raised her chin, and, looking defiantly into Sandra's eyes, said, "I presume I'm the 'she' you're looking for," and held out her right hand. Sandra shook it and smiled sweetly. "I'm sorry. I didn't intend to be rude."

The three sat at the dining room table and Sandra opened the conversation by saying, "Dick told me that you had just moved in, and he seemed quite upset that he wasn't able to provide you with proper accommodation. I must admit that I was also surprised, but I have been giving it some thought. Only men could have thought up this ridiculous situation, and you have my wholehearted sympathy and support."

This seemed to soften the atmosphere considerably and Majaka responded, saying that she had been given no instructions or advice on where she would be living, only that she was to report to Inspector Starling at Umbedzi police station this morning. "And here I am, with two suitcases and not a clue what to do next."

"Well, until a better solution can be found, I suppose you'll have to make do," replied Sandra. "You have your own room, a shared bathroom, a house servant, and a job. Have you figured out how bathroom sharing is going to work?"

Dick decided he had better chip in at this point and said, "Yes. Well, at least I have given that some thought. After all, if I had a sister or a mother, and they were to visit, we would have a similar situation. The bathroom door has a lock on it, and we'll have to use it in turns."

"And what about if you have other visitors? Is Majaka supposed to lock herself in her room or just go out and wander the streets until they've left?"

He gulped, not knowing what to say or how to say it, but eventually heard himself say, very meekly, "Well, I don't have any visitors, so that's not an issue." Hardening his attitude, he added, "But if I did have a visitor, so what? You've met Majaka and can see that she is a new-age Waranian. Intelligent, well-spoken, and articulate, and she will probably become an inspector like me when independence is granted." She gave him a cold, hard stare.

Gloomily, he walked Sandra back to the hotel, thanked her for coming over, and walked home thinking 'there goes another one' as he glumly climbed the steps to his front door. So much for 'softly, softly catchee monkey'.

Chapter Twelve

Making sure that Majaka was well out of the way, Dick phoned Taffy and explained that he had been told to accommodate an African policewoman in his spare bedroom and was at a loss as to how to handle it.

Of course, he should have expected Taffy's response. "You lucky bugger. If you don't want her, send her over to me. I'm not one to look a gift horse in the mouth." With that, he laughed and rang off.

Woman Constable Majaka settled in quite well at the police station. She appeared more than content with her bedroom once she had cleared out the rubbish and had Shadreck give it a thorough cleaning. Shadreck wasn't at all pleased with this arrangement. Looking after the bwana was quite acceptable to him but doing the same for a Mfasi was ridiculous. It should be the other way around. However, when confronting the bwana with his dilemma, he was told once again that his wages would be increased and for that he was thankful.

Dick allocated Majaka's duties to manning—or should it be womaning—the charge office desk from eight to five each weekday, with weekends off. He noticed that when on duty she was always smartly dressed in her police uniform of flat black brogues, gray knee-length skirt, and crisply ironed shirt with epaulets displaying the brass letters RWP.

They had adopted a routine whereby he used the bathroom first, making sure he locked the door securely, and then she would follow suit. They began by taking their breakfasts separately but after a few days ate breakfast at the same table, indulging in light conversation.

Dick continued his regular visits to the Umbedzi Hotel and Sandra's indignation began to thaw to the point that she even began making suggestions of where they could rendezvous from time to time. He took this to mean that there would be no heavy petting and certainly no beast with two backs for the foreseeable future, if ever, and was at a loss to come up with any ideas. In the meantime, Dick was getting more and more randy and sick and tired of punishing Little Tommy night after night, especially with a leather belt gripped between his teeth lest he make a noise that awakened Majaka.

Taffy came over that weekend, but with no spare room at Dick's place, he was forced to stay the night at the Umbedzi Hotel. Taffy had the opportunity to meet Majaka and as soon as Dick had shepherded him out of the house and back to the Waterhole, Dick was astounded to hear Taffy say, "She's a bit of alright, that one. I wish I had one. She's quite a looker."

"But Taffy, yes, she's nice-looking, but what about, you know, the rules? No miscegenation."

"C'mon, man. She's a woman, and we're stuck out here in the sticks. Lighten up a bit, no one will know, and you can't keep pulling your plonker forever. And anyway, do you think you'd be the only one?"

Fortunately, Taffy left town the next morning and on Monday the calamity occurred.

It all started quite innocently. He had already shaved, showered, and donned his uniform, but wanted to pee before heading off to town for a stroll around. The bathroom door was ajar, but as he walked in, it was full of steam and Majaka, who was lying in the bathtub up to her neck in bubbles, screamed. "What are you doing bathing at this time of day?" he demanded.

She replied, "I thought you'd gone to town, and I decided to pamper myself." She was completely covered with smelly soap suds, with only her head appearing above the foamy waterline. Apart from her initial scream, she didn't appear particularly perturbed.

Thinking that he could hardly pee while she was in the bathroom, he decided to try to hold it until later. He noticed that she was beginning to sit up, exposing her breasts. And try as he might, he couldn't take his eyes off of them. He had seen hundreds of African women's breasts before and couldn't understand why he was so interested in this pair. Admittedly, they were quite perky and firm, but what drew his attention was that like the rest of her body, or at least the arms, legs and face that he had already seen, they were not black but a beautiful, light coffee-colored brown with her dark nipples thrust forward almost half an inch beyond large areolas as though stimulated.

She smiled at him, a beautiful smile the likes of which he had not seen since her arrival, and said quite brazenly, "You obviously came in here to pee, so go ahead, I don't mind." He shrugged and stepped over to the toilet but had a job getting Little Tommy out of his underpants and shorts. It was so erect that he couldn't pee anyway. With his back still turned toward Majaka, he had one hell of a struggle to get Tommy back where he belonged and zipped up tight.

Before turning around and heading for the door, he heard her say, "Well, if you're not going to pee, would you mind washing my back for me?" As he looked over his shoulder, he saw that she was holding out a sudsy sponge. Without speaking, he knelt down beside the tub and began slowly and methodically sponging her flawless and quite muscular back while still gazing at those marvelous breasts.

Dick, now well aware that he had entered into dangerous territory, began sponging her armpits, then her breasts, before descending to her pudenda and underneath to her bottom. Then, all was lost.

Turning her face up toward him, Majaka, still smiling, whispered, "Have you never heard the expression 'You haven't tasted sweets until you've tasted chocolates?'"

Curling her hand around the back of his neck, she drew his face down toward hers and kissed him softly on the lips. She then stood and began drying herself off before taking his hand and leading him into his bedroom.

What followed was beyond Dick's belief. To begin with, the African woman who was lying naked on top of his bed with him was warm, soft, yet muscular. He had thought that her light brown facial coloring was due to a daily application of Ambi-Extra skin-lightening cream that most young Africans used but now realized that she had naturally pale skin. Her lips and nipples were dark; her eyes were golden brown; and her features delicate. She was, in fact, quite beautiful.

Having struggled out of his shorts and shirt, he lay back as Majaka stroked him lightly from the top of his head to the tips of his toes until Little Tommy was at a bursting point. She then straddled him and, with those delightful breasts hanging above his head like ripe pawpaws, slowly began to post. Then, just like riding a horse, she increased her rhythm to a canter, then a gallop, all the while laughing and squealing until he burst, adrift in a world of starlight, moonlight, and shadows. A well-satisfied feeling of placid contentment embraced him, and he began to see things from Taffy's point of view.

Two conflicting thoughts crossed his mind. The first, "What have I done?" was followed by the second, "Why have I waited so long?" Compared with this woman, the likes of Melissa and even Miss Annabelle Delaney were nonstarters.

Dick didn't go to the Umbedzi Hotel that evening, nor the next nor the next. Instead, after work, he would sit with Majaka at the kitchen table, eating whatever meal Shadreck reluctantly cooked for them before sending him back to his quarters and climbing into bed with her.

Chapter Thirteen

The thefts, assaults, and even one or two murders that had occurred in the nearby Umdenga African township had become a normal part of the daily police reports, but one morning Majaka came to him, perfectly composed and as usual dressed immaculately in her RWP uniform, to report that a woman was in the charge office with the strange complaint that her two-year-old son had been stolen.

Dick interviewed the woman, a considerably overweight and obviously distressed native whose husband worked as a waiter at the Umbedzi Hotel and to whom she had been married for slightly over three years. Aided by Majaka acting as interpreter, she told him that early that morning three strange little men had burst into her small house in the township, grabbed her two-year-old son, and had run off into the bush with him. She described the men as being very short, almost naked, and speaking in a tongue that she had never heard before.

This didn't sound like one of the usual groups of ruffians that occasionally caused trouble in the township and being completely puzzled, Dick called in a few of his men to ask their opinion. One man, in particular, seemed familiar with a group of people living at the extreme northwest edge of their territory, which bordered what everyone referred to as the Congo. He said that the area consisted of a deep rainforest and was inhabited by strange and very short people who never left their steamy and damp habitat. They were members of the very primitive Mbuti tribe, who wore animal skins rather than modern clothes. He added that they were wild and vicious and that no one ever ventured into their territory.

Dick recalled talk that he had overheard in the bar and had brushed off as nonsense, talk that centered around a band of pygmies that had been stealing maize from a farm over to the northwest of his territory and almost one hundred miles from the township. He reluctantly decided that he should pay a visit to these Mbuti pygmies as much out of curiosity rather than having any expectations of recovering the complainant's son.

The following morning, accompanied by Majaka and Sergeant Zibando, all three dressed in their WRP uniforms, they loaded the Land Rover with enough provisions to last them for a week, along with tents, sleeping bags, his trusty .303 rifle, and backpacks in case they had to travel part of the way on foot. They drove through Umbedzi and out onto the long road, first in a westerly direction before turning northward. The road soon turned from a blacktop to a dusty corrugated dirt surface that hadn't been graded in months.

The Land Rover threw up clouds of dirt and dust behind them as they trundled further into the unknown until, thoroughly shaken, they pulled over to rest. No rain had fallen for weeks and the bush all around them was barren and dry. When they continued their journey, they noticed a distinct change in the terrain. The bush became green and lush and the trees were larger and more plentiful as they ascended the slowly rising dirt road and over to the left Dick saw some farmland with several acres of very healthy-looking maize.

Dick thought that perhaps this would be a good time to pay a courtesy call on the farmer and his family, as he had never ventured this far north before. Dick turned left off of the dirt road onto a narrow but well-maintained dirt track that presumably led to the farmhouse. Dick could see a neat-looking building ahead and with no other buildings in sight, decided that this must be the farmer's home and gazed approvingly at the carefully manicured lawn and flower beds that surrounded it.

All three climbed out of the Land Rover and when Dick went up to the door he was startled when a white man suddenly appeared brandishing a shotgun, a growling bull mastiff at his side. "What do you want?" he said, and when Dick explained that he was patrolling his territory and was calling in as a matter of courtesy, the man put the shotgun aside, smiled as he shook Dick's hand, and invited him inside.

Majaka and Zibando were left standing in the driveway and Dick asked if they could be provided with some food and water. He then looked around the cabin, noting that it was well-furnished, clean, and had the most impressive and decorative parquet flooring Dick had ever seen. The floor was made up of literally thousands of pieces of exotic wood and had been buffed and polished to a gleaming shine. He was reluctant to even step on it, but the farmer just smiled, saying, "One of my little hobbies. It took me months, but it's all hardwood grown on this farm, and you won't damage it by walking on it."

Dick noted that even though there were a few hunting trophies hanging on the wall, it was nothing compared to Taffy's collection.

"Salty DuPlessis." the farmer introduced himself, offering Dick his hand. "Sorry about the rough introduction, but being this far from civilization, I'm not used to visitors." Dick studied Salty. The man was of average height with a stocky build. He hadn't shaved for a few days and the stubble that grew on his face and chin did nothing to enhance his appearance. He wore the usual shorts and bush shirt, sturdy leather *veldskoens*, and thick woolen socks up to his knees. Thick, curly hair that was gray in places hung over his shirt collar.

Casting his arm toward the window he said, "The farm consists of about five thousand acres, most of which is overgrown bush. I have four hundred acres of maize and two hundred head of cattle at last count unless those little buggers from across the border have been up to their tricks again."

"Tell me more about 'those little buggers', Salty. I'm actually looking to have a chat with them about an incident back in Umbedzi where a little piccanin was kidnapped. And please call me Dick. Everyone else does."

"Okay, Dick, I'll tell you, but you're not going to like it. The Mbuti live inside the rainforest on the Congolese border. They're pygmies, wear no clothes, hunt with poisoned arrows, and are cannibals. That's what's probably happened to your little piccanin if they took him. Anyway, let's have a cup of tea."

And, with that, he clapped his hands and called out, "Winifred. Belinda." Two African women came running in from the back of the cabin. "Let's have some tea for me and the inspector, and while you're at it, look after the two police officers that he brought with him. They're standing outside."

Salty explained to Dick that although he was South African by birth, he had lived most of his life in Warania, and having spent most of his time living with Africans, he had adopted some of their ways. For instance, he had five African wives and seventeen colored children, all living in a compound behind his shack. He visited Umbedzi and Chimuka very infrequently, only to buy provisions or to deliver harvested maize to the granary or cattle to the abattoir, and was mostly self-sufficient. A diesel generator provided electricity, and there was plenty of fresh running water from a multitude of springs only a short distance up the hill. A five-ton truck and an old Land Rover got him to town and back.

He told Dick that if he was intent on visiting the Mbuti, he would have to go on foot as the dirt road only extended for a few more miles before petering out. He suggested taking one of his teenage sons, a boy named Stephen, who could speak some of the pygmies Bantu language and would be able to assist him.

Stephen was brought in and introduced to Dick. The lad looked to be about seventeen, was quite tall, well-spoken, and, of course, of mixed race. When apprised of the situation regarding the abducted two-year-old from Umbedzi township, he pointed out that if the pygmies were the ones who had taken the child, it would be several days before they could get back to their rainforest settlement for they had no means of transport other than on foot.

Stephen made absolute sense, but there was still no reason why he shouldn't visit the pygmies and reconnoiter the lie of the land. Salty enthusiastically agreed to Dick's request to set up camp for a couple of nights on his farm, and Dick, Majaka, and Sergeant Zibando erected three tents adjacent to Salty's cabin on his immaculate lawn, one for each of them.

The three made good use of their host's hospitality, particularly in relation to his extensive knowledge of the pygmies who lived up in the mountainous rainforest less than forty miles from his farm.

On day three, leaving their Land Rover and much of their equipment with Salty, each carried a backpack containing some food, plenty of water, and a few essentials. Before beginning their trek up into the forest, Dick made sure that he was carrying his .303 and plenty of ammunition.

With Stephen leading the way, they made good time. They were all fascinated by the abundance of shade supporting a variety of shrubs and bushes, while tall trees, which included mahogany and African pearwood, reached for the sky. The dry heat of the savannah was rapidly replaced by intense dampness in the air and a slight fogginess all around them.

After a grueling hike up into the forest, Stephen estimated that they had walked over fifteen miles, so they made camp. With no tents, the best they could manage was to string four tarpaulins between the trees to serve as bivouacs under which they laid their light sleeping bags. Due to the sticky and stifling heat, they chose to lay on top of their sleeping bags rather than inside them, and after each had consumed a tin of corned beef and some water, they spent an uncomfortable night being eaten alive by insects and getting very little sleep.

Day two was pretty much the same as day one as they continued to climb using game trails that meandered here and there, but Stephen seemed to have a built-in compass and pressed forward at a determined pace.

Day three was when Stephen expected to reach the area where the pygmies lived. They walked slowly, casting their eyes left and right, but saw nothing all morning. They stopped around noon to rest and drink some water when, out of the dense forest, five small, dark, and almost naked men appeared, each one aiming a primitive bow and arrow at their small group.

Stephen began jabbering at them in what Dick presumed to be their local Bantu language, and he was relieved to see them slowly lower their bows although he noted that their arrows were still notched and ready to shoot. While Stephen and a man who appeared to be the leader of the group continued to converse, Dick studied the pygmies. Although small, perhaps around four feet tall, they were all perfectly proportioned.

After what seemed an interminably long conversation, Stephen explained that he told the pygmies of the child's abduction back in Umbedzi township, but they shied away from the subject and totally denied any involvement. They agreed to take these strangers into their small village where they could see for themselves, but, of course, Dick and company all knew that it would be days before the abductors would return with the child. They agreed, however, to visit the village and after several hours of trekking through heavy and damp undergrowth, they arrived at a collection of the most primitive forms of huts any of them had ever seen. These huts, if they could be described as such, were no more than a pile of sticks covered in grass and leaves with a small hole as an entrance. *Similar in many ways,* Dick thought, *to the bird nests that he had seen hanging in trees.*

All four of them were relieved to unburden themselves of their backpacks, which they laid on the ground beside them. The small pygmy village seemed quiet and peaceful and the pygmies themselves weren't at all hostile.

Several women and children stood or sat staring at them, the children completely naked and the women with only scraps of animal skin draped around the waist, their breasts hanging loose with the older women's breasts no more than empty flaps of skin.

In the center of the rough circle of huts was a large patch of cleanly swept earth in the center of which was a small fire pit, and Dick noted with alarm that the circumference of the fire pit was made up of bones, several of which were clearly recognizable as human. Skulls, hipbones, ribs, and other pieces of the human anatomy clearly brought home to Dick the realization that these pygmies were indeed probably cannibals.

Gripping his .303 tightly, Dick pointed the fire pit out to the others and suggested that they leave. Stephen tactfully thanked the pygmies for their help, but the three of them noticed with growing concern that several more men had joined the five who had escorted them to the village and all were pointing their small bows and arrows at them.

After a brief conversation in Bantu, Stephen solemnly advised his party that the pygmies would allow them all to leave except for the woman who, apparently, they wanted to eat for supper. While trying to absorb this distressing news, two of the pygmies ran forward, snatched up all four of their backpacks, and ran off into the forest.

Majaka broke into tears and went to stand behind Dick, who had thoughtfully loaded and cocked his rifle before entering the village. Realizing that they were in peril of their lives, he raised his rifle and fired one shot into the fire pit, causing bone shards to fly in all directions and startling their captors who had appeared not to have seen a firearm or heard a gunshot before.

Quickly loading another round into the chamber, he fired a second shot at one of the bowmen, aiming for a body shot but being the marksman that he was, striking the man's foot instead, causing a howl of pain and indignation as he dropped his bow and hopped around on one leg.

"Back away slowly," said Dick to his three companions. As they did so, Dick loaded a third round into the chamber knowing that he only had seven more left in the magazine. The bowmen did nothing as their hostages slowly backed away and when they were at a safe distance, the four turned and fled, regrettably leaving their backpacks behind.

They made a hasty escape, first at a run and later at a fast walk, continually looking behind them to ensure that they weren't being followed.

Once they had been running or walking for about an hour and considered that they were a good five or six miles distant from the village, Dick topped up his magazine with cartridges, and they slackened their pace. Then Stephen let out a shriek, as from out of nowhere, an arrow struck him in the forearm. He quickly and bravely pulled it out but the wound was deep. Looking at his companions, he told them through gritted teeth that the pygmies covered their arrow tips with poison obtained from the skin of colorful little frogs living in the rainforest. He told them to put a tourniquet on his upper arm quickly or he would be dead.

While Dick searched in vain for any sign of their attacker, Majaka whipped off her belt, wrapping it around Stephen's bicep twice before she could buckle it. Snatching a stick from the ground, she forced it between his arm and the belt and twisted it round and around, tightening it in an attempt to stop the flow of blood from his lower arm to the rest of his body.

Dick could see no sign of the bowman and anxious to put as much distance from him as he could, Dick and Zibando helped Stephen to his feet and headed downhill as fast as possible.

Stephen was keeping up the pace for the first couple of miles but then began to grow weaker. They stopped to rest and despite Majaka's tourniquet, Stephen began shaking uncontrollably and then began having convulsions. Eventually, his face turned a blueish gray, and he stopped breathing. He was dead.

No one spoke. The sight of so much trauma unnerved them all, and they stood looking at Stephen's corpse and Dick shuddered. What to do now? He was now the leader of this pathetic threesome and had to make some decisions.

Continually casting nervous glances all around, Dick said, "Well, we can't carry him all the way back to Salty's. We'll never make it and will die trying. Let's take him a mile or two farther and then do the best we can to bury him and make haste to get out of this godforsaken place." With Dick taking Stephen's legs and Zibando his shoulders, they struggled on down the slope before Dick, thoroughly exhausted, called a halt.

"This is hopeless, we'll all die at this rate." They then set to work scraping and digging with their knives and any useful scraps of wood they could find until they had made a hole about two feet deep and long enough to lay Stephen's body. Majaka retrieved her belt from Stephen's arm, and Dick and Sergeant Zibando laid the body into the small grave that they had dug. All three then packed damp soil over the body, making a small but significant mound on which they piled as many stones as they could find, hoping that this would keep wild animals at bay. No one could think of anything appropriate to say, so they all departed with Dick muttering an almost silent "Thanks, Stephen" as they left.

The three of them walked all day and all night. They had lost their backpacks, sleeping bags, tarpaulins, food, and water in their haste to get away and all they could do was continue to walk, stagger, or crawl downhill, hoping it was in the right direction until hopefully they would reach Salty's farm.

Chapter Fourteen

As they continued to descend, Dick noticed that the trees were becoming sparser and the undergrowth thinner until, with relief, he saw ahead of them the familiar golden-gray colors of the vast savannah that lay below. "Not far now," he said to encourage his small party to keep going. After another three hours of shuffling forward, they could see Salty's fields of green maize a mile or so ahead.

Staggering along Salty's dirt driveway, all three collapsed on his front stoep. Salty's dog started barking and Salty appeared out of nowhere. "What the hell happened to you lot?" he exclaimed. "Where's all your stuff?" Then looking around and counting only three of them demanded, "And where's Stephen?"

The three of them, parched beyond belief, could only croak out a request for water and when it came it tasted like pure nectar. Salty quickly snatched the water away from them, insisting that they sip slowly or it would kill them.

Sergeant Zibando and Majaka, having already collapsed, fell instantly into an utterly exhausted coma, and it was left to Dick to explain what had happened to them during the preceding six days. While Dick tried to explain, his mind was so confused and his speech so slurred that Salty could see that none of them was in any condition to explain anything, so he had his wives find some pillows and blankets and allowed them some time to recuperate while the women cooked up some food for them to eat when they woke.

Seated around Salty's table after twelve hours of sleep, more water, and a hearty meal of something called *bobotie*, a South African dish consisting of curried minced meat baked with an egg custard topping, they were ready to talk. Salty was infuriated when hearing that his eldest son had been killed by the pygmies and was not at all happy that he had been buried in a shallow grave not far from the pygmy village.

"Well, we'll be going back to sort those little bastards out. And we'll bring Stephen home for a decent burial if the little buggers haven't already eaten him."

Dick didn't like the sound of 'we' for he had no intention of ever going back into that miserable, murky, bug-infested hell. But before he had a chance to protest Salty was already spouting off about how they were to form and provision a hunting party to wipe out the tiny village and retrieve Stephen's body.

Majaka, he said, could remain behind, but Dick and Zibando would go, along with three of his other sons, one aged fifteen and two aged sixteen, to avenge their brother's murder. Each would have a firearm, either a rifle or shotgun, as well as revolvers, and they would take plenty of ammunition and enough water and provisions for eight days, plus a litter to bring Stephen's body home on.

Dick explained that, much as he would like to accompany them, he needed to get back to Umbedzi, as he had urgent work that needed attending to. To his dismay, at this point Salty produced a large .45 revolver from beneath the dining room table and pointing it directly at Dick advised him that like it or not, he and Zibando were returning to the rainforest where they would help annihilate the pygmies and lead them to Stephen's grave.

Realizing that Salty had lost his mind from grief and would blow him away in an instant if given half a chance, Dick quickly changed his tune. "Of course, of course," he muttered timidly. "I was quite forgetting you would need us to show you Stephen's grave, but perhaps Sergeant Zibando could do that. You don't really need me. You can even take Majaka."

Unfortunately, both Zibando and Majaka, who were seated at the table with them, stared at him with hooded eyes and gave him a look that is sometimes referred to as 'the hairy eyeball'. He realized that he was stuck between a rock and a hard place. Also, there would be no more nooky with Majaka, so resigned to his fate, whatever that may be, he tried to worm himself back into everyone's favor by declaring that he would indeed return to the scene of the crime.

It took two days for Dick, Majaka, and Zibando to recover from their ordeal and for Salty to get backpacks, firearms, tarpaulins, food, and water organized. Then they were off, once again trudging into the rainforest, only this time very wary of any forty-eight-inch jungle bunnies that might be waiting in ambush for them. Two days into their climb through the dense and misty undergrowth, they began hearing some distant grunts and barks unlike any of them had ever heard before.

On their third day, the noises became louder and closer, and then, not twenty feet ahead of Dick, who was leading the group, loomed a huge and forbidding silverback gorilla. "Don't turn or run," said Dick, knowing that the monster would be upon him in seconds. Instead, he just stood staring at this gigantic beast, with his mouth hanging open in shock. The gorilla continued barking and grunting but made no attempt to draw any closer, and its face changed to a curious rather than hostile expression.

They were staring at each other while the rest of Dick's party shuffled up behind him, none of them speaking but all with the same curious sensation that the gorilla was not intent on harming them. Dick estimated that the silverback must have weighed between three and four hundred pounds and dreaded to think what it could do to them if it decided to attack. Salty, standing right behind him, had his rifle loaded and ready, but Dick waved at him to lower it.

The gorilla cocked his head from side to side and then shuffled off the game trail, apparently no longer interested in them, and they proceeded on their climb deeper into the forest. The following day Dick guided them to Stephen's grave, which thankfully was undisturbed. After Salty had some time alone at the graveside, he joined the rest of the party, saying they would recover the body on their return. Continuing toward the pygmy village, they could still hear the barks and grunts of their gorilla companion who was obviously keeping a close eye on them although they never saw him again.

Dick warned everyone that they were drawing very close to the cluster of pygmy huts, and they all, Dick included, had their weapons cocked and loaded until there before them stood the small pygmy village. The shattered fire pit looked the same as when Dick had left it and not a soul was to be seen. They went from hut to hut, Salty muttering under his breath, "Come out, you shitty little bastards," but it was obvious that the camp, village, or whatever it was called had been abandoned. Salty then began smashing and tearing the little huts apart, ordering his three sons to help him. Piling all the debris into one great mound, he then set fire to it and watched it burn until nothing was left but smoldering ashes.

The dejected group of six then began the long walk home, and Dick was certainly not looking forward to the disinterment of Stephen's remains. Setting the litter beside the grave, they took turns removing the rocks and carefully shoveled away the damp soil until the corpse was completely exposed. Although it had been only just over a week since Stephen was buried, worms and maggots had found the body and were feasting on the softer parts. His eyes, lips, ears, and nostrils were infested with crawling maggots, intent on their feast, and his body was bloated almost beyond recognition.

Dick had seen several cases where bodies had been left to rot. One incident, which Dick had the misfortune to attend, concerned a man who had died from syphilis while squatting behind a bush attending to the call of nature. His genitals and stomach were crawling with maggots and the smell was so nauseating that Dick had vomited time and time again. Hardened to such incidents, he was able to look upon Stephen's corpse and steel himself to remain stoic.

Dick watched as the boy was rolled into a tarpaulin, tied in tightly, and lifted onto the litter to be carried through the forest and down the hill as they headed for Stephen's home and final resting place. They expected this journey to take at least three days, possibly four, but they had done what they had set out to do, had plenty of provisions and, with the obvious exception of Salty, were well satisfied that much had been accomplished.

Making a bivouac on the first night, they lit a small fire and were making tea while they each ate a tin of bully beef when they heard a cry, a human cry—in fact, what sounded like a child's cry—just below them. They immediately threw dirt on the fire and crawled to the side of the game trail, setting an ambush for whoever was coming up the incline.

The child's cries became louder and before they knew it, three little pygmies came into view, one carrying a screaming and struggling infant. "It's those little buggers that kidnapped the toddler from Umbedzi township," whispered Dick. Salty remained silent, merely nodding his head. As they drew level, he fired three perfect shots, one into the head of each of the three pygmies. Sergeant Zibando rushed forward and grabbed the terrified child, and holding him close told him, in his own Waranian tongue, that he was safe now and would be taken home to his mother.

They were welcomed back as heroes upon returning to Salty's farm two days later. Dick took Majaka aside saying, "I think we did all we could. I tried to help Salty and take charge of things, but I have to admit that everyone pulled their weight remarkably well."

Majaka, to her credit, paid more attention to the two-year-old toddler that they had rescued. But once Dick was fed, bathed, and dressed in clean clothes, she did deign to snuggle down with him in his tent and engage in some frantic intercourse before they both fell asleep in each other's arms.

The following morning, Dick, Majaka, and Zibando bid farewell to Salty, his five wives, and sixteen children and drove home to Umbedzi with huge sighs of relief. Little did Dick know what was in store for him, for if he had, he would most certainly have stayed at Salty's for a few more days.

Upon their arrival at Dick's house, Majaka retired to her room to unpack what was left of her belongings before heading straight for the bathroom. Sergeant Zibando went home to his wife and daughter, anxious to tell them about his recent adventure, and Dick, sitting in the small charge office with his two-year-old ward, sent one of his constables into the township to locate the child's mother.

The mother appeared shortly afterward and delightedly swept the child off his feet, making a huge fuss of him, before thanking Dick for rescuing him and then departing. Dick, noticing for the first time a nasty smell emanating from his clothes and body, decided that he would join Majaka in the bathroom to take a shower but when he tried the door it was locked. Banging loudly on the door and demanding to be let in, Majaka replied that he would have to wait.

Several minutes later the door opened and as she appeared, wrapped in a large bath towel, he noted a sour expression on her face and a huge frown that did not bode at all well. When he asked what was wrong, she replied, "You stink. Go and get cleaned up, then we have to talk."

Suitably bathed and shaven, Dick dressed and returned to the small sitting room which, by mutual agreement, they now comfortably shared. Majaka was already seated, looking both worried and sad, and announced that she thought she was pregnant. The look of horror spread across Dick's face, and he stupidly asked, "Who's the bounder? I'll have him flogged."

"It's you, you idiot," she replied. "I haven't been with another man for months. It must have been that first time we did it when you taught me all those naughty things. That was two months ago, and I've missed two of my monthly periods. What shall we do?"

"But weren't you using anything? One of those Dutch caps or something?"

When she answered, "What are you talking about? What's a cap got to do with anything?" he realized that she probably wasn't familiar with Annabelle's fancy forms of contraception.

"Well, I thought you were taking some precautions. After all, we've been doing it pretty regularly for the past couple of months. It was bound to happen. I don't know what to do."

In a daze, Dick walked to the small cabinet where he kept a few drinks for special occasions and poured himself half a glass of Johnnie Walker Black Label. Knocking it straight back, he exclaimed slowly and resolutely, "I can't marry you if that's what you're thinking. I'm not supposed to even be sleeping with you. They made it clear when I first joined the Force that miscegenation would not be tolerated. Anyway, you were the one who started it. You left the bathroom door open while you were lying naked in the bathtub."

Majaka rose swiftly, grabbed a tumbler from the cabinet, filled it to the brim with his precious Johnnie Walker, and tipped it all over his head. Dick roared in protest and grabbing her by the front of her shirt, he yelled, "You stupid cow. What did you do that for?" Slowly, he calmed down, then began laughing uncontrollably and within seconds, she joined in. Together they sank slowly to the carpet where they gently removed their casual, and in Dick's case, whisky-soaked clothing, and began to dance a horizontal tango.

By morning, back in Dick's bed, they discussed their dilemma in a more mature fashion. They came up with a few solutions. One was to both leave the RWP and move to another country, probably the United Kingdom, where they could get married. Another was to find someone locally who would perform an illegal abortion.

Thirdly, they could brazen it out, get married locally, and live with the consequences. In the end, they decided that Majaka would seek out someone in the township who would perform an abortion. With their decision made, they copulated one more time before she bathed, dressed in civilian clothes, and went into the township to find a suitable abortionist.

Dick watched her leave, thinking how brave she was. To watch her, so smart and self-assured with her chin held high, her knee-length skirt swinging freely with the motion of her hips, and her light green woolen sweater blowing gently in the breeze, no one would ever think that she was walking into the jaws of hell. Now dressed in uniform, Dick went to inspect the horses and found them in good health and well groomed. Shadreck, as well as being cook, houseboy, garden boy, horse groomer, and general dogsbody, had proved, to the best of Dick's knowledge, to be excellent at keeping his personal life a secret, and Dick's considerable backhand bribes had been successful, he hoped, in keeping the romantic goings on at the household private.

While Dick had been away, several incidents had come to the attention of the police force at Umbedzi and had been dealt with efficiently by the officer on duty. Dick waded through piles of property crime report forms and complaints of assault. One report of rape turned out to be a case of nonpayment of wages, and there was an interesting case of bestiality where an African man was caught in the township rogering his goat and offering onlookers a piece of the action for two shillings each.

Majaka was taking a long time to come back from the township, but Dick assumed that she had found someone who would take care of business and was resting quietly before taking the bus home.

When Shadreck placed a shepherd's pie on the table shortly after six o'clock, Dick became seriously worried. After eating, he became even more concerned when a man came into the charge office claiming that he had found a dead woman lying in the long grass beside the road.

Dick immediately drove to the scene to find Majaka lying in a small pool of blood at the roadside, her skirt rucked up around her thighs and, mysteriously, a large tear in the right sleeve of her green sweater.

He lifted her, placed her in his Land Rover, and drove back to the police station, a tear trickling from his eye, for he knew what had happened, and he knew that he was to blame.

The following day, filled with remorse, and with Majaka loaded into the body box, he took her to the morgue in Chimuka, filled in the request for a postmortem, and tied the requisite tag to her toe. Returning to the station, he couldn't stop the visions circling around in his head—some cackling, dirty old woman, prying and poking around in Majaka's most private parts with a collection of rusty bits of wire, probably coat hangers, while Majaka tried to stifle the screams that were involuntarily escaping from her mouth. How could he ever forgive himself?

Once again, he phoned Taffy with his tale of woe, and this time, his friend sounded truly worried.

"I think I'd better come over there. You sound in a pretty bad way, and with good cause, I might add. Hang tight, and I'll be there in a couple of hours." True to his word, Taffy arrived and tried to console the man who had become a good friend. Sitting opposite Dick at his small, shabby table he said, "Dick, man, you've got to pull yourself together. No one made her do it. It was her decision. In any case, you don't know for certain that she had an abortion. Wait until you've received the postmortem report before jumping to conclusions. I don't like the sound of the way you found her. You said her clothing was rucked up and torn. Sounds like she was attacked or beaten to me."

Taffy spent the evening trying to convince Dick that Majaka's death may have been nothing to do with her seeking an abortion and ended up spending the night in Majaka's bed before heading off back to Zumba in the morning.

Five days later, Dick received a telephone call from the coroner's office. The deceased had been thoroughly examined and the cause of death was deemed to be severe trauma due to being struck by a heavy metal object on the lower back. He also added that her right arm was broken and suggested that taking into consideration the location and position of where and how the body was found, he suspected that she was probably struck by the front mudguard or bumper of a vehicle that failed to stop. "Was there any indication that the woman was or had been pregnant?" Dick asked.

"None whatsoever," came the reply. She hadn't been pregnant in the first place, Dick realized. She just wanted a new way of life and saw Dick as the answer.

Retiring to his small living room, Dick once more turned to his dwindling supply of Johnnie Walker, sat in his overstuffed and lumpy sofa and wept softly.

Chapter Fifteen

Eventually pulling himself together, Dick decided to visit the scene again, taking one of his constables with him. As they searched back and forth along the roadside, the constable called out, "Sir, come over here. I think I may have found something." When Dick looked, he saw a flashy, chrome-plated wing mirror lying in the tall grass that somehow looked familiar to him. Before touching it, he searched his memory until he remembered exactly where he had seen such a mirror before. Taking his handkerchief from his shirt pocket, he carefully wrapped the mirror and when he got back to the station, he sent it off to police headquarters to be dusted for fingerprints.

Several days later, he received a call from the fingerprint bureau saying that they had lifted a fingerprint from the mirror that matched a known previous offender currently wanted for a series of offenses, ranging from assault to robbery and theft. The name, Joshua Zambuti, meant nothing to Dick, but what did interest him was that the caller also mentioned that they discovered traces of blood on the mirror. Dick explained how and where the mirror was found and asked that they send the mirror and blood samples to their forensic laboratory for a comparison to the deceased policewoman Allison Majaka, upon whom the mortuary recently conducted a postmortem.

Two days later, Dick received a phone call from an excited forensic analyst who told him that, indeed, the blood on the mirror was a perfect match with blood taken from Majaka's corpse.

Now Dick was on the hunt for an old, rusty Ford Cortina with a missing left-side wing mirror. He phoned Taffy, saying, "You were right, Taffy. She didn't have an abortion. In fact, she wasn't even pregnant. The whole pregnancy issue was a ruse. What actually happened to Majaka was a hit-and-run road accident, and I might know of the car that was responsible. I think it was the same one that was used to abduct me when I arrived in Warania."

"It was a beaten-up old Ford Cortina with flashy chrome wing mirrors, identical to the mirror that I found at the scene. The blood sample that was taken from the mirror matched Majaka's, and they found a fingerprint on it that belonged to a wanted criminal named Joshua Zambuti."

Taffy cursed, saying that he knew of a local troublemaker named Zambuti who drove a clapped-out old Cortina and that he would go to the local township immediately to check it out. "No," said Dick, "I'll come over, and we'll go together. I'll see you in about two hours." He called one of his constables to go with him and within minutes they were in the Land Rover and off to Zumba.

Pulling into the Zumba police station, Taffy was waiting for them and climbed into Dick's Land Rover, along with one of his own constables, and directed Dick to the Zumba township. "Got your rifle?" asked Taffy jokingly, their differences over the hunting debacle long forgotten. Dick smiled as he pointed to the gun rack behind him. "Never without it, thanks to you."

Zumba's African township was laid out in neat rows of little brick houses with small gardens neatly arranged in front of some, and scraggly patches of bare earth in front of others. Dick noted that derelict cars were parked haphazardly in front of other houses. They eventually drew up in front of an untidy and uncared-for building with a rusty old Ford Cortina parked outside. All four policemen climbed out of the Land Rover and Dick went to inspect the vehicle more closely. Sure enough, it had the same flashy chrome-plated wing mirror on the driver's side, but there was only a hole on top of the left mudguard where the other mirror should have been.

Upon closer inspection, Dick found some threads of green wool that appeared to match the color of the sweater that Majaka had been wearing, tangled in the rusty bumper. He also found a small dent at the front of the passenger side mudguard, but the vehicle was so full of scratches and dents that this was probably of no significance. "We've got the car," said Dick as he placed the tiny threads in an envelope. "Now, let's get the driver."

Taffy and his constable went around the back of the house while Dick hammered on the rickety front door. When he heard a shout from behind the house, he ran around to find Taffy's constable holding his right shoulder, with a nasty stab wound bleeding profusely, and Taffy disappearing in a cloud of dust. Dick and his constable chased after him, and they soon passed Taffy, who at about two hundred and forty pounds, couldn't run to save his life. "Go back and look after your constable," shouted Dick. "I see the bugger. We'll get him." With that, they ran after the fleeing culprit for all they were worth.

Although the man was wearing a bright orange shirt that stood out clearly among the subdued browns and grays of the township, he was still fifty or sixty feet ahead of them and gaining ground. He dodged between two brick pillars into a cemetery. They followed, but he was nowhere to be seen. Hundreds of gravestones varied in height from two to five feet, and as they stopped and gazed across the graveyard Dick said, "He's in here somewhere, hiding behind one of these gravestones no doubt, and he must be very close. Be careful. Remember he's got a knife, and he's not afraid to use it."

They split up, moving cautiously from grave to grave, when a sudden movement only a few feet from where Dick was standing, gave the man away. The next thing Dick knew, the man was running at him, knife pointing forward and held above shoulder height. Dick waited for the onslaught that was about to come, thinking of the judo and aikido that he had learned back in London. *Use your attacker's momentum to thwart his attack,* Dick thought, and as the knife came down, he stepped aside, grabbed the man's sleeve, then the collar of his jacket, and swung him further forward in the direction that he was already heading. The man shot past him at a full run and then, as he fell, cracked his head on a convenient headstone and dropped, totally stunned. His knife sailed on ahead of him before clattering to the gravel pathway.

When Taffy caught up to them, Dick's constable already had the man in handcuffs. Upon searching him, he found a wallet containing a driver's license showing a photograph of his ugly mug and pronouncing the holder to be none other than Joshua Zambuti. "We have our man," exclaimed Dick, and the five of them, having recovered Zambuti's knife, returned to the Land Rover. When Zambuti later appeared in court charged with the hit-and-run killing of Woman Constable Allison Majaka, the abduction, robbery, and attempted murder of Inspector Starling at Chimuka Airport, the stabbing of Taffy's now fully recovered constable, and a multitude of other offenses, he was sentenced to a total of thirty years hard labor with no time off for good behavior.

Following Zambuti's trial, Dick received the much-coveted Commissioner's Commendation for the successful outcome of his investigation. The commendation included a framed certificate to hang on his bedroom wall and a pleasant addition to his record of service at headquarters.

Having replaced his original bottle of Johnnie Walker Black Label, Dick sat quietly, contemplating his future with glass in hand. He was over twenty now and took a mental tally of his several short-lasting romances and the thrills and spills encountered during almost two years of serving in the RWP. He had become accustomed to life in the sticks and enjoyed the level of authority that the member in charge of a rural police station was accorded. He would certainly not be suited to city life and had no desire to delve into any type of business venture. Besides which, he had no money to do that if he wished to.

In any case, the Queen's representative to Warania, the right honorable Sir Roy Johnston, governor general of the Colony, was due to visit Umbedzi on his newly announced tour of the entire country by train. Apparently, Sir Roy was to bring with him his new bride, a lady he recently married in Britain.

Chapter Sixteen

Umbedzi had no hall of any size in which to entertain Sir Roy and his new wife, so it was decided to hold a welcoming reception at the railway station upon his arrival. The mayor, Jimmy Abbots, who was also the proprietor of Umbedzi's one and only grocery store, would be resplendent in his mayoral chain of office to welcome Sir Roy. He had invited virtually the entire white population of Umbedzi, along with a few prominent black citizens, to come in their Sunday best to celebrate this momentous occasion. Chains of bunting adorned the railway station and the station's small waiting room was a profusion of flowers, food, and drink carefully arranged by the local Women's Institute. Dick would be present in his traditional uniform of jodhpurs, boots and leggings, shirt and tie, barathea tunic, belt and brace, and, of course, his cap bearing the proud lion and assegai badge of the RWP.

As the reception committee waited on the platform, the Garratt steam locomotive drawing Sir Roy's ancient but beautiful wooden carriage came into view with dark puffs of steam and smoke belching from its funnel. All those assembled, most of whom had already taken advantage of the vast array of liquor, cold beers, and punch that had been laid on for the occasion, began waving and cheering.

The train drew to a halt with a great hiss of steam, the carriage door opened and everyone gasped in open admiration as out stepped Sir Roy, resplendent in a dark blue button-down high-collared jacket with gold oak leaves embroidered on the collar, chest, and cuffs. The jacket, with its long tails, was set off with white breeches, and finishing the ensemble was a cocked hat decked with long white ostrich plumes.

No doubt in his day, Dick thought, *he would have cut quite a figure, but now, well into his seventies with rounded shoulders, a pot belly, and a stoop, he looked plainly ridiculous.* Nonetheless, everyone cheered and clapped as Sir Roy shook hands with Mayor Abbots but Dick was more interested in the woman who stepped down behind him. With a shock, he recognized the governor general's new wife to be none other than Miss Annabelle Delaney. Anna, or rather Mrs. Annabelle Johnston, looked as radiant as ever with her shock of red hair and captivating figure, and Dick noted that on this occasion she was again wearing glasses.

She smiled at the crowd there to meet them, and although casting a glance in Dick's direction, she showed no sign of recognition. But why should she, he thought? Clad in his police uniform, with a weathered face, bent nose, sideburns, and a rather splendid mustache, he looked nothing like the callow youth she had seduced two years ago.

Dick sauntered over to the tables laden with an assortment of finger foods and beverages and selected a cold bottle of Chimbuka before standing aside and watching Annabelle meet and greet the interesting collection of citizens that were there to welcome them. All the local business owners were there, along with several farmers, and not all were British. Many were born and bred Waranians, several were from various European countries, and of course, there were many South Africans, some Rhodesians, and even two couples from Kenya.

Some of the women, Dick couldn't help noticing, looked much better, younger, and more animated than usual. Gone were the baggy dresses, jeans, T-shirts, and blouses that they usually wore, and in their place were stylish hair-dos, high-heeled shoes, nylon stockings, and tight, form-fitting outfits including quite a few of the new and popular mini-skirts. He noted that two of the younger women had arrived braless with their nipples pressing proudly against thin tops. As he gazed at them, he could feel a stirring in his loins that usually meant trouble and muttered to Little Tommy under his breath, "Down boy, down."

After allowing a respectable amount of time to pass, Dick drew closer to Annabelle until he stood right next to her. When there was a suitable pause in her conversation with the wife of the local butcher, he whispered quietly in her ear, "Remember me, Anna?"

Curious, she turned around, looked him straight in the eyes with a frown, and said, "No, I don't. Should I?" Then the frown slowly disappeared as she began to realize that she did vaguely recognize the rugged tan policeman beside her. As recognition dawned, she broke into a smile. "Oh, my God. Surely, you can't be Richard. You've become a man! Oh, I have so much to tell you, and I can see that you will have much to tell me. We must get together, but we're only here for two nights, and I am sleeping on the train."

"What the dickens are you doing with that old windbag?" he asked in surprise, nodding toward Sir Roy who was stuffing his corpulent face with small sausage rolls as he chatted pompously with a group of men nearby. Unfortunately, neither of them noticed that Sandy Cartwright, editor-publisher and news journalist of the local weekly rag.

The Umbedzi Gazette was standing nearby and listening to every word while pretending to struggle to open a bottle of beer. "Oh, but Richard, he's the governor general, and we live in a big house with lots of servants and plenty of money. He's too old to do anything in bed, but we get lots of invites to fancy events, and I get to meet the most interesting people. Even my two pussy cats love this life. Do you remember them? Christmas and Easter."

She quietly took his hand in hers as if shaking hands in farewell but stroked the inside of his palm softly with her index finger, the age-old indicator meaning "I will if you will." After a momentary pause, and speaking very quietly, she continued, "Come back to this platform at eleven tonight. He will have passed out by then, and we'll figure something out." She then turned away and began circulating again, and since there was nothing to keep Dick at the reception any longer, he left and returned to his quarters. Neither Dick nor Annabelle noticed that Sandy Cartwright, erstwhile editor-publisher and news journalist, left the reception right after Dick had gone.

Back at his quarters, Dick disrobed, had a quick shower, and stretched out on his bed for a couple of hours nap, dreaming of the evening's encounter with Annabelle.

Shadreck had prepared one of his favorite dishes, an East African curry with rice and sambals, and Dick set to in earnest, building up his strength for the night to come. Once he had thoroughly demolished Shadreck's delicious meal, he enjoyed a couple of cold Chimbukas before dressing in a pair of shorts sans underwear, his lavender-colored Hawaiian shirt, hoping it would bring him better luck than the last time he wore it, and a pair of light leather slip-on shoes. At 10:30 sharp, he left the house and took a casual stroll down to the railway station.

Shortly before eleven o'clock, he entered the deserted station and took a seat on a platform bench, anxiously waiting for events to unfold. At precisely

11:00, he saw Anna climb quietly down from the governor general's carriage and approach him. She was wearing a flimsy dress that fluttered in the cool breeze, a pair of flat-heeled shoes, and no glasses. As soon as she saw him, she quickened her pace and flung her arms around his neck, giving him an affectionate kiss before taking his hand, and, in the dark and silent railway station, save for the buzzing, chirping, and squeaking of crickets and Christmas beetles that were rampant at that time of the year, she led him into the empty waiting room.

All the bunting, flowers, and food had been removed, and it was once again a small waiting room with a large center table and a dozen or so wooden chairs.

Dick took a step back and asked "Anna, there are a couple of things that I've been wondering about for the past two years. One is pretty stupid, the other quite serious. Firstly, why is it that you sometimes wear glasses and other times you don't?"

She giggled before replying. "Well, I wear glasses to appear more professional and intelligent. They're just plain glass, and I can see perfectly well without them. Now, what was your other question?"

"Who was that bloke who burst into your flat? He acted like your husband or that he owned you."

"Oh, yes. That was Steve. He wasn't living with me and wasn't my husband, but he thought he was my boyfriend. As you know, or should know, I like my sex, and Steve often satisfies my needs. It was terrible what happened that evening, and I'm so, so, sorry. Now forget about him and let's have some fun."

She then took a step toward him, raised her arms above her head, and let her flimsy dress drop, revealing her beautiful and voluptuous figure. The sight of her red tuft of pubic hair and her proud and magnificent breasts aroused Dick immediately and unzipping his fly, he gave Little Tommy free rein to explore the undergrowth.

"Not so fast, Dick," smiled Anabelle. "Let's try something a little different that I haven't done for a long time." She led him to the table in the center of the room and slowly unbuttoned and removed his shirt. She then pulled down his shorts, saying, "Oh, no undies. You really came prepared. I think they call that going commando."

She gave his cherry a little kiss, then climbed onto the table, lay on her back with her legs akimbo, and said, "Tonight I'm going to introduce you to the sixty-nine position." She then made him crawl on top of her, pushed his head between her legs, and took him in her mouth.

"Oh, this is wonderful," he mumbled. "I've never done this bef…aaagh," and heard Annabelle scream as a huge flash lit the room for a split second. As they scrambled off the table, Dick heard the sound of running feet.

Quickly pulling on his shorts and shirt while Annabelle slipped into her dress, he muttered, "Someone's just taken our photo." They ran out onto the platform, but no one was in sight, and they stared at each other in dismay. They were alone once more but in no mood for any more monkey business.

"Who do you think it was?" she asked, not really expecting an answer, and nor did she get one. They sat down despondently on the platform bench once more, holding hands and pondering their future, especially hers. Eventually, they parted, Annabelle back to her carriage where Sir Roy was sleeping in their bed, sawing logs, and Dick back to his quarters where he poured himself a stiff scotch and pondered the outcome of the night's foolishness.

Chapter Seventeen

It was well after midnight when Sandy Cartwright, the editor-publisher and news journalist of the Umbedzi Gazette stood in his darkroom developing and printing the very clear and excellent black and white photograph that he had taken earlier. "This is dynamite," he said with glee, thinking of all the possibilities that the photograph would offer him.

He was, of course, thinking of the monetary value that this once-in-a-lifetime scoop would bring. Should he go to the national radio and newspaper bigwigs or instead blackmail Sir Roy, who he knew had access to plenty of cash? After a few minutes, he decided that the latter course of action would be his best bet, and sitting before his typewriter, he prepared a note that would knock the silly old bugger's socks off.

Early that morning, having had very little sleep, he left a sealed envelope addressed to Sir Roy, marked personal and confidential, with one of the flunkies who was employed on the great man's railway carriage. The message merely said: "Dear Sir Roy. I am in possession of an item that will cause extreme embarrassment to you and your wife should it be made public. If you wish to see it, meet me at the extreme western end of this railway platform at ten this morning."

The attendant on duty outside Sir Roy's carriage door handed Sir Roy the envelope at the earliest opportunity and the great man frowned as he opened it while indulging in an enormous fried breakfast and read the neatly typed message. *Am I being blackmailed?* he thought. Impossible, I've never stepped out of line and have done nothing wrong, and he eventually concluded that this was just some chancer thinking that he or she could make some money or, worse still, try to assassinate him at the western end of the platform at ten o'clock. He decided to summon his aide de camp and alert the police.

Dick groaned when he was summoned and shown the note. After discussing it with Sir Roy, it was decided that Dick and two of his constables would arrive at the platform before ten, wait for the blackmailer to appear, and then arrest him. However, Dick had other plans. His plan was to show himself and pretend to give chase in the hope that he could identify the culprit before he or she was allowed to escape. He would deal with them later.

Just before the appointed hour, Cartwright, wearing dark sunglasses, a trilby hat pulled down well over his face, a light raincoat, and a scarf, stood out like a sore thumb when he arrived at the designated spot and was alarmed to see not Sir Roy, but Police Inspector Dick Starling and two police constables coming toward him. Dick deliberately made a botch of the chase, allowing the man to quickly disappear from view, and much to Cartwright's relief, he was not pursued. Dick, on the other hand, having been shown Cartwright's letter, knew perfectly well what 'the item' was, and was as keen as Anna that it not come to light.

He was pretty sure that he recognized the blackmailer as being none other than Sandy Cartwright and decided that he would have to deal with the blighter himself in order to keep the photo a secret. Cartwright, now shaken to the core by his narrow escape, knew that he had to revert to Plan B. Returning to his office, he immediately telephoned the editor of the Warania Herald in Chimuka and informed him that he possessed a photograph of Sir Roy's wife having some exotic kind of sex with a white male who was certainly not her husband. The editor sounded interested and suggested that he bring or mail the photograph to Chimuka, so they could perform due diligence before making it public. Cartwright agreed, immediately jumped in his truck, and headed for Chimuka in great haste to begin negotiating a substantial reward for his scoop of the year.

Upon arrival at the editor's office after lunchtime, Cartwright proudly presented him with his photograph but the editor merely laughed at him. "Yes," he said, "they're doing the sixty-nine all right, but her legs are covering his face and his are covering hers. How can anyone prove who they are?"

"B-but I saw them, and I know who he is too. He's the member in charge of our local police station. And she's a redhead, recognizable to anyone."

Again, the editor pushed the photograph back to him. "A fat lot of good that will do you with a black and white photograph. They could be just about anyone. No, I'm sorry Cartwright, we're not interested. Close the door on your way out." And with that, Cartwright silently left the editor's office, returned to his truck, and drove home.

I'll get them somehow, he thought. Cartwright, with his mind on revenge instead of on his driving, wavered across the center line and was struck head-on by a huge cement truck and killed instantly. When police later attended the scene, they discovered a dirty picture among his personal effects. They all laughed at it and pinned it up on the tea room wall.

Meanwhile, back at the offices of the Warania Herald, the editor called in his top news reporter, Jeff Spencer, and gave him a rundown of the conversation he had earlier with Cartwright, telling him to pay very special attention to Sir Roy's wife as they toured the country in their railway carriage. "We might have a hot one here," he said with a chuckle.

Dick, still fretting over the close call he'd had, thanked the Lord that Sir Roy, silly old bastard that he was, had immediately come to him with the letter rather than deal with it himself. From the brief glimpse he had of the man standing at the end of the platform, he was still pretty certain that it was Sandy Cartwright. Having given considerable thought as to how he would approach Cartwright, it was mid-afternoon before he went into town to see him. On his arrival, he found Cartwright's only employee, a pretty young woman of about nineteen or twenty, sitting at her desk in tears.

"Whatever is the matter?" he asked. Between lots of blubbering and crying, she told him that she had just received a telephone call from the police in Chimuka saying that Sandy was dead. Killed in a motor car accident on the road from Chimuka to Umbedzi.

He knelt down beside her and put his arm around the girl's slender shoulders to help comfort her and was surprised when she lay her head against his neck and continued to quietly sob. "What's your name?" he asked.

Between sobs, she murmured, "Valerie, Valerie Cross." Once again, Dick was torn between comforting this distraught young woman and rushing off to the crash scene in the hope of recovering the photograph. Common sense won out over lecherous opportunity, and he bade her farewell, rushed to his Land Rover, and headed south toward Chimuka in the hope of encountering the scene of the accident before all was revealed.

When he got there, the body had already been removed from the wreckage. Cartwright's vehicle, a surprisingly new Ford F100 half-ton pickup truck, was totally mangled and Dick could see, from the amount of blood and gore across what was left of the dashboard, that the man had not been wearing a seat belt and had catapulted straight over the steering wheel and through the front windscreen. The cement truck and its driver were still at the scene, the driver sitting at the roadside, cradling his head in his hands and visibly shaken.

Dick spoke with the sergeant in charge at the scene and asked him if Cartwright's vehicle had been searched for any valuables or personal effects, feigning concern that the tow truck personnel, who were on their way, would certainly purloin anything of value. The sergeant smiled, saying that the deceased's wallet, wrist watch, and briefcase were back at the Chimuka police station. He then sniggered, saying that Cartwright must have been a dirty old man, and went on to describe the photograph they had found in his briefcase, which now adorned the notice board in the police tea room.

Dick, attempting to conceal the horror that swept over him, addressed the problem with what he considered to be abject disgust saying "Sergeant, regardless of the humor that you all seem to have found in this photograph, it was totally inappropriate to use it as a means of demeaning the poor fellow even further. I will go and recover this photograph and ensure that his wife or family never become aware of it." And with that, he jumped into his Land Rover and made a hasty exit.

On arrival at the Chimuka police traffic department, he found the tea room, and there, resplendent on the cork noticeboard, was a picture of him and Annabelle, totally naked on the table, with their heads buried between each other's legs.

He quickly removed the photograph and left, now headed back to the Umbedzi Gazette office, where he hoped to retrieve any other prints and the negatives before anyone else discovered them.

Young Valerie Cross was still in the small office when Dick arrived and was now more composed than she had been when he left. "Hello, it's me again. I've come from Chimuka, and I'm sorry to say that you were correct. Sandy didn't survive the accident, and it looked like it was his fault as he was on the wrong side of the road when he hit the cement truck. God knows what happened, perhaps he had a heart attack. But whatever the cause, I have to go through his office. You never know, it could have been suicide and the accident was, in fact, deliberate. Perhaps he left a note."

She took him through to the office and left him to search through Sandy's desk and filing cabinets, but after over two hours of searching, he still hadn't come across any prints or negatives of the photo in question. He did, however, notice that Cartwright's Cardex system was open to a card headed the Warania Herald.

Once more, he questioned Miss Cross. "Is there anywhere else that Sandy might have kept stuff, any stuff, documents, photographs, negatives?"

She looked at him blankly and then, as though a light was suddenly switched on, said, "Of course. He has a dark room that has all his photographic stuff, and there are some filing cabinets in it too. I should have thought of it before." She led him to the back and indicated the door to the darkroom but didn't enter.

He thanked her and when he entered, he found a conventional light switch. The room was quite small and had a sink and various trays and bottles of fluid. Hanging on clothes pegs were a number of developed strips of film and Dick meticulously held each strip up to the light and eventually discovered the one he was looking for. He immediately pocketed it and was about to leave when he noticed that some of the prints laid out on the small metal table were of couples fornicating.

Upon closer inspection, he recognized some of the participants. There was Umbedzi's mayor Abbots, totally starkers and getting a blow job from the wife of the guy who owned the local garage, and plenty more residents of their small town having it off with each other. Some Dick knew; others he didn't.

Sifting through the files stored in Cartwright's filing cabinets, he found even more revealing photographs. After gathering them up, he returned to the front office where he thanked Valerie Cross for her help.

"But what am I to do?" she asked him. "Who's going to print the Gazette and who's going to pay my wages? Sandy's not married and has no family that I'm aware of."

Dick replied that he would give it some thought and get back to her. Returning home, Dick took a last look at the incriminating photo before burning it and the roll of negatives that could so easily have been the ruin of him and Annabelle both. Then he sat and enjoyed studying Sandy's collection of pornographic photographs, trying to identify as many of the subjects as he could and making notes on the back of the photographs once he was sure he had identified someone. He finally came across some unbelievable full-frontal photographs of a naked and obviously quite happy Valerie Cross, smiling at the camera while clutching her ankles high above her head. He could almost see what she'd had for breakfast.

***

The following morning his telephone rang as he was still having breakfast and when he answered he heard, "Did you happen to come across any photos of me in Sandy's darkroom?" Even though she didn't identify herself, it was clearly Valerie. "As a matter of fact, I did. Quite revealing to say the least."

"Oh." A long pause was followed by, "Can I have them back, please? If I come over personally?"

Gazing at her photograph again he quickly replied, "Sure. But make it around six this evening, and I'll treat you to dinner."

"Okay, I'll be there, and I'll bring a bottle of wine to boot," and rang off.

Dick summoned Shadreck and told him that he was expecting company that evening and to prepare something special. Then he quickly went through the rest of Sandy's photographs and found a total of seven of Valerie in the altogether and in a variety of revealing poses.

Promptly at six, Valerie arrived at the house. She had obviously gone home to change after work and was wearing a pair of high heels, a short turquoise mini-skirt, and a very low-cut and tight-fitting white top that revealed a large expanse of flesh.

Dick welcomed her in and asked her if she would like some wine. "I have a very nice Nederburg Cabernet or, if you prefer white, there's a bottle of Chardonnay cooling in the fridge."

"Oh, I'll have the white, thank you," she replied, sitting comfortably on the well-worn sofa. She crossed her legs, revealing even more of her thighs in the process.

Dick joined her in a glass of Chardonnay, they chinked glasses, and Dick, got straight to the point, asking, "Why did you let Sandy take those photographs?"

Her reply was equally straightforward. "I've been selling them to a magazine company in the United States and so far, I've earned nearly five thousand US dollars. No one knows me there, so it's quite safe and Sandy was really a very good photographer and very discreet. I hope you're not going to tell anyone. After all, it's not breaking the law, is it?"

"No, it's not breaking the law." Then she moved closer to him, placed a hand on his knee, and asked, "You promise you won't tell anyone? I'll be very nice to you." Upon hearing this, Dick's eyebrows weren't the only things that shot up. Just as he was about to pounce on her, Shadreck emerged from the kitchen announcing that the food was ready, and they reluctantly retired to Dick's small and rickety dining room table. Shadreck had prepared a shepherd's pie, which Dick had to admit was even better than his previous effort, and the pair of them quickly demolished it. Dick told Shadreck to leave and clean up in the morning and the pair returned to the sofa.

This time, Valerie sat on Dick's lap and stroked his neck as she began kissing him. He, in turn, placed a hand on her thigh where it crept higher and higher. Suddenly, a gentle tapping on the front door startled them.

Sighing, she climbed off his lap and straightened her skirt while Dick went to see who was there. No sooner had he opened it than Annabelle Johnston née Delaney barged in, threw her arms around his neck, and hugged him so tightly he thought he would suffocate.

As he desperately tried to fend her off, his thoughts were in turmoil. It seemed his love life was one of either feast or famine. "Anna, what in heaven's name are you doing? What's wrong? I thought you were supposed to have left this morning."

Annabelle began to cry softly and then, turning toward the living room, began bawling as she saw a young and pretty girl with great big eyes staring at her.

"Augh, everything's gone wrong. First, you had no sooner left than a porter turned up to see what all the fuss was about and then ran to wake my husband. Fortunately, I was dressed and able to fluff it off when Sir Roy arrived. I told him I couldn't sleep and went out to get some fresh air. Then he told me that we would be staying an extra day in Umbedzi, and we'd been busy all day. This is the first chance I've had to catch up with you. I've left him sleeping in the carriage and have walked all the way here only to find you cozying up with some floozy."

At this point, Valerie jumped up and shouted, "Hey, old lady, who are you calling a floozy?" They flew at each other like a pair of hellcats.

Dick stared in horror as the two women bit, scratched, and clawed at each other. *This was madness,* he thought, and tried to intervene but soon backed off after first one, then the other, set about him. After a minute or so, things calmed down, each woman collapsing into a chair. Valerie was gripping a big chunk of Annabelle's red hair in her left fist and sporting three deep scratches down the left side of her face, which were trickling blood. Annabelle was nursing a nasty bite on her right wrist and had blood running into her eyes from where the chunk of hair had been torn out.

Dick, with a few scratches and one bite, strangely in his pelvic region, where his shirt and shorts had been partially torn off, stood between them, not knowing what to say. Eventually, Annabelle broke the ice and, looking over at Valerie, calmly suggested that perhaps she had overreacted and that they should move over to the table, sit down and have a drink. Relieved that some semblance of order had been restored Dick rescued the two glasses of wine which miraculously had not been knocked over, poured a third for Annabelle, and set them on his shabby dining room table.

With the three of them sitting around the table, Annabelle told the other two that she was dreadfully frustrated. While living with Sir Roy provided many luxuries and advantages, he was far too old to engage in sex, something that she really missed. When she found Dick in this lonely and godforsaken outpost, she thought it was just too good an opportunity to miss. Of course, she didn't know that he had a girlfriend, and was shocked when she saw that Valerie had beaten her to the punch. Valerie said that she too was frustrated and admitted that she wasn't really Dick's girlfriend, she was merely doing him a favor.

They both laughed at this and the women each gave the other a knowing nod, stood up, and each taking one of Dick's hands led him to the bedroom. What followed was, to Dick's way of thinking, beyond marvelous. For the first time in his life, he had participated in a ménage à trois and as he lay there, between two naked and beautiful women, he considered that this was perhaps the happiest and most idyllic moment of his life. All of a sudden, he was struck with the realization that today was his twentieth birthday, and he smiled all the more.

Chapter Eighteen

At 2:00 in the morning, with all three thoroughly worn out and sated, the two ladies decided that they should leave. Annabelle went first as she was anxious to get back to the railway carriage before Sir Roy noticed her absence. Valerie decided to leave a little later and snuggled up to Dick saying with a kiss and a whisper, "We'll have to do this again, and soon."

Life was not so simple for Annabelle. She had just left Dick's house when a suspicious-looking man, dressed all in black, approached her. "Good morning, Mrs. Johnston, out rather late, aren't we?"

"Who the hell are you? And leave me alone," she said as she stormed off.

But he determinedly kept pace with her, saying, "Jeff Spencer of the Warania Herald. And unless you become a bit more civil, you'll be reading all about your late-night exploits in a day or two in the newspaper." She stopped, stared directly into his eyes, and decided on a course of action. Without uttering another word, she grabbed him by the right sleeve of his black windbreaker, pulled him toward her until he was on tiptoes and slightly off balance, then swung to her left, bending slightly. Tugging on his sleeve so that he was pressed against her right hip, with one deft motion she straightened her legs as she hurled him over her right shoulder.

In the dojo, she would have eased his fall onto the mat, but in this instance she slammed him down, head first, onto the stony road surface, fracturing his skull and breaking his neck. Dusting herself off, she walked away and fifteen minutes later she was in bed with Sir Roy snoring away beside her.

When Valerie eventually and very reluctantly climbed out of Dick's bed, he went to his desk, sorted through Sandy's photos, and placed several in a large envelope. "Don't forget these," he said as he handed her the envelope. "You might want to look through all of Sandy's negatives and destroy them or your secret will be out. You're much nicer in real life, by the way, but I'll always remember those delightful photographs." He gave her a quick smile, which earned him another kiss, and then she was gone.

Dick wandered back to his bedroom, thoroughly exhausted, and was climbing back into bed when he heard someone scream, followed by a hammering at his door. Putting a towel around his waist, he ran to open it, and there stood Valerie. "There's a man, a dead man, lying down the road," she screamed.

A puzzled Dick put some clothes on and followed Valerie out onto the road where, sure enough, a European man was sprawled across the narrow gravel roadway. Upon closer inspection, Dick saw that his head was at an unnatural angle, and there was a small pool of blood beneath it. As he searched through the man's pockets, he found a wallet that identified him as Jeffrey Spencer, a news reporter with the Warania Herald. In another pocket, he found a small notebook containing some brief notes about Lady Annabelle Johnston and her activities during the past twenty-four hours.

Pocketing the notebook, Dick recalled the open Cardex in Cartwright's office, guessed what had happened, and knew without a shadow of a doubt that Anna had been accosted by this reporter and had used her judo skills to settle his hash once and for all.

He did some quick thinking before telling Valerie and a couple of police constables who had arrived on the scene, "This has obviously been a hit-and-run road accident. Valerie, I think you'd better head home, and I'll contact you later for a statement." Then, shaking his head, he said, "I've got some work to do." And turning to the constables he continued, "Let's take some measurements and a few photographs. Then we'll put him in the body box and take him to the mortuary in Chimuka."

An hour later, and now in an almost comatose state, Dick was driving the Land Rover to Chimuka where he would deposit Mr. Spencer's corpse in the mortuary, complete with a toe tag, and open an investigation.

He decided to stay well clear of Lady Annabelle Johnston for the few hours that remained of her stay in Umbedzi, thankfully reminding himself that her train would leave at nine o'clock for Zumba.

Upon returning home, he crawled into bed but rose later that day and telephoned the editor of the Warania Herald to inform him of the death of his reporter Jeff Spencer. The editor was understandably shocked and seemed unable to comprehend how this could have happened. He claimed to have no idea what story Mr. Spencer was working on or what he would be doing out on a quiet road in Umbedzi in the middle of the night. Dick wasn't surprised when the editor asked only one question, "Were Sir Roy Johnston and his wife still in Umbedzi last night?" When Dick confirmed that they were but had left earlier that morning, the only response he received was a thoughtful 'Hmmm' as the editor rang off.

Dick went into the backyard where a forty-four-gallon drum sat, which was used for burning rubbish. He threw in some paper and wood and tossed in a lighted match. When he had the fire going, he tore Spencer's notebook apart, one page at a time, and fed each page into the flames.

He then commenced to open a docket on the 'hit-and-run accident' that had occurred the previous night that killed Mr. Spencer. He sent the undeveloped film of Spencer lying on the road off to Chimuka to be processed and drew a meticulous diagram of the 'accident' scene depicting the body, the blood, and the immediate surrounding area.

The following afternoon, as was his way, he shrugged the whole episode off as simply being part of the life of a police inspector in the RWP, donned his breeches, safari jacket, and pith helmet, and took Wayward out for an afternoon ride. He was sure not to forget his trusty .303, loaded and with the safety catch on, and secure in the holster on his saddle.

Turning off the gravel road after a mile or so, he allowed Wayward to walk across the *vlei*, a dried-up seasonal marsh where the undergrowth was sparse with very few trees, and the sun, now beginning its slow descent in the west, began turning everything a glorious golden hue. He decided that despite a few hiccups along the way, he enjoyed life in Africa and couldn't believe how far he'd come, both in distance and more significantly in his transformation from a totally ignorant, aimless—and yes, clueless—youth, into a man of the world. He would stay, he decided, whatever the outcome.

True to form, his complacency was shattered when, as he passed beneath a small cluster of trees, he was startled by the rattle of machine gun fire off to his left. He and Wayward were showered with twigs and leaves from the overhanging trees and the thoroughly panicked horse broke from his casual walk into a flat-out gallop in seconds. Dick was so startled that he crouched low over his neck, quite content to stay low and get out of there as quickly as possible.

Eventually, he was able to slow his horse down and returned to his house, taking an entirely different route. Shadreck was nowhere around, so he unsaddled Wayward and put him back in his stall before going straight to the telephone where he called the Chimuka police headquarters. Of course, no one of any senior rank was available, so he decided that he would have to wait until the following morning to report the incident.

Speaking with the assistant deputy commissioner for his area the next day, he described what had happened and the response was alarming. He was told, "Yes, we've had a couple of these incidents in the past week or two, Starling. It appears that the Warania Independence Party, or WIP as it's come to be known, is dissatisfied with the progress being made in gaining Warania's independence from Britain. They want it now and, aided by some eastern bloc countries, they have been supplied with arms and ammunition and, in some cases, training."

The assistant deputy commissioner went on to say that the WIP guerrillas were, in fact, terrorists and that neither the Waranian government nor the government of Great Britain was prepared to give in to that type of pressure. "Therefore, the RWP as well as the country's small but well-trained military are going on the offensive. New, more modern equipment will shortly be issued, along with intensive training for all RWP personnel. Send in a report of yesterday's incident and stand by for further instructions." With that, the telephone conversation ended.

Shadreck put in an appearance once the conversation ended and Dick asked him to make a pot of tea. He then went over the morning's events in his head and concluded that he was obviously the intended target of the attack. However, the shooter was hopelessly incompetent, and he would have his sergeants and constables in for a group discussion to find out what they could tell him.

Calling for a meeting at three o'clock that afternoon, he then had a quick lunch and told Shadreck to put a dozen or so chairs in a circle beneath the large marula tree behind the house.

When everyone was assembled, Dick gave them a rundown of the last evening's events, repeated what he had learned about the WIP and its recent guerrilla activities, and asked for some input or observations. No one spoke for a minute or two.

Then Sergeant Zibando, the senior of the three sergeants, said, "Sir, we are all aware that there is a small group of troublemakers within the WIP who are spreading the word in the township that they are in the process of forming an army. This army will not wear uniforms and will be comprised of volunteers drawn from the general public. They will continue their normal day-to-day activities but will be supplied with guns, which they will hide and keep their whereabouts secret. Then, from time to time, they will take these guns, go out to nearby farms or isolated houses where the white people live, kill them, and then hide the guns and return to their normal activities."

Zibando continued, "They believe that in this way the white people will leave Warania, and we, the black people of Warania, will be able to run our own country. They tell the people that the Waranians will then live in big houses, like the white people do now, and will drive big motor cars and earn much more money."

"Thank you, Sergeant, for being so straightforward with me. I really do appreciate that. Does anyone else have anything to add?" A young constable, probably in his early twenties, raised his hand. "Yes, sir, we have all heard of these WIP *tsotsies*; they're just criminals. Most people take no notice of them but the very young men, often encouraged by their girlfriends, seem to be taking a lot of interest. I think there is going to be a lot of trouble."

Dick nodded his head, deep in thought, before asking, "Do any of you think these people are right? Do you believe that things will become better if there is a violent takeover of the country? If the white people, who operate large farms, farms that provide the food for most Waranians, are killed or driven out, will Waranians be able to run them efficiently, if at all?"

"If the white people who run the railways, keep the electrical grid operating, and look after Warania's economy all leave or are killed, how will the Waranians continue to operate their country? I'll tell you how. The Russians will do it, and they will be far less benevolent than Britain, which has already agreed to grant independence to Warania but is trying to do so in a slow and organized manner so the transition, instead of being abrupt and chaotic, will be smooth and well organized."

Dick went on, speaking slowly and looking intently into each man's eyes as he spoke. "Waranians will not all have big houses like the white people have, there simply aren't enough houses. Nor will they all drive around in big motor cars. Firstly, there aren't enough cars. Secondly, where is the money going to come from to buy, maintain, repair, and fill them with petrol? These WIP skellums are just taking advantage of simple people who understandably want a better life for themselves and their families and think that this approach will result in them getting it."

Feeling that he had said enough, he asked for questions and was surprised to see Sergeant Zibando raise his hand again. "Sir, all of us here, sitting under the marula tree, are worried. The WIP knows us, they see us in the township and in the beer halls, and they know that we work for the government. They see us as supporting the continuing white dominance of our country. We know that they will come after us and our families. They want us to support them and if we don't," he shook his head and swallowed, "if we don't, we will suffer."

Again, Dick paused before replying. He understood implicitly what Zibando was saying. These men of his were in a far worse situation than he was, for they had nowhere to run and were clearly in danger of being persecuted and intimidated, or even worse, by their fellow Waranians if they didn't toe the WIP's line.

"Okay. We must take extra precautions to protect you and your families. I will discuss the matter with headquarters immediately and make sure that you are adequately protected. This meeting is now over, but we will have another in a day or two."

Returning to his office, Dick made copious notes of ideas and proposals that he would make the following morning to his superiors. He then retired to the table for some steak, egg, and chips that Shadreck had prepared, and chased the meal down with a couple of cold Chimbukas.

The next morning, Dick was on the phone to headquarters, speaking with the assistant deputy commissioner again. "Sir, I've had a meeting with my staff here in Umbedzi and realize that the terrorist threat that we spoke of yesterday is far, far worse than I was led to believe. Intimidation is rife in the township, and my African police are frightened for themselves and their families. We need to do something quickly."

"Yes, yes, Starling. Don't go getting your knickers in a knot, lad. What sort of thing do you have in mind?"

"Well, for starters, sir, we should erect an eight-foot security fence around the entire police camp, enclosing my quarters that also doubles as the police station and the African police accommodations. Secondly, I would like permission to train all my personnel in the use of the Browning semi-automatic shotgun and place two men on perimeter patrol twenty-four hours per day."

"Well, Starling, I think you might be jumping the gun a bit there. After all, we've only had three incidents reported so far, including your one yesterday evening. Let me give this some thought, and I'll get back to you in a day or so."

Satisfied to some degree, Dick went about his usual duties, sorting paperwork and studying the few dockets pertaining to offenses that were still under investigation. Shadreck brought him a cup of tea at ten o'clock and all seemed well until he noticed that Shadreck was favoring his right shoulder, carrying things with his left hand even though Dick knew he was right-handed. "What's wrong with your shoulder?" asked Dick. All he got in reply was a shy giggle as Shadreck left the room. Dick shrugged and thought no more of it.

Later that morning, he received a phone call from Valerie at the Umbedzi Gazette. "Hey, Dick, how are you? That was fun the other night, but boy that woman friend of yours is certainly a wild one. I've got bumps, bruises, and scratches all over the place. Is she really the governor general's wife?"

"No, no, no. Don't even let anyone hear you say that. Think of her as an old friend who came by unexpectedly and was surprised to find you here. Anyway, what's going on in the newspaper? Will it close down?"

Valerie lowered her voice to say, "No, there are two blokes here at the moment who apparently own the paper and several other small publications all over the country. They're talking about bringing in a new manager to replace Sandy, and they also want to enlarge the business to encompass a new stationery shop. There will be no edition of this week's Umbedzi Gazette of course, but one of these gentlemen will be staying here to get next week's edition printed. After all, there's been a lot happening in Umbedzi during the past few days and everyone's asking about it."

"Well, when do I get to see you again?" Dick asked and the words were no sooner out of his mouth than she said, "Tonight. I'll be there at six, and don't worry about food. My treat."

Valerie's treat turned out to be two small pizzas to be warmed in the oven, a small basket of strawberries, and a fancy pressurized can of whipped cream topping. Once they were finished with their meal, they disappeared into the bedroom where Valerie came up with some ingenious uses for what was left of the whipped cream and Dick fell asleep with a smile on his face.

Chapter Nineteen

The Waranian government acted fairly quickly in its response to the threat of terrorism. Dick had an eight-foot security fence erected and four additional constables were posted to the police station to help with the twenty-four-hour foot patrols. His small charge office was now manned throughout the day and night and the front gate was locked from dusk to dawn with an intercom speaker mounted at the gate for late-night callers.

Additional Browning semi-automatic shotguns were installed in a beefed-up gun cabinet and Dick's old Lee Enfield .303 was replaced by a FN semi-automatic rifle.

Dick now felt that he was in a stronger position to deal with the oncoming threat and called Taffy to check how he was getting on in Zumba. "We have had no problems over here yet," Taffy told him, "but I'm sure it's only a matter of time. I heard from general headquarters that there have been several more attacks recently."

"Same here," replied Dick. "How about getting together the weekend after next for a few Chimbukas?" He had plans for Valerie this weekend.

"No, can do, sunshine. I'm going out with a pal that weekend to look for a marauding bull elephant that's been causing havoc up in the tribal trust lands about thirty miles from here. But I can make it this weekend if you're free. This elephant is an old bugger with only one tusk, but it's torn up three kraals and killed one of the elders who tried to chase it off."

Dick reluctantly agreed, deciding that he would have to cancel the arrangements he'd made with Valerie. Perhaps he could postpone it until the following weekend when Taffy was out hunting.

***

Growing more concerned with the increase in terrorist activities, Dick had taken the unorthodox measure of appointing two of his constables to gather information on possible guerrilla activity in his area. Dressed in civilian clothes and instructing them not to disclose that they were policemen, he sent them out separately to visit the tribal areas, calling on individual kraals, talking to the natives living there, and inquiring subtly if they had heard or seen any suspicious activity. He sent them out for periods of one to two weeks and when they returned, he would debrief them to find out what they had learned.

The first to return, Constable Elias, reported that he visited over a dozen kraals and spoke with the headmen but had nothing of value to report. Constable Phineas returned a few days later, telling him that one of the children in a kraal that he had visited had been running around with a stick, pointing it at the other kids and shouting out 'bang, bang, bang', as though he were shooting a rifle.

Phineas said that he gave the child some sweets, took him aside, and told him that he liked watching his game very much. "I asked him, 'Where did you get the idea from? What kind of stick makes those funny noises?'"

"The child replied that he had seen men from nearby kraals meet from time to time. They have sticks wrapped in blankets hidden in the hollow trunk of an old dead baobab tree and sometimes they take them out and play with them. They are very loud and one even makes a noise like 'rat-a-tat-tat' and sometimes sparks and smoke come out."

"I asked him to show me the tree, which he did. It is very old and hollow with a slit about five feet high and a foot wide, easily big enough for a man to slip in and out of. I did not go inside, but I am sure that if these men are practicing with firearms in that area, then the villagers know about it. They are either frightened of these men or implicit in their plans. I told the boy not to speak to anyone about this and gave him some more sweets. I then came directly back to the station."

Making copious notes on this very convincing account of guerrilla activity, Dick told Phineas that he had done an excellent job and that they would return immediately to this baobab tree and search for the weapons. If found, they would leave them there, report the find to headquarters, and call in the military to lie in ambush and wait for the guerrillas to return. Dick armed Phineas and another constable with semi-automatic shotguns and brought out his own FN rifle. The men climbed into the Land Rover, driving about thirty miles into a particularly desolate area of the tribal trust lands. Phineas told him that they would have to leave the Land Rover and walk another mile to the baobab tree and since the area ahead was rocky and overgrown, he would lead the way.

After picking their way along the trail for about fifteen minutes, Phineas startled Dick by dashing off the small game trail that they had been following into the thick undergrowth, shouting loudly in his native language. In the next instant, the air was filled with automatic gunfire. Dick and the other constable were showered with leaves, branches, and twigs as it dawned on them that they had been led directly into an ambush.

Dick recalled from his recent anti-terrorist training that the best response to a surprise ambush was the dreaded death or glory 'immediate action drill', which meant charging directly into the ambush, firing low until behind the attackers, and then, provided that they survived the ambush, blow the attackers to pieces from behind. He reacted before thinking, firing a single shot, time and time again until miraculously he was through. Turning around, he saw the three of them, lying flat on the ground with their Russian-made AK-47s pointing at the spot where he and his constable had stood just seconds earlier.

With their weapons on fully automatic, they had idiotically emptied their magazines in seconds, losing complete control in the process and firing most of their ammunition into the treetops, as an automatic weapon is likely to do unless held down firmly. While they were desperately trying to load fresh magazines, and with his marksmanship considerably improved in recent months, Dick shot all three of them, one in the back, another in the head and the third he shot in the shoulder, intending to neutralize him but keep him alive for questioning.

He loaded a fresh magazine in his FN and called out for his constable but received no response. Having first relieved the two dead guerrillas and their wounded comrade of their AK-47s, he unloaded them and then went back to the game trail, searching for his constable only to find him lying dead, his body shredded by several bullet wounds. *Of Constable Phineas, there was no sign, and no doubt,* thought Dick, *there never would be.*

Then he began to shake as uncontrollable tremors racked his body. He sat down on the ground and took a long drink of water from his canteen as he tried to regain his composure. He had to give credit to Phineas for the incredible story he had concocted to lure Dick into the ambush. There was, of course, no piccanin and no hollow baobab tree. He had been taken for a sucker, and it had almost paid off.

Once he had collected his thoughts, he made a more thorough check of each of the terrorists and found that two were most certainly dead and the third was lying on his stomach, his shoulder bleeding profusely, and realized that he had a problem. There were three dead bodies to dispose of, a wounded terrorist to get back to the station where he could be properly interrogated, and five rifles that he obviously couldn't carry. And there was also the renegade Constable Phineas, armed with a semi-automatic shotgun, somewhere in the vicinity.

Deciding to tackle one issue at a time, his first concern was his own safety and, in that regard, he again carefully inspected his FN and replaced the depleted magazine with a full one. With one round up the spout and the safety catch released, he was ready for action. Then he gathered up all the firearms and buried them beneath a tree that he would recognize when he came back to retrieve them later. He piled up the three bodies after searching the two dead terrorists' clothing. He discovered nothing noteworthy except that each had a supply of cannabis pellets, no doubt to give them Dutch courage before the ambush. They also had two hand grenades and a number of full magazines.

He buried all the ammunition and drugs in a separate location from the rifles and then approached his injured captive. Before getting too close, he told him to roll over for he presumed the man was still in possession of two hand grenades, just like each of his comrades. He was aware that terrorists with more extensive training had been taught that if injured and incapacitated, they were to pull the pin on one of their grenades and then lie on it to keep the handgrip depressed. When their adversaries rolled them over to check if they were dead, the hand grip would be released and the grenade would explode, killing or maiming anyone in close vicinity. It was well known that when high on cannabis, these men would think nothing of killing themselves in the process.

The terrorist stared at him but did not move, giving Dick a hard stare and keeping his lips tightly sealed. *This will be a hard one to crack,* thought Dick, but I'll give him one more chance. "Move or you're dead," he said, but the man continued to stare at him. From a distance of about thirty feet, Dick reluctantly shot him between the eyes.

The impact of the shot lifted the man off the ground, and there beneath his chest was a hand grenade, the pin removed and the hand grip now released. Dick took a dive behind a nearby tree before the grenade exploded with a deafening roar, sending pieces of flesh, clothing, and dirt in all directions.

"Okay," thought Dick, "now I don't have to worry about getting that one back to the Land Rover." After retrieving the man's second grenade, he dragged his shattered corpse over to where the other three lay and began a slow and wary fifteen-minute walk back to his vehicle. Thankful that its reliable four-cylinder engine started like a dream, he returned to Umbedzi.

When he reported the incident to headquarters, they sent out a team from the Criminal Investigation Department, accompanied by an officer from the Special Branch, a newly created division of the CID that specialized, among other things, in politically motivated activities. Dick took them back to the scene of the ambush where they recovered the four bodies, the arms, ammunition, and drugs. A smarmy-faced individual from Special Branch, who identified himself as Detective Inspector Weeks, merely looked down his nose at Dick and sneered, "Why the hell did you have to kill him? Now I have no one to interrogate."

The following day, his old friend from the annual inspection, Superintendent Billings, arrived in Umbedzi and once settled on Dick's uncomfortable sofa with a cup of tea, began to brief him on the latest developments.

"You had a very nasty and troubling experience, Starling. Unfortunately, you were not the only one. There have been five serious terrorist attacks across the country in the past week. In two of those incidents, lonely farmhouses were attacked at night by groups of seven or eight terrorists armed with AK-47s, hand grenades, and in one case, with an RPG or rocket-propelled grenade. In both cases, the farmer and his wife were murdered and in one case a two-year-old infant was slaughtered as well."

"The other three attacks took place in small villages or kraals where terrorists demanded food and women. In one case, the headman refused and was bayoneted to death after being horribly tortured and mutilated in front of the entire village. There have undoubtedly been other incidents where the villagers have complied and are too afraid to report it. The obvious intent is to frighten the living daylights out of our rural Africans, who are now living in fear of these WIP terrorists. Oh yes, in the future, these animals will not be referred to as guerrillas. We're now calling them terrorists."

"We are, therefore, instituting a new series of procedures. Firstly, every physically fit white male in the country will be conscripted to serve on a part-time basis in either the military or the RWP. Those conscripted to the RWP will be issued police uniforms similar to those worn by our regular members but with the letter R attached to both collars. These reserve officers will be required to assist in manning all of our police stations, including this one, and will perform regular patrols of their station's region."

"A similar arrangement will be made with our African police officers although in their case reservists will not be conscripted but will be selected by senior African police personnel from locals who are known to be loyal retainers of the old school. They will wear a camouflaged overall, helmet, and black ankle boots. Unlike their European counterparts, they will be paid for the hours they put in."

"With regard to the limited number of African inspectors presently on the force, they will be increased twofold with all additional new inspectors being promoted from senior sergeant ranks, men who have proved their loyalty and integrity in the past."

"In the case of Umbedzi, and several of our other smaller outposts, builders will shortly be arriving and will make some alterations to your building. The increased manpower will necessitate larger premises and a proper armory. Until these structural changes take place, you'll just have to make do with what you've got."

"Oh, and by the way, your Land Rover will be having some major alterations done to it, which will take a week or so. You will have to make do with an old replacement vehicle from the central vehicle pool for a couple of weeks, and your horses will be withdrawn from service."

It took Dick took a while to assimilate all this information. It all seemed very practical and none too soon in coming, but he couldn't help asking, "How is all this conscription and selection of police reservists to be initiated? Am I supposed to do it?"

"No, no, no. Headquarters will handle all of that. Be prepared to allocate duties to these individuals when they arrive. Your reservists, both black and white, will be drawn from the local population, so you won't have to worry about accommodating or provisioning them."

"Now I must be off. I have to drive over to Zumba and run through the same stuff again with Inspector Lloyd-Jones. Have a think over what I've told you and give me a call at HQ if you have any questions." With that, he climbed into his police issue Austin Cambridge and drove off.

In a daze, Dick thought that it was definitely time for a cup of tea. Retiring to his office, he called on Shadreck, who he noticed was no longer favoring his right shoulder, to make tea. While sipping the brew, he thought of his two undercover operatives, Constables Phineas and Elias. Phineas was obviously in league with the terrorists, but what about Elias? Elias was due back from his patrol in a day or two and Dick gave serious thought as to how he would handle his debriefing.

When the man eventually arrived, Dick sat him down in his office and asked what intelligence he had gathered. "Not very much, sir," the man said. "But there is something very strange going on. The villagers are not their usual friendly selves. They seemed subdued and even frightened. Although they did not realize I was a policeman, they were not behaving normally. It seemed as though they didn't want visitors and did not offer me any food or a place to sleep. Very strange."

Dick briefed Constable Elias on the earlier incidents while he had been away and warned that he should be extremely vigilant when going about his duties. He advised him to identify himself as a policeman in the future and to inform the villagers that a reward would be given to anyone giving the police information regarding the identity or whereabouts of any suspected terrorists or their cache of weapons.

Some hours later, Dick got a call from Taffy, who had received a visit from Superintendent Billings. "What do you think, Dick? Think maybe it's time to pull up sticks and return to Blighty?"

"Maybe," replied Dick, "but let's wait awhile and see how things pan out. We'll talk some more tomorrow; there's lots to talk about."

Dick's next phone call to Valerie was rather awkward. "But Dick, you promised. And I've been looking forward to it all week. Now you're telling me I have to wait another week. I think I'll have to find myself a new boyfriend."

"No, no, don't be stupid. You can come over one evening during the week, and we'll still have next weekend to look forward to."

"Okay, I'll come over on Monday evening, but I want you to do the cooking. Perhaps a nice braaivleis and a couple glasses of wine. Then we can have some fun."

Chapter Twenty

Taffy arrived at Umbedzi police station shortly before noon on Saturday and found Dick seated in his living room, pen and paper in hand, and furiously scribbling.

"Well, hello. Still at work, are we? Time to knock off and go for a couple of beers."

"Hello, Taffy. I'm just making some notes here. Things seem to be getting worse by the minute, and we're going to have to make some big changes or the shit will really hit the fan. We're not equipped, manned, or properly trained to deal with these constant terrorist incidents."

"You're right there. We've had a couple of problems this past week in the township. Young chaps with AK-47s are swaggering around the beer halls and telling everyone to support the WIP. By the time I heard about it and went out there, taking my FN and a couple of constables with shotguns, it was too late, and they were gone."

"Okay. Well, we said we would talk about it this weekend and decide what we should do, so let's go down to the Waterhole and discuss it over a beer."

They sauntered down to the Umbedzi Hotel and Dick noticed that the Waterhole was busy and that the new bartender was a black man. He was smartly dressed but a disappointing alternative to the likes of Melissa or Sandra. They ordered their beers and sat in a corner seat near the door.

Taffy asked, "So, what do you think? Should we take the chicken run? For that's what everyone is calling it. Or should we stick it out? This place is my life, and I love it, but I'm damned if I'm willing to die for it. The trouble is, where would I go? I know nothing except police work in the African bush and game hunting, hardly a prime candidate for the Metropolitan Police, am I?"

"Do you have family back in the UK?" Taffy simply laughed. "Yes, I have family alright, but they wrote me off years ago, and I don't think I'd be welcomed back. Perhaps I could try Rhodesia although they're going through the same stuff that we are, so it would be more like jumping from the frying pan into the fire. What about you?"

"No, no one. My folks were killed in a car crash years ago, and I was living with an old aunt before coming out here. She was on her last legs then, and I haven't heard from her since I left, so she's probably kicked the bucket. I've no reason to go back. Maybe South Africa would work, but I haven't got much money and don't speak Afrikaans, so I doubt that the SAP would want me."

The two of them sat quietly, deep in thought, before Taffy said, "Bugger it. I'm not going anywhere. I'll just play it day by day and if I'm left with no choice, I'll return to the UK and see what awaits me. I have a few bobs that will tide me over until I can sort something out."

Dick said "Okay, if you're staying then I'm staying," and the words were hardly out of his mouth when the quiet comfort of the bar suddenly erupted into automatic gunfire as three Africans burst through the door, AK-47s held at their hips, spraying the entire bar room with shells.

Dick and Taffy, seated right next to the door, were initially out of sight of the gunmen and watched in horror at the carnage being created as shells ripped into the numerous bar patrons. Chairs toppled over, men were dropping like flies and the bar was being ripped to pieces along with the men sitting there, but there was no sign of the barman.

Dick and Taffy's immediate reaction was to dive to the floor but Dick realized that as soon as the terrorists turned to leave, they would be sitting ducks. He reacted without thinking and leaped onto the back of the nearest terrorist, swinging him toward his two comrades.

The man was stunned and stopped firing his gun as he twisted around, trying to shake off his assailant. Dick hung on tight and when the other two saw what was happening, they turned their guns on him. Seeing that Dick was protected by their comrade, they held their fire.

They obviously couldn't shoot him and stood, apparently baffled until seconds later they were both sent flying by Taffy, who, at somewhere around two hundred and forty pounds, bowled them over like ninepins and sent their rifles skidding across the floor.

Taffy immediately grabbed one of the AK-47s from the floor, turned it onto the two terrorists, and shot them both in the head at point-blank range. Dick, meanwhile, still clinging to the back of the third terrorist, managed to put him in a choke-hold, ferociously squeezing the life out of him until he dropped his rifle and tried to pull Dick's forearm away from his throat. Dick was so enraged that he found strength that he did not know he possessed and continued to squeeze until the man dropped unconscious to the floor.

As soon as the blood stopped pounding in his ears, he became aware of the groans and screams that filled the room and looked around in horror at the scene that surrounded him. Glancing toward Taffy, he saw that he had a dazed and bewildered look on his face. "Taffy, are you okay?"

"No, I'm bloody well not. Get me a chair, quick, before I fall down."

Dick grabbed a chair, sat Taffy down, and then went looking for a telephone. Finding one behind what was left of the bar, he called the local hospital, told them briefly what had happened, and said that they should get some ambulances and medical staff over to the hotel pronto.

Then he set about triaging the bodies that were scattered all over the room. Some people were not injured, and he asked them to help. "Check to see which ones are dead. There's nothing we can do for them. Then try to figure out who are the most seriously wounded and do what you can for them until medical help arrives."

He went first over to the unconscious terrorist, who he could see was starting to come around.

"You bastard," he shouted and viciously kicked him in the face. Then rolling him onto his stomach, he removed the man's bootlaces and secured his wrists tightly behind his back with one lace and his ankles with the other lace. Using a rag that he found in the carnage at the back of the bar, he tied the wrist and ankle restraints together tightly, almost breaking the man's back in the process. "Now you can learn what it's like to really suffer."

Within minutes, the hospital's only ambulance arrived containing one doctor, a casual acquaintance who Dick knew to be Dr. Harold Salter, and two nurses. One appeared to be an East Indian girl and the other a young blonde woman. The two paramedics who normally worked the ambulance came in and surveyed the situation.

"It's a mess," Dick told Salter, "we've hardly started sorting out the wounded from the dead but some of the wounded look to be in very bad shape."

"Okay, Starling. You take it easy and go and look after your pal over there. We'll take it from here." He turned to the two nurses and the paramedics and began the triage in earnest.

Dick walked over to where Taffy was seated and found him slumped in his chair with tears streaming down his cheeks.

Dick could think of no words to say, so just stood beside him with a hand resting on his shoulder and waited for him to recover.

Eventually, Taffy wiped his face, shook his head, and in a shaky voice said, "Dick, I'm ashamed. I was frozen in fear until I saw you tackle that son-of-a-bitch. Where did that come from? You saved our lives."

"I don't know, I suppose I acted before thinking." Trying to lighten the mood a bit, he added, "A wise man once asked me when I got into trouble—where was my gun? Never go anywhere without your rifle and keep it close by. There's wild game everywhere." But there was no response from Taffy, not even a smile.

While they were talking, Sergeant Zibando arrived with a couple of constables. Zibando told him that someone had reported the attack, and he had come straight over. "Agh, baas. This is terrible."

"Yes, it is and if you look over there, you'll see the three bastards that caused it. Two are dead and the one tied up like a Christmas turkey is unconscious. Get them back to the police station. No, wait; let me go and get the Land Rover. You stay here." Hoisting Taffy to his feet, they made a slow walk back to the Land Rover.

Once home, Dick seated a still semi-comatose Taffy in his living room before taking the Land Rover back to the hotel.

With the assistance of Zibando and his two constables, he threw the two bodies and his trussed-up and half-conscious prisoner into his vehicle, drove back to the police station, and locked his prisoner, still hogtied and complaining miserably, in one of the cells.

He then checked on Taffy, who had managed to find a glass of water and was looking marginally better, before telephoning the inspector in charge at Chimuka police headquarters and describing what had happened. "There could be as many as a dozen dead and several more with serious injuries.

They need some help over at the hospital, so organize something as quickly as possible and get them up here."

When finally getting back home, he poured himself a stiff whisky, sat on his lumpy sofa, and tried to come to grips with what had just taken place. The discussion with Taffy about their future, the sudden terrorist attack and the carnage that followed, and Taffy's emotional collapse. He found his pulse was still racing as he sat there, confused and troubled.

Taffy spent the night in Dick's spare bedroom and the following morning said he'd better get back to Zumba. "I did some serious thinking last night and didn't get much sleep. There are some things I have to attend to, and they can't wait, but Dick, thanks again for what you did yesterday. You were a real brick."

Once Taffy had left, Dick walked back to the hotel. Several CID and Special Branch officers were there going through what was left of the Waterhole and, of course, Detective Inspector Weeks was at the forefront of the proceedings.

"Hello, Dick, quite the hero I hear. Congratulations. A couple of my men have been talking with our prisoner back at the station. You made quite a mess of him, but he's singing like a canary now and giving us lots of information. We'll be taking him back to Chimuka when we leave later today. The bodies of his comrades and those poor buggers who were killed are being taken away as we speak. The death toll was actually nine, with another four in critical condition at the hospital. A terrible business."

Dick nodded and walked back home, wondering how much worse things would get before he had to leave.

Chapter Twenty One

On Monday, a clapped-out old open-topped Land Rover rolled into the station, an apparent replacement for his relatively smart and much newer model, which was taken away for some work to be done as per Superintendent Billings' instructions. Shortly afterward, Sergeant Zibando informed him that he was being promoted to inspector and would be traveling into Chimuka on the bus to be fitted with his new uniforms.

That evening Valerie arrived as promised, bringing with her an assortment of sandwiches and drinks and relieving him of the responsibility of preparing the braaivleis, which he had completely forgotten about anyway. "Oh, Dick, isn't it terrible what happened at the hotel. I've heard that you were so brave." She wrapped her arms around him, smothering him with kisses saying, "Everyone's talking about it, and in fact, I've heard several people say that they've had enough and are leaving. What do you think?"

He only shrugged. "Well, Taffy and I were talking about that just before it happened and decided that we would stick around and see how things pan out. I think I'll take it one day at a time. Perhaps being that the attack was so close to home has made things appear worse than they really are."

They sat at the table, ate her sandwiches, drank her wine, and spoke very little. When they had finished eating, she stood up, took his hand, and led him into the bedroom, saying, "I think I know what you need."

***

When Zibando returned a couple of days later, he informed Dick that he had been instructed to recruit twelve suitable men from the Umbedzi township as reserve constables and have them equipped and trained in the basics of the police work that they would be undertaking.

Builders soon began arriving at the Umbedzi police station and within a month they had constructed a very impressive extension to Dick's thatched cottage. The new charge office had a more modern appearance with tiled flooring, two small windows with protective screening, plenty of room for his small desk and filing cabinet, and a walk-in armory equipped with several FN rifles, several Uzi submachine guns, six new .38 revolvers and a plentiful supply of ammunition.

No improvements had been made to his living quarters, which was a disappointment but at least it was now separated from the new charge office by only one stout, lockable door.

No sooner had these additions been made than a number of his acquaintances from the small town of Umbedzi began turning up at the station. The butcher Ted Fletcher, the owner of the local garage Tommy Crystal, and the town mayor and owner of the local supermarket Jimmy Abbots, to name a few, showed up in their khaki drill uniforms, adorned with the insignia that identified them as reserve inspectors in the RWP.

Realizing that he had to put their disorganized comings and goings into some kind of order, Dick drew up a duty roster that required each of his seven reserve inspectors to report for duty one evening per week for four hours. They would man the charge office and deal with any reports that came in, as well as make periodic patrols of the Umdenga township, accompanied by one of his constables. His Land Rover was eventually returned but now looked more like a battle wagon. All the windows were covered with stout wire mesh with the exception of the front windscreen, which had a wire screen hinged at the top which could be quickly dropped into place in an emergency.

A large two-door hatch had been installed on the roof, presumably so that two men, with their heads and shoulders protruding, could better utilize binoculars, firearms, and tear gas grenades. With all these developments taking place, the week flew by and before he knew it, it was Friday, and he and Valerie could spend the whole weekend together.

He gave her a call and when she answered she sounded very bright and breezy, telling him that she had been very busy with the new editor. The Umbedzi Gazette was up and running again. Apparently, construction work had already begun on extending the building for the new stationery shop and wasn't it all so exciting!

He told her to come over that evening instead of waiting until the following day, and he would cook up some steaks and *boerewors*, the local sausages, on the grill. She eagerly agreed and said that she would bring a bottle of wine and see him at six.

With his mind filled with the delights of the evening and the weekend ahead, he completely forgot about the reserve inspector, who would be occupying the charge office right next to his living quarters.

Valerie arrived punctually at six with a bottle of wine, as promised. Entering the front door, she saw the local butcher, Ted Fletcher, smartly dressed in his KD uniform, behind the small counter.

"Hello, Valerie," greeting her with a friendly smile, "what can we do you for?"

"Oh, I'm here for dinner with Dick. I know the way." She breezed past him, through the living room and kitchen, and out into the backyard where Dick was busy getting the charcoal barbeque started.

"What's Ted doing here?" she asked. "I thought it was only going to be the two of us."

"It will be. There's been a bit of a shake-up with all this terrorist stuff going on. What I used to call a cottage with a small charge office attached is now a proper police station with living quarters attached. It will work out okay, but there will be a lot more policemen around in the future. Anyway, Ted will only be here until ten. Then we'll have the building to ourselves."

With that said, he put his arm around her shoulders, and they shared a long and passionate kiss.

Dick noted with delight that Valerie was dressed to kill. She was wearing a pair of the tightest and shortest pair of shorts he had ever seen. They looked like they had been painted on, and she informed him that they were the latest craze and were known as hot pants. As she pirouetted to give him a three-hundred-and-sixty-degree view of her latest acquisition, he had to smile. The bottoms of her cheeks were exposed and, from the tightness of the material, he guessed she was wearing no panties. Her tank top revealed that she wore no bra either, for both her nipples were prominently outlined beneath the thin fabric.

While he was otherwise engaged, the briquettes in the barbeque began to glow and Dick returned to his duties as a chef. The steaks were soon sizzling and the boerewors, with a few pricks of a fork, began dripping fat onto the hot coals. While he had been busy with the barbeque, Valerie had tossed a salad and buttered a couple of buns. They opened the wine and began their meal, seated opposite each other at the small table, while busily playing footsie at the same time.

"That was delightful," said Valerie. Dick relaxed in his chair and felt her bare foot creep between his legs as she wriggled her toes into his crotch with an evil little smile spreading across her lips.

As Dick predicted, Ted Fletcher went off duty at ten o'clock. The front door and front gate were locked and the happy pair retired to Dick's bedroom.

Chapter Twenty Two

That same Saturday morning, Taffy Lloyd-Jones was packing his Land Rover with sufficient gear for a two-day foray into the bush in search of the rogue elephant that had been creating such havoc. Instead of the fellow he had originally intended to take, he took his trusty Constable Jonas Mtembe, who often accompanied him on safari and acted as his gun bearer. In any case, Mtembe was a much better tracker than the pal that Taffy had originally planned on taking. His dog, Bentley, seeing the Land Rover being loaded up, was the first one into the vehicle, his tail wagging in anticipation since on these occasions he was always assured of some good, raw meat.

Taffy also took his personal .458 Winchester, a single-shot, large-bore rifle that he'd used on many occasions when hunting elephants.

Once in the area where the elephant had last been sighted, they drove aimlessly around, looking for spoor in the form of elephant droppings, damaged or toppled trees, or flattened undergrowth. After about three hours of slow, careful driving, Mtembe pointed to the left, where a group of small trees had been pushed over. Stopping the vehicle, Taffy and Mtembe got out and approached the trees warily. Sure enough, they found several great mounds of elephant dung, half-digested fiber which bore easily recognizable bits of grass and leaves. When he pushed his finger into it, Taffy found that it was still reasonably warm.

"He must be close by," Taffy told Mtembe, '*Hamba gashle*', a common phrase meaning to go carefully. He had no need to shush Bentley, for he was well-trained to keep down and stay quiet when on the hunt.

Mtembe, being a far better tracker than Taffy, led the way, studying the spoor carefully as they progressed stealthily forward until Mtembe raised his hand, silently indicating that they should stop. He then pointed to the three o'clock position, and there Taffy could see through the thick bush, no more than three hundred feet away, the vague outline of a massive gray elephant with one huge tusk, swaying slightly from side to side as though sleeping.

Signaling Mtembe to hand him the Winchester, Taffy pushed his palm down and backward, indicating that Mtembe should remain behind, and then slowly crept forward, careful not to step on a twig or create any noise that would alarm the beast. When he was barely one hundred feet away, he slowly raised the rifle to his shoulder and aimed for a heart shot, low down and directly behind the shoulder. As he took up the slack on the trigger, the animal turned toward him, obviously having heard something with those incredibly large ears.

Taffy had lost his chance of the heart shot and realized that he had made some sound or movement that the elephant had noticed. It began to lumber toward him, and he knew that this was no mock charge; this was the real thing. The great bull elephant was charging, and he was the target. Realizing that he had no hope of outrunning it, he decided on taking an incredibly difficult headshot, aiming for the area just behind or into the eye.

He squeezed the trigger, the rifle bucked and the animal faltered but kept coming. Taffy tried to dive sideways but tripped and fell backward as the massive animal tumbled forward and the head of the dying elephant fell on top of him. Its huge tusk impaled his stomach, crushed his spine, and exited through his back before sinking into the soft sandy soil below.

Mtembe, horrified at what he had seen, ran to Taffy to find that both he and the elephant were dead. He gathered Taffy's rifle and returned to the Land Rover where, although he had little in the way of driving skills, managed to get the vehicle started. In a jolting, stop-and-go fashion, he regained the dirt road that eventually led him back to Zumba. Taffy's faithful dog Bentley remained behind with his master, and lay down beside his crumpled and bloody remains, whining with grief. Once back at the Zumba police station, Mtembe reported the incident to the reserve inspector who was on duty at the time, and he in turn telephoned Umbedzi to ask Dick for direction.

At that very moment, Dick was snuggled beside Valerie, happily content and enjoying every minute of his weekend of domestic bliss, when he was awakened out of his warm and cozy complacency by the sound of someone sharply rapping on the bedroom door. "What is it? What the hell's going on?"

he yelled as he sprang out of bed and wrapped a dressing gown around his naked torso.

"Come quick, sir," shouted the constable. "Big trouble, sir. Big trouble."

As Dick staggered out of his bedroom, the constable stumbled over the words before he announced, "The inspector in Zumba, sir, Inspector Lloydie-Jonesie. Sir, you must go there quickly, The mad elephant, it has killed him." Bewildered, Dick asked, "How do you know this?" The constable replied that he had just received a telephone call from the Zumba police station.

As he hastily put on his uniform, he explained to Valerie, now sprawled naked across his bed in a most unladylike fashion, that Taffy had been in some kind of hunting accident and that he had to leave immediately. She pouted a little but conceded that his duty must come first, and he rushed out of the door to the Land Rover with his constable in tow.

Having loaded a body box onto the roof of the Land Rover, Dick drove like a maniac, making record time before reaching the Zumba police station, only to be told by a clearly ruffled Constable Mtembe that Taffy's body was another hour's drive away in the tribal trust lands. Taking Constable Mtembe with him, the three headed in the direction that Mtembe indicated. After about ninety minutes of driving over atrocious dirt tracks, they came upon a group of over one hundred Africans—men, women, and children—crawling all over the carcass of the massive bull elephant, tearing strips of hide from its flesh and carving great chunks of meat from its body. To Dick's amazement, one man was actually inside the animal's massive body, with his head sticking out from a huge hole in its side and grinning with glee as if he'd won a fortune.

"What in heaven's name is going on?" asked Dick, and Mtembe explained that the death of this marauding elephant would not only provide fresh meat but some parts of it were also considered an appetizing delicacy for the local tribespeople for days if not weeks to come. It would also put an end to the fear that had been haunting them after the death of their headman.

As Dick drew closer, he saw Taffy's body, skewered to the ground by the elephant's one gigantic tusk and being totally ignored by the numerous meat-gatherers surrounding him.

"Stop," roared Dick, "get them away from that animal, Mtembe. Tell them that there will be no more meat until they help roll the carcass off of Inspector Lloyd-Jones' body and free it from that tusk." Mtembe and Dick's constable began shouting and gesticulating at the mob until they reluctantly backed off, and then, with a great deal of effort and using a chain attached to the Land Rover's tow bar, they helped lift, push, and roll the carcass high enough off the ground to extract Taffy's body, but it was still impaled on the tusk.

Dick and his two constables seized Taffy by his arms and legs, unceremoniously slid him off the tusk, and carried him away to a small clearing. Taffy's guts and sinews clung to the tusk and were dragged across the dry, stony ground, but at least he was free. Bentley lay down with a cloud of gloom hovering over him and watched the proceedings from a distance.

The next thing was for Dick to remove the tusk from the animal's head and knowing full well that up to one-third of it was buried in the head, this would be no easy task. Directing the constables to put the tribesmen to work, he made sure to promise the tribesmen that once the tusk was removed, they were free to take all the meat and hide they could carry.

They set to with a vengeance and after hacking with axes, saws, knives, and anything else at their disposal, they finally freed the tusk from the animal's huge head. To Dick's amazement, the tusk measured almost nine feet from root to tip and must have weighed over one hundred pounds, for it took all three of them to load it into the back of the Land Rover. Even then, they had to leave the back door hanging open. With Taffy's body safely ensconced in the body box, and with the help of a few tribesmen, they loaded the box onto the roof of the Land Rover and left the scene. They returned to the Zumba police station, where they explained the situation to a reserve inspector and dropped off Mtembe, and then drove on to the Chimuka morgue, where they deposited Taffy's remains.

Dick was not sure what to do with the tusk or, for that matter, Bentley, who jumped into the Land Rover immediately after the body box was loaded. Dick took the tusk and the dog back to Umbedzi and had Shadreck and a couple of helpers carry the tusk into the backyard. Once he had cleaned poor Taffy's blood and gore off it, perhaps it could be used as some type of memorial to Taffy Lloyd-Jones, RWP Inspector and Great White Hunter.

Bentley, it appeared, was to become an uninvited member of the household.

Chapter Twenty Three

A postmortem examination was performed on Taffy's remains and Taffy's next of kin had been located. Flying into Chimuka's small airport in a Boeing 707, his middle-aged sister, a spinster named Gwyneth Lloyd-Jones, told the authorities that she wished to have Taffy's body flown back to Wales, where he would be given a burial in the family crypt below Saint Mary's Church near Pontypridd in the Rhondda Valley.

Dick made a point of finding out from police headquarters where she was staying and called to offer his condolences. On the spur of the moment, he suggested that he drive down to Chimuka the following afternoon and take her to dinner as he was probably the closest friend that Taffy had, and he would like to give her a summary of Taffy's recent accomplishments and interests. She enthusiastically agreed and confirmed that she would meet with him in the dining room of the King George Hotel at six o'clock the following day.

When he met her, Dick found her to be quite a few years older than Taffy. A distinguished-looking woman with a rather horsey face, she was quite tall and slim, totally unlike her overweight and slovenly brother, and was extremely well-spoken and obviously intelligent and well-educated. She wore a gray, knee-length gabardine suit, a silk scarf tied around her neck, and sensible brown leather brogues. It was a totally inappropriate garb for hot and clammy Warania, but no doubt eminently suitable for the colder climate of Wales.

Dick was relieved that he had chosen to wear his unaccustomed blazer and tie, long gray flannel trousers, and well-polished shoes. Over a glass of wine or two, he was surprised to learn that Taffy came from a wealthy land-owning family. According to Gwyneth, Taffy and his twin brother had both disgraced themselves in their youth, Taffy by getting one of the Lloyd-Jones' servants pregnant, an event which, at the time was so unthinkable that the family went to considerable expense to cover up. Gwyneth also told Dick that Taffy, whose Christian name was actually Hywel, and his brother David were both heavy drinkers, which Dick already knew in the case of Taffy. They were always getting into fights or minor skirmishes and were constantly in trouble with the local police; it was a total embarrassment to the family.

Consequently, their father suggested that they both emigrate somewhere far away from Wales and that they would be paid a handsome monthly remuneration to stay there. *In other words,* thought Dick, *he was the same as a few of the other colleagues that he had encountered in the RWP and elsewhere.* Taffy and his twin brother were what was locally referred to as remittance men.

Gwyneth went on to describe how the two brothers had then separated. Taffy went to Warania, where he joined the RWP, while David emigrated to Australia. She said that while Taffy did write the occasional letter home, they had completely lost contact with David, and they didn't know his present whereabouts. Both brothers had bank accounts in the British Channel Islands and that is where, to this day, their monthly remuneration, paid regularly from the family coffers, was sent.

Dick told her that Taffy had never spoken of his family, nor that his brother was a twin; he presumed that the two brothers had long since lost touch with each other.

He told Gwyneth of Taffy's love for big game hunting and, exaggerating a bit, told her that he had become a well-known conservationist, intent on protecting the health and safety of African wildlife in the region and using his own hunting expeditions as a means of preventing a dangerous imbalance of the species.

Gwyneth seemed to accept Dick's somewhat glowing account of Taffy's almost two decades of life in Warania with approval, obviously pleased to be able to return home with some pleasant facts to recite when giving the eulogy at Taffy's funeral.

Considering the evening to be a considerable success, Dick bade Gwyneth a sedate farewell and wished her a safe journey home. He was surprised when she suggested that, when next in Britain, he spend a few nights at the family home near the ancient town of Llantwit Major, which lies west of Cardiff on the Bristol Channel, and insisted on giving him her address and telephone number. He didn't appraise her of the fact that he had never returned to Britain since leaving in 1962 and had no plans to do so.

***

While the month-long construction of Dick's new charge office had been going on, living conditions in what Dick originally considered his house and home were bedlam. There was no question of having Valerie over for social comfort, and she was lodging with a family where all she had was a bedroom and access to their bathroom and kitchen. They did sneak away for a dirty weekend in a motel in Chimuka, but on his miserly inspector's pay that almost broke the bank.

Now that the construction was coming to an end and things were settling down, the charge office was regularly manned by either a reserve inspector or one of Dick's African sergeants. Valerie became a frequent visitor again and Dick became quite enamored with the domesticity of it all.

Bentley also seemed quite at home, content with a corner bed made up of old blankets, and well-fed by a surprisingly considerate Shadreck. In fact, he seemed to prefer Shadreck's company to Dick's, which irritated Dick, but then why would Bentley bite the hand that feeds him?

Valerie's job at the Umbedzi Gazette became more interesting as a new girl had been employed to work in the recently completed stationery shop, and her new editor, publisher, and news journalist, someone called Frederick Erasmus, was apparently an easy bloke to get along with. She also received a small pay rise and began looking for an apartment or basement suite that she could call her own.

Then another hammer dropped. Constable Elias, Dick's loyal undercover operative who had recently brought in several items of interest regarding local terrorist activity, arrived in his office with some alarming news. He reported that an informant that he had been cultivating claimed that Shadreck, Dick's houseboy, cook, and general factotum who had recently taken two weeks' holiday to visit his family back in the Tribal Trust Land, had actually attended a terrorist training camp across the border in neighboring Zambia. The informant, to whom Elias had paid a generous reward, claimed that Shadreck was only one of several household employees in the town of Umbedzi, who, along with other groups scattered across the country, had formed small gangs of terrorists aiming to slaughter their employers one night. This was something along the lines of the planned Night of the Long Knives by the Mau Mau in Kenya, which was foiled and culminated with the Mau Mau terrorists killing not white people but more than three hundred sleeping Kikuyu whose only offense was a desire to live in peace.

"Can your informant provide the names of the other members of this group?" asked Dick. Elias nodded, saying, "Yes, but he wants much more money."

Dick immediately telephoned the sour-faced Special Branch Detective Chief Inspector Weeks, who had been so critical of Dick killing all three of his ambushers earlier in the year but had become much more considerate after the attack on the Waterhole. When Dick explained the information Elias had given him, he became almost servile and said that he would be arriving shortly with his African counterpart and plenty of cash.

When Shadreck served Dick's lunch at midday, a bowl of soup and a toasted cheese sandwich, Dick waited until he had returned to his quarters before tipping it in the bin and making something himself.

Shortly after two o'clock on Friday afternoon, Detective Chief Inspector Weeks arrived in an unmarked police car and surprisingly, he was quite friendly as he shook Dick's hand. He introduced his African Colleague Detective, Inspector Chibanda, and said that they would like to speak with Constable Elias immediately.

Dick called for Elias and when he arrived, all four of them sat together, going over every part of Elias' report. When finished, Weeks said, "We better make damn sure that none of this information leaks out. Elias, can you visit your informant on your own, ensure him of his personal safety, and arrange for us to meet with him as soon as possible? Tell him that he will be well rewarded if his information turns out to be accurate, and we must act quickly."

Elias then left, followed by Weeks and Chibanda, who said they would arrange accommodation at the Umbedzi Hotel.

The following day, Elias again met with Dick, Weeks, and Chibanda. He told them that his informant had agreed to meet with him and Detective Inspector Chibanda in the township that night, but obviously, Weeks could not come. "We will meet my informer at six o'clock in the main beer hall."

Weeks, chagrined at not being able to meet the informant himself, agreed that it would be impossible. Chibanda dressed down for the occasion in baggy khakis and a T-shirt and left the station with Elias just after five.

The main beer hall in Umdenga township was quite crowded. Friday meant the end of the work week for many of the township's residents and the main beer hall was a natural gathering point where friends could get together and chew the fat.

Elias and Chibanda each purchased a bottle of Chimbuka and sat at an empty table, waiting for their informant to appear. They tried to keep up a casual conversation, talking about their wives and families in an attempt to appear inconspicuous, and shortly after six, Elias' informant appeared. The man sat down at the table, a bottle of Chimbuka in hand, and joined in their rather stilted conversation. He was a man of about thirty, sporting a rather scraggly beard and wearing a grubby white singlet, frayed and torn jeans, and shoes made from an old car tire.

After downing their drinks, he nodded slowly to both men and then beckoned them to follow him. They shuffled along behind him and walked for a few hundred yards to a small shelter made of pieces of derelict corrugated iron, scraps of plywood, and, in some places, merely cardboard.

Once inside this tiny hovel, and speaking in their native tongue, the informant, who identified himself as Moses, first asked for money. Chibanda came well prepared and handed the man one hundred Waranian pounds, telling him that there would be more, much more, if his information was correct.

Moses shook his head, reminding them that his life would be in peril if he were discovered and Chibanda reluctantly handed him another one hundred pounds. Moses then began to recite seven names and the addresses of those in the terrorist group that he knew of, which included Dick's houseboy Shadreck. He then went further, detailing where they had hidden their firearms, ammunition, and explosives which, of all places, was in a secret basement below the new stationery shop in Umbedzi.

Moses had discovered that the entire group was being organized and coordinated by a white man, Mr. Erasmus, who was now running the Umbedzi Gazette newspaper office in Umbedzi. Chibanda was more than impressed as he scribbled all this information down in his notebook and told Moses that he would be well rewarded if even some of this information turned out to be true. "Is this where you live?" asked Chibanda, for the grubby little squat in which they were seated was abysmal, even by primitive African standards.

"No," he replied. "My home is better than this and so are my clothes. I am not only telling you this for the money. My sister and brother, my mother and father, have all been killed by these WIP murderers while living peacefully in our kraal back at home. My sister and mother were both raped many times and my father, who was the headman of the village, was beheaded. I want you to catch them and kill them. All of them."

Chibanda promised Moses that the police would soon act on this information and repeated that he would receive a generous reward for all his help if the operation was a success.

Reporting this information to Dick and DCI Weeks when they returned, Constable Elias was excused and a plan of action was immediately put into place. Shadreck's small kia at the back of the police station, along with the homes of the other six men that Moses had identified, would all be raided simultaneously, along with the Umbedzi Gazette's new stationery shop. Before doing so, Dick would try to find out from Valerie more about her new editor, Frederick Erasmus, and the company that was now publishing the Gazette.

DCI Weeks was busy on the telephone well into the night and was back at the station early the next morning with surprising news. Apparently, Erasmus was a member of the banned Warania Communist Party and the company he worked for was a front for that same organization.

Dick had, in the meantime, met with Valerie and asked her about Erasmus. "He is obviously a South African and has a strong Afrikaans accent, but doesn't seem to know much about operating a small-town newspaper. His writing is so awful that I'm doing most of the final layout and editing myself. I should be paid more money, a lot more."

When Dick told him this, Weeks nodded, saying "It all fits, but we'll soon sort him out."

The raid on the Gazette was to be a joint police and military operation and, in addition to the seven members of the WIP's terrorist gang and the Gazette's stationery shop, they would also raid Erasmus' house. The raid would take place the following night at 0300 hours and would be coordinated by Weeks, using several walkie-talkie radios brought in with the military personnel. Each raiding party would consist of four individuals, two police officers, and two members of the military. Everyone would be armed with either a .38 revolver or a Walther automatic pistol. DCI Weeks would be in overall command.

Dick was told that he was to raid the stationery shop with one of his own men and two members of the military, all of whom would be arriving at midnight in military transport. It was emphasized that no one other than the three of them must be aware of these plans until shortly before they were put into action.

On the night of the raid, Dick had selected the newly promoted Inspector Zibando to accompany him, keeping the reason to himself. He only informed him that he was required to be at the station, in uniform, on the night in question, together with eight uniformed constables at 0100 hrs.

At around midnight, two army trucks rolled into the Umbedzi police station's forecourt and twenty or so uniformed soldiers silently disembarked led by a white officer, Lieutenant Charlie Soames. He had brought with him a dozen handheld radios and a trunk containing an assortment of pistols, semi-automatics, and plenty of ammunition.

Additional policemen were brought in on the same vehicles and Lieutenant Soames and DCI Weeks sorted them into groups of four and issued radios, firearms, and ammunition. The DCI then addressed the group.

"You've been brought here to conduct a series of simultaneous raids on a number of different buildings in which it is suspected that you will find nine or more WIP terrorists or their organizers. The names and addresses are here." He distributed a sheet of paper to the leader of each group. "A thorough search of each building will be performed. You are seeking firearms, ammunition, and subversive literature and all persons present will be arrested. Men, women, and children. Bring them all to the Umbedzi police station. Any questions?"

No one spoke, and he turned to Dick. "In your case, the Gazette building will be locked and presumably unoccupied, so you will have to force your way in and locate the basement. It will be interesting to see what you find there."

Shortly after two o'clock, the military vehicles left the police station and transported the teams to points in the Umbedzi township from where they would proceed on foot. Dick's Land Rover would drop a team close to

Erasmus' house before traveling on to the Gazette building, while DCI Weeks and Lieutenant Soames would remain at the police station to coordinate the raids.

Chapter Twenty Four

At three o'clock, all the teams were in place. They were concealed in quiet, shadowy locations well away from their targets, silently waiting for the go-ahead. When receiving the command, they simultaneously burst into action.

Two of Dick's constables quickly seized Shadreck, who was sleeping in his kia at the rear of the police station, while at the six houses in the township, doors were kicked or broken in while two team members remained at the rear of each of the buildings to arrest anyone trying to escape. The team at Erasmus' house was a little less impulsive, ringing the doorbell and knocking loudly on the door to announce their presence. At the Gazette building, Dick used a crowbar to force open the back door, led his team through to the stationery shop, switched on the lights, and began searching for an entrance or trap door to the basement.

After a brief search, one of the soldiers called Dick over and showed him what he had found, rolling back a corner of the room's loosely fitted carpet. A solid and hinged door with a recessed handle was set into the wooden floor. When Dick lifted it and shone his torch down, he saw a ladder leading into the basement.

Instructing Inspector Zibando and one of the soldiers to remain up in the store as lookouts, Dick led the other soldier down into the basement with a torch, searching for a light switch. What met their eyes when the lights came on was beyond belief, for lining one wall was a rack of at least twenty AK-47 rifles. They counted seventeen metal ammunition boxes, which judging from their weight, were full. There were also cases of hand grenades and four rocket-propelled grenade launchers, along with three cases of rocket-propelled grenades.

"Can you believe this?" asked Dick of his soldier companion. The fellow shook his head and said, "I think we'd better get back upstairs and inform

Lieutenant Soames." Dick agreed, and they climbed out of the basement and radioed the police station to report what they had discovered.

"Roger, Starling," came the reply from DCI Weeks, "remain where you are and stay alert. Most of the raids went off without a hitch, but in two cases, one in the township and the other at Erasmus' house, things didn't go so well. Erasmus shot two of our men, one dead. He escaped out of the back door and is still on the loose with an automatic assault rifle. The other, a WIP terrorist named Isaac Taware, shot one of our men dead and wounded two others. He got away and is still armed with an AK-47 but may be wounded. Both men may be on their way to your location. As soon as we have some of the teams back here, we'll send reinforcements."

Dick decided that their best bet was to stay inside the Gazette building until those reinforcements arrived. They would be sitting ducks out on the street, but inside they were concealed and could cover both entrances and the several windows at both front and back.

Briefing his three men, they took up positions inside the building, remained silent, and awaited reinforcements. Instead, they received a rapid delivery of bullets through the glass front door, one of which tragically struck one of the soldiers in the head, killing him instantly.

Dick, startled by the sudden eruption of automatic gunfire, watched in disbelief as a white man, presumably Erasmus, burst through the shattered glass door, spraying the entire shop with bullets in a controlled fashion, keeping his weapon low, striking Zibando in the chest and Dick in the thigh. This was no amateur.

Despite the leg wound, Dick, who already had his Walther in his hand, cocked and loaded, fired three quick shots toward Erasmus, none of which appeared to have hit him although the man seemed to be having difficulty inserting a fresh magazine into his rifle. An African, naked except for a pair of ragged shorts, immediately appeared in the doorway, AK-47 in hand, casting his head in all directions as he attempted to find a target.

Dick and the second soldier sought shelter, Dick behind the shop counter and his colleague in the small hallway that led to the newspaper offices.

Dick's leg was bleeding badly and hurt like blazes. Zibando was calling out weakly for help and the fourth member of the team lay motionless on the floor. As the terrorist entered the shop, Erasmus called to him, "Hey, man. Over here, I need some help."

The African ran to him, dragged him to his feet and the two escaped through the completely demolished doorway, followed by a couple of wild shots from the soldier hiding in the hallway.

DCI Weeks' reinforcements arrived in time to see the two men leaving the building and disappear around the corner. They gave chase and were amazed to see both men climb onto two bicycles that they had obviously arrived on and pedal off down the road. The frantic shots fired at them didn't appear to have hit their mark. Within minutes, the shop swarmed with police and military personnel. Dick and Inspector Zibando were taken to the local hospital and the dead soldier was dispatched to the Chimuka mortuary.

DCI Weeks was up to his neck in challenges. What to do first? The Umbedzi police station was totally inadequate for the task at hand. He phoned headquarters for more Special Branch personnel to be sent immediately. He then ensured that all the men that had been arrested were separated from each other although in some cases this amounted to no more than handcuffing them to a tree outside, each with a guard who was instructed to club anyone who spoke or gave even the slightest hint of trouble. With three of his men dead and another two wounded, this was not going to go over too well at HQ.

One item of news that he considered to be something of a double-edged sword was that the dead body of Frederick Erasmus was later found at the side of the Chimuka Road, lying next to his stolen bicycle. It appeared that a chest wound, probably a punctured lung sustained when Dick had fired at him, had turned out to be fatal, much to the displeasure of DCI Weeks. While ridding Warania of a formidable enemy, Dick had again denied him the opportunity of interrogating another important prisoner. There was no sign of Isaac Taware, Erasmus' African accomplice, so another bandit was beyond his reach.

Thankfully, Lieutenant Soames and his men remained in Umbedzi with the additional police personnel that they had brought in for the raids. Two of the police were inspectors and took charge of police activities, using Dick's newly renovated Land Rover and the two military trucks to patrol Umbedzi township, where they picked up rumblings of unrest following the raids. On several occasions, their vehicles were pelted with rocks and bricks by unruly crowds of protesters and the new screens on Dicks Land Rover proved their worth over and over again.

Meanwhile, Dick was enjoying first-class service at the local hospital. His wound was dressed, and although still in pain, he was able to hobble around a little with the aid of a walking stick after a day in bed. The nurses, both black and white, were treating him very well, especially when it came to giving him a bed bath. Two nurses in particular, an East Indian girl by the name of Ushadevi (just call me Debbie), and a pert little blonde named Connie, both of whom he had first encountered with Dr. Salter after the Waterhole attack, took especially good care of his family jewels, giggling and laughing as they took turns lathering them up, then rinsing them off. *Well, this is a treat,* he thought.

Although he didn't realize it at the time, Debbie and Connie were to become an integral part of Dick's life in the not-too-distant future. The girls appeared to be around Dick's age and had come from England on a three-year nursing contract. Debbie was born in the town of Eastleigh, not far from Southampton, where she lived with her parents and was English to the core despite her Asian appearance. She had short dark brown hair and skin the color of a milky latte, a beautiful smile with dimpled cheeks, and deep brown eyes that seemed to sparkle whenever she spoke. She claimed that she weighed 120 pounds although Dick suspected that she'd shaved a few pounds off that estimate for she had a strong, mildly muscular build and an impressive bust.

Connie, by contrast, was blue-eyed with shoulder-length wavy blonde hair usually worn in a ponytail and had a mischievous smile. She was the slenderer and taller of the two, with a tiny waist and an appealing figure. She hailed from Chiswick, West London where she had lived with an aunt before moving to Warania.

While in hospital, he received several visits from Valerie who was so full of news that he had no opportunity to tell her how brave and commanding he had been during the attack.

"They have me working my fingers to the bone," she said without pausing for breath. "Every piece of paperwork in the entire office had to be examined and refiled. Then the girl who was working in the stationery shop was arrested and questioned but was finally released when they found that she knew nothing of the basement or its contents. I don't know what's going to happen with the Gazette now. The owner has apparently been arrested and all his other small newspaper offices have been raided and closed down, but that nice Detective Weeks has told me that I will be paid for the time being."

Dick told Valerie that he would contact her as soon as he was released from the hospital although he secretly hoped that it would not be for some time.

After one of the best weeks of his life, Dick was discharged and returned to Umbedzi police station. It was a rude awakening to find his bedroom occupied by DCI Weeks, his spare bedroom occupied by Lieutenant Soames, his houseboy Shadreck in one of the two cells and his police quarters swarming with policemen from all over the district. He was finally able to convince DCI Weeks and Lieutenant Soames that they would both be better off moving into the Umbedzi Hotel. Shadreck was shipped off to a prison in Chimuka and Dick was able to return the station to some semblance of normality.

His next priority was to contact Valerie. "Dick," she cried, "how are you, sweetheart? Are you at home?" He told her he was but with Shadreck now under arrest and heading for prison and him with a gammy leg and in great pain, he had no one to look after him.

"Oh, you poor thing. I'll move in and look after you. Then I can move out of my dump and won't have to look for a small flat, after all. I'll be over straight after work with all my stuff. Bye." Dick groaned. Yes, it would be very convenient for both of them, but he was hoping to develop his relationship with the two nurses and that obviously wasn't going to happen in the near future. Blast!

Slowly, things began to return to normal. Weeks and Soames left town with their prisoners, the African township settled down and his police compound was once more a relatively peaceful and quiet haven where the off-duty police officers could enjoy their normal pursuits.

The Umbedzi Gazette offices and the stationery store were closed down and shuttered and Valerie, who was now out of work, became his full-time, live-in lover, cooking his meals, making the bed, and keeping his section of the house clean and tidy. His leg wound healed nicely, and he was pleased to see his old friend Inspector Zibando almost fully recovered from his bullet wound and back at home with his wife and children. Fortuitously, Zibando and his family had adopted Bentley and were feeding him well, giving him plenty of exercise, and provided him with a comfortable pile of old blankets for a bed.

This happy state of affairs lasted for several weeks and Dick was becoming quite accustomed to this life of domesticity. Valerie was a charming companion and an enthusiastic lover. She cleaned and cooked much better than Shadreck ever did and, Dick, a naïve young man, gave no thought to where this might be leading. The bubble popped when Valerie, snuggling next to him on his disgusting old sofa, asked, totally out of the blue, "I love you, Dick, and I love being around you. Do you think we should get married?"

He sat bolt upright and, before thinking, blurted, "Me? Marry you? Are you nuts? Where did this come from? I can't get married. I'm too young. What's wrong with us living together like we are?" He continued to bluster in this fashion until he saw that she was no longer snuggled up to him. In fact, she was no longer sitting next to him but instead was standing before him bawling her eyes out.

Then, a strange look came over her. Her tears stopped, her eyes hardened, and she let him have it with both barrels. "You miserable, selfish bastard," she shouted "I've cooked and cleaned for you. I've kept this dump of yours clean and tidy and looked after you while you whined and crawled around like you were really hurt. We both know it was a sham. I'm not staying here a moment longer."

To emphasize her point, she bent forward so that her nose was almost touching his, looked him unblinkingly in the eyes, and searched for a suitable comment on which to end her tirade. "I wish, oh how I wish, that the fleas of a thousand camels would infest your arsehole."

With that, she packed up her few belongings, stormed out of the building, and he never set eyes on her again. *Thank goodness I didn't marry her,* he thought.

The following morning, he engaged a new houseboy named Elijah, who came with a very good reference from a doctor in Zumba but to be on the safe side he had him fingerprinted and vetted as best he could and was satisfied with the results. It turned out that Elijah was a better cook than either Shadreck or Valerie. He didn't possess any AK-47s that Dick knew of and hopefully didn't wish any unpleasantness on his new employer.

It was quite a relief to be rid of Valerie, Dick thought. He admitted to himself that he was all the things that she accused him of and more although the snide remark about the camels' fleas even now stuck in his craw. He still had a hankering for those two nurses at the local hospital, however, and thought they might be interested in seeing how his bullet wound was healing up.

Admiring his face in the mirror that morning, he trimmed his rather impressive handlebar mustache and curly sideburns and thought that with his sunburned face and crooked nose, he looked quite dashing.

Going through the previous night's occurrence book, he noted that it had been a pretty busy evening. Both of his cells were full, one with a collection of battered and bruised drunken brawlers who had been dragged in from the nearby township, the other occupied by a solitary woman who was being sheltered from a brutal husband who had beaten her and was still being sought. When he went to her cell, he was even more surprised to find that it was a white woman, and she appeared to be sleeping soundly on the cell's lumpy and smelly spring mattress.

"Bring that woman to see me when she wakes up," he told the desk sergeant. "And get Elijah to make her some tea and toast."

Fifteen minutes later, the woman was brought into his office. She looked to be about forty, with long dark and horribly tangled hair, brown eyes, a puffy face, and a dress that was more suited for a scarecrow than a member of the European elite. She said that her name was Allison Freemantle.

Once Elijah had brought her tea and toast, accompanied by some butter and marmalade, Dick asked, "What's your story?" Between sips of tea and mouthfuls of thickly buttered toast, she explained, "My husband works at the local asbestos mine. We've a house at the mine, provided by the owners, and there are several other mine employees living out there. We've lived there for about a year and things seemed to be going quite well to start with."

"But then Ted, my husband, started complaining about the job and about several of the miners getting sick, mostly with some kind of cancer. He wants to move back to England, but I was born and have lived my entire life in Warania and don't want to go. We had a row, he was drunk and hit me in the face with the back of his hand. That's why it's so swollen. I ran out of the house to one of our neighbors, and they brought me to the police station."

"Well, you can't stay here, not in our cell anyway. Did you bring anything with you?"

She shook her head and began to sob.

Dick thought, *Now, what am I supposed to do?* He was sick of the sight of women crying. Then a thought struck him. Nurses are empathetic people; perhaps Debbie or Connie could help. And with that in mind, he telephoned the hospital and fortunately for him, Debbie was on duty. When he explained the situation, she said that she and Connie would come over later that day and try to help.

The two girls turned up as promised and spoke with Allison Freemantle, whom Dick had placed in his spare bedroom. After about half an hour, they emerged from the room to tell Dick that they would gather a few items of clothing, cosmetics, and a toothbrush for her, and would bring them back later. They then left and Allison remained in the bedroom with the door closed.

That evening, Debbie and Connie returned with a small suitcase and went into the spare bedroom, then into the bathroom, and finally back to the spare bedroom.

While this was going on, Dick instructed Elijah to prepare a meal for four people and soon the three women emerged from the spare bedroom. Debbie and Connie, still in their nurse's uniforms, looked crisply attractive, as usual, but Allison had been transformed. He could now see that she was only in her late twenties, and by wearing light make-up and being clean, fresh, and slim, he had to admit that she was surprisingly attractive despite her slightly swollen face.

She came straight over to Dick and kissed him on the cheek. "Officer Starling. I'm so very grateful to you and these two girls for your help. I've decided that I must leave the mine. I'll go to my parent's house in Chimuka after collecting some things from my house. Would you please come there with me and protect me from Ted? I know he'll beat me again if I go alone."

"Well, certainly, Allison. And please call me Dick, everyone else does. First, eat some supper, then sleep here tonight, and we'll gather your things in the morning. Then I'll take you to the station and put you on a train to Chimuka."

"Oh, thank you. Yes, that would be perfect."

They all sat down at Dick's rickety table to eat Elijah's roast chicken, baked potatoes, and salad and over dinner and several glasses of wine, Debbie nudged Connie with her foot and said, "Dick, seeing as we're here, perhaps we should have a look at your leg wound." Allison asked about the wound and the two nurses gave her a vastly exaggerated account of his bravery and fortitude during the earlier raids.

"Can I look, too, please? I always wanted to be a nurse, and I've never seen a bullet wound before." Connie looked at Debbie and shrugged her shoulders. They smiled at each other and Connie replied, "Why not?"

After Elijah cleared away the table and completed washing and putting away the dishes, Dick told him that he could return to his quarters. Dick then went into his bedroom with the three ladies thinking, "Are they genuinely concerned about my bullet wound or am I in for another pleasant surprise?"

"Well, in order to make a full evaluation of your condition, you'll have to remove all your clothes and lie on the bed," Connie said briskly.

At this point, Dick thought he knew what was coming but felt rather embarrassed with Allison present. He also recalled his stupid presumptions when taking Sandra out on their first date, so just to set things straight he asked, "Are you okay with this, Allison?"

She smiled at him saying, "D'you think I haven't seen a naked man before?"

He slipped off his shirt, shorts, and sandals and lay on the bed, Little Tommy already rising to the occasion. "Oh my," said Debbie, "it looks like you're not the only one wanting some attention."

Debbie and Connie carefully examined his bullet wound and claimed that it had healed quite nicely, while Allison looked on. Then she joined the other two, reached out, and said quietly to the two nurses "D'you mind if I do this? I feel I owe it to him." Taking hold of Little Tommy in a gentle grip, she began slowly stroking him up and down.

Leaving Allison to her ministrations, Debbie said to Dick, "I think we'll be leaving now seeing that you're in good hands," And with that, she started to giggle. "No pun intended, Dick."

After the two nurses packed their small suitcases and left, Allison released her grip on Little Tommy and slipped out of the clothes that Connie had loaned her before returning to the bed and sliding in beside him.

Thus, the evening proceeded well into the night before Dick fell into a deep and trouble-free sleep. When waking up in the early morning, they took one more turn around the block before Dick escorted Allison back to her house at the mine where, thankfully, there was no Ted Freemantle to deal with. She gathered her belongings and Dick dropped her off at the railway station with a farewell kiss.

Contemplating the past twenty-four hours, he couldn't help but wonder how a perfectly innocent and unplanned incident could turn out so wonderfully. He thought his life was just getting better and better but, if he'd had a crystal ball, he may have viewed things differently.

Chapter Twenty Five

A couple of weeks passed with only the usual run of complaints. The police reservists, both white and black Waranians, adjusted well into their routines. Some of the reserve inspectors were respected members of the black community, and there was no apparent animosity between the ranks. Their duties were generally limited to working evening and weekend shifts at the station's new charge office, while the African police reservists carried out patrols in Umbedzi's township in groups of four or more during the hours of darkness.

Weekend activities in the township usually included friendly football matches between the six or seven local teams and were attended by up to three thousand supporters from the Umdenga township and outlying areas. The three so-called beer halls in the township were not really halls at all but large open areas of ground, surrounded on all sides by six-foot wire mesh fencing and with one large central building from which beer was served. Concrete tables and benches were scattered throughout the grounds, some beneath trees, others out in the open but covered with concrete shelters that provided a degree of shade from the harsh sunlight and protection from the occasional shower.

Although no hard liquor was sold, bottles of Chimbuka and one-gallon buckets of traditional African beer were available, the latter a creamy type of traditional and nutritional low-alcohol brew shared among the groups seated around the table in a take-a-swig-and-pass-it-on manner. While no food was served inside the beer hall, an assortment of snacks were sold by hawkers, who laid the tasty offerings on sheets of newspaper immediately outside the gates. These snacks ranged from fried caterpillars, grasshoppers, huge flying ants, and even locusts when in season and were considered a succulent delicacy by the African population.

The treats reminded Dick of his amazement at the first time he had seen swarms of green locusts flying around the lampposts at night, obviously attracted by the light. The African policemen and their entire families, would rush out onto the street, all carrying plastic grocery store bags or some type of container, grab handfuls of locusts, and squish them into their bags for an after-dinner treat, while at the same time stuffing the large insects into their mouths, grinning in delight.

He watched in disgust as they pushed three or four-inch-long live locusts into their mouths, legs, and wings still wiggling and kicking as their juice trickled down their chins. "Try some, baas. They taste like butter," they said. He laughingly relented only to discover that they did indeed taste like butter and later learned that they were also extremely nutritious.

Dick had discovered over the past two years that most of the Africans he had encountered were very sociable people and generally good-natured, so it was with considerable disappointment to see their pleasant and happy dispositions slowly eroded by a handful of malcontents.

Political unrest was becoming a major issue within the African community at large. The Waranian Independence Party, the WIP, was being challenged by another party calling itself the Rawanian Independence Party, the RIP, using the country's original name of Rawania before the British colonization some seventy years previous. For some reason, the colonizers had difficulty pronouncing the word Rawania; it always seemed to come out as Warania, so they called the country Warania instead.

At the time of colonization, there were no national boundaries, only tribal boundaries, so in common with many colonized countries in Africa in those days, the colonialists used natural boundaries, such as rivers or mountain ranges where they existed, to define the country's borders. Where they didn't, they drew straight lines across a map with a ruler to determine a national border and Warania was no exception to this. They paid little heed to tribal areas, which were often split in two, but with no fences or physical barriers, the natives continued to cross these invisible lines with impunity, mostly to visit friends or relatives who lived on the other side.

This ridiculous situation, however, had little impact on the two rival Waranian political parties as their supporters were generally divided along tribal lines. The WIPs were stronger in the north, while the smaller tribes supporting the RIP were mostly in the south. As is often the case in Africa, both candidates vying for power were determined that once they won the election, they would declare the country to be a one-party state or dictatorship, thus relegating the loser to permanent insignificance. Violence and intimidation became the popular means of campaigning for both parties, and this situation was becoming more and more prevalent in the township and the tribal trust lands. To add to the problems facing the country, the Russians had given their support to the training and arming of the WIP terrorists, and now China was doing the same for the RIP. Both superpowers were seeking Warania's virtually untouched mineral resources.

Football games in Warania's African townships became venues for political rallies by both the WIPs and the RIPs, and this, in turn, became the all-out warfare that the RWP had to deal with.

Thus, it turned out that Dick, accompanied by Detective Inspector Elias Chibanda (who had remained in Umbedzi permanently after the earlier raids), Reserve Police Inspector Tom Crystal, and three African police constables, piled into the stout, screen-protected Land Rover, and drove over to the township stadium to attend a Saturday afternoon football game. There was a crowd of close to three thousand spectators, almost all men, cheering or booing as the play drifted from one end of the pitch to the other. The Tigers, a team sponsored by the local asbestos mine and wearing striped orange and black jerseys, were playing against the green-clad Chamber of Commerce-sponsored Tomcats. In the closely contested game, the Tomcats came out as the winners with a score of three goals to two.

Under normal circumstances the crowd would then disperse, many drifting off to the beer halls to toast their heroes or to drown their sorrows but on this occasion, a dark-suited individual strode to the center of the pitch with a large megaphone and addressed the crowd in English. Although the native Waranians were divided into several different tribal entities, each with a different language or dialect, most of them spoke or understood English quite well.

"Who is that man?" asked Dick. Chibanda answered, "Agh, that is Solomon Chiweshe, the leader of the Waranian Independence Party. He is from Chimuka and is very anxious to become President of Warania when it becomes independent." Chibanda then busied himself setting up his reel-to-reel tape recorder before saying, "Now let's listen to what he has to say," as he pressed the 'record' button.

"Comrades, friends, ladies, and gentlemen," Chiweshe began, "before you leave, I have something very special to say to you. We, the people of Warania, have been patiently waiting for a long time for the British government to grant independence to our country. We have heard promises time and again, but still, their Queen rules over us. We toil in the fields and in the factories, we wait at their tables, cook their food, and weed their gardens while their countrymen live in luxurious houses, drive beautiful motor cars, and send their children to schools to which only a very few of us true Waranians are allowed to enter."

"We must protest, we must demonstrate, and we must overcome this disgraceful situation. Look up there on that hill. You see one police car containing only a few men, half of them true Waranians and the rest are Governor Johnston's gestapo. And they think that they can control us, the thousands who are seated here below. The time to act is now."

The crowd roared and turned toward Dick's police Land Rover, shaking their fists and making so much noise that they drowned out any further words of wisdom coming from Chiweshe's megaphone. As the crowd of spectators started to run toward them, Chibanda scrambled to pack up his equipment. Dick, worried that the mob would descend on the police station, started the engine, made a quick three-point turn, and, with Chibanda and his recording equipment safely in the Land Rover, withdrew. The two-mile journey to the station was enough to gain the safety of the police enclosure and to close and lock the gates long before the arrival of the inevitable frenzied mob.

Dick called on all the African police in the compound to report to the station in uniform, and he equipped them with an assortment of weapons, some with batons and shields and a few with shotguns. As expected, the crowd descended on the police station and could be heard long before they were seen. When they eventually arrived, who should be leading them but Chiweshe, the character in the suit, still brandishing his megaphone.

"Forward," he shouted. "Show these invaders that we have had enough."

Inspector Elias Chibanda, having re-activated his recording equipment, armed himself with a megaphone, and shouted back first in the vernacular and then in English, "Go back. Don't listen to this troublemaker. Go peacefully to your homes. Please." But all to no avail. The mob reached the fence and began shaking it and hurling rocks, bricks, bottles, and stones over the fence at the police station. Windows were broken, policemen were injured, and Dick realized that there was only one way to stop it. Their leader had to be taken out.

He called upon Tom Crystal, whom he knew to be an excellent shot. "Tom, you're a good shot, and I want you to shoot that Solomon Chiweshe. Try to bring him down without killing him if you can. Hit him in the leg or something. Can you do it?"

"Yes," Tom calmly replied as he raised his FN semi-automatic rifle to his shoulder.

"Very well. Chibanda, give them one last warning." Chibanda complied but his voice could barely be heard above the noise of the crowd and the crash of missiles surrounding them.

"Tom," Dick said, "take aim at the man in the dark suit. One round. Fire."

A loud crack split the air, and Chiweshe crumpled to the ground. The crowd immediately stopped shouting and when Crystal fired a couple more shots into the air, they turned and fled.

Dick sent two men out of the gate to retrieve Chiweshe and bring him inside, where his injuries were examined. He was not seriously hurt. Tom's shot had struck him in the thigh, but it was an in-and-out wound, and he was bleeding profusely.

Chiweshe was proving to be quite a handful and making a big fuss, not certain whether to scream because of the bullet wound or protest loudly about police brutality. Rudimentary first-aid was administered to his wounded leg, while little notice was taken of his screams of pain or his protests.

Dick phoned DCI Weeks of Special Branch and told him of the afternoon's incident and the shooting of Chiweshe. Weeks told him that Chiweshe was to be held in custody for inciting violence, taken to hospital for treatment, and he, Weeks, would arrive later in the day.

Once Chiweshe was treated and placed under guard at the local hospital, Dick took two police reservists and three of his constables on a tour of the township. He realized that this was the equivalent of waving a red flag at a bull, but the alternative was to cower behind his eight-foot wire fence. And that would never do.

Driving slowly through the township, it was apparent that few people were out and about. The streets were almost deserted, the beer halls almost empty and the sun was slowly setting over the western hills. Then from nowhere came a loud crack as a brick smashed into the Land Rover's door, and another fell onto its roof. As darkness descended, their vehicle was being pelted with rocks, bottles, and stones from all directions but still no one could be seen.

"Okay," said Dick, "they're lobbing at us from behind the houses. Let's go to the township square, so we can see them." As they drove on, their attackers began to show themselves, some running behind the Land Rover and still throwing bricks and stones as the Land Rover quickly outdistanced them.

At the township square, they were confronted by a mob of two or three hundred rioters and dozens of dustbins, metal beds, and old cars blocked their way. Once again, they were pelted with an assortment of missiles, fortunately from a mob that was gathered fairly close together, presumably egging each other on. Dick stopped the Land Rover and, having checked the wind direction, told the two constables seated in the back to open the roof hatch and begin throwing tear gas grenades toward the front of the mob.

This tactic worked well, as once the six-second time release had expired, the grenades began discharging tear gas, which drifted slowly into the crowd, and they began to back off and disperse. Unfortunately, one smart individual picked up one of the grenades before the six seconds elapsed and tossed it back at the Land Rover. The perfect lob fell between the two constables, through the hatch, and straight into the center of the vehicle, which meant all six police officers quickly disembarked while scrambling to put on their gas masks.

In the confusion that followed, the police officers were coughing and spluttering, and when most of the tear gas had drifted away, they tore off their masks and rubbed their eyes; all six of them severely affected by a dose of their own medicine. Fortunately, the mob had retreated a considerable distance away, which meant that they offered no immediate threat. The gas eventually dissipated, their eyes recovered and after leaving all the doors of the Land Rover open for a few minutes, they were able to resume their patrol with no further incidents.

Upon returning to the police station, an inspection of their Land Rover revealed serious damage. Mechanically, the vehicle was sound but the bodywork was badly battered and torn. In some cases, the bricks and rocks had left gaping holes in the doors and metalwork, and while the screens had protected the windows, the screens were seriously twisted and bent. Dick's trusty Land Rover would have to be returned to the central vehicle pool and a replacement sought.

From now on, Dick realized he would need more than one vehicle patrolling the township on a twenty-four-hour basis if he was to retain control over its residents. In record time, he managed to procure three more Land Rovers to constantly maintain a presence in the township, while the fourth would remain at the station for normal police duties.

Meanwhile, the WIP's leading light in the party was recovering well from the gunshot wound to his leg and was awaiting the Crown's pleasure to appear in Magistrates Court on a number of charges.

After several similar attacks on isolated police stations and police vehicles, the government decided that political dissidents such as Chiweshe would be confined in a camp well away from the general population until Britain could decide what to do about the situation. A suitable desolate location was selected and, after erecting some fencing and housing, many known dissidents and political activists were detained and held there. These were referred to as containment camps by some and as concentration camps by others, but they succeeded in keeping the ringleaders separated from the general population, and peace was seemingly restored to the small town of Umbedzi and to the country as a whole.

***

The Commissioner of the Royal Warania Police Force was a man of many years' experience and dedicated to upholding the rule of law in Warania. He called a meeting in Chimuka of all the officers in charge of police stations throughout the country and Dick although only a lowly inspector, was in attendance and listened with growing concern as the commissioner addressed them.

"Gentlemen. As you all know, policing the black community of Warania has become more and more difficult over the past year, and it has been decided by our government in London that the situation has become intolerable. The British Parliament has reached a point where it feels that Britain, regardless of whether the country is ready for it or not, can no longer resist granting independence to Warania, free of British control. Therefore, every man and every woman in this country will be entitled to vote for a new government in a newly independent nation."

"Voting will take place four weeks from today for it is felt that the situation has become so volatile that the sooner a transfer of power is effected the better. Polling stations will be established at virtually every school and public office in the country and the newly elected president will be entitled to form a cabinet of his choosing."

"We all know that the two main opposing parties will be the RIP and the WIP. We also know that we can expect many incidents of brutal intimidation by supporters of both parties."

"It will be your job to maintain law and order to the best of your ability. But know full well that whichever party wins, you are all likely to find yourselves out of a job, myself included. I'm sorry to have to put this so bluntly, but I feel that it is only fair that you fully understand the situation that you and I are facing. I have been assured by Her Majesty's government that if you remain until the end of your tenure, you and all those who hold ranks of inspector and above will be rewarded with six months' salary from the day of your resignation or dismissal."

"Leave before then, in other words, desert, and you get nothing. Those of you with over ten years of service will receive a gratuity of five thousand pounds and those with over twenty years of service will receive a pension from Britain. RWP Associations here in Warania, in Britain, and around the world, which as you know are made up of former members, will assist those of you needing help in relocating or finding alternative employment. If you have any questions or need further assistance, contact the personnel department at HQ. Thank you all and good luck."

Following the commissioner's speech, there was much mumbling and grumbling before everyone dispersed. Dick walked back to the parking lot with Barry Merriweather, the inspector who had taken over the Zumba police station after Taffy's spectacular demise. It was well known throughout the force that Merriweather was a homosexual and thus nicknamed Marigold. However, he was an efficient police officer and generally accepted as being just a little different, never imposing himself on his colleagues. No one questioned his periodic visits to a certain club for gentlemen of a different persuasion in Chimuka once in a while.

"So, Marigold, what do you make of that little bombshell?"

Merriweather paused before replying, "Well, I might call it quits and return to the UK. There's really nothing here for me and life will be much easier back home. My family has a small home-furnishing business in Liverpool that they've been pestering me to join and help them with. So I might do a bunk and to hell with their six months' wages. By the way. I had to sort out a load of documents and rubbish when I arrived in Zumba."

"Taffy was not the most organized of people and things were in an awful mess. I came across a couple of curious items that will be of interest to you. I should have given them to you earlier, but I brought them along today knowing that you'd be here. God knows what they're all about." Having said that, he handed Dick two sealed envelopes, a thin one and a bulky one, both bearing the words 'For the attention of Inspector Richard Starling. Only to be opened upon my death'.

Dick frowned as he accepted the envelopes, shook hands with Marigold, and they went their separate ways. When Dick returned to Umbedzi, he was met at the door by Tom Crystal, the garage proprietor/reserve police inspector. Dick was anxious to open the mysterious envelopes but Tom appeared flustered saying, "Have you heard the news, Dick? It's been on the radio. One man, one vote in a month's time. Christ, what am I going to do?"

"Well," replied Dick, "you probably won't be required as a police reservist in a month's time and people will still need their cars fixed, so I don't think you have to do anything. I think our main priority will be to help me stop these silly buggers from killing each other for the next four weeks. Then, I'm sure things will settle down."

Although he was curious to know what Taffy had written, Dick decided to deal with the envelopes when he had more time. They probably should have gone to Taffy's sister Gwyneth. If Marigold hadn't been so slow in producing them, they would have. He placed them in one of his desk drawers, alongside his British passport, birth certificate, and the note that Gwyneth Lloyd-Jones had given him with her address and telephone number. He called in the newly promoted Inspector Zibando and told him what he had learned from their commissioner. Zibando said that he was pleased that the country was to gain independence but thought that the weeks leading up to the election would be troublesome.

Dick thought of the danger that Warania's white population may be facing and particularly Debbie and Connie. The hospital switchboard managed to connect him with Debbie. "Hello, Debbie, I presume you've heard the news. I think we should talk. Would you and Connie like to come over this evening? I'll get Elijah to rustle something up."

Her reply put a smile on his face. He summoned Elijah and asked him to prepare bangers and mash for three and opened his first Chimbuka of the day. While sitting and enjoying his beer, Dick realized that the situation in Warania was only going to get worse and was concerned for his own safety and for the safety of the two nurses. When they arrived, he told them what he had learned from the commissioner and said, "I think things are going to get pretty nasty. Perhaps it's time to think about your own safety. More incidents of violence and terrorist activity will inevitably follow once the WIP and the RIP start to campaign."

He showed them some of the weapons kept in his small police armory, particularly the FN rifle, and suggested that he give them some rudimentary instructions on their use. They each took a weapon and Connie said, "I've used guns before. Back home, Daddy would take me grouse shooting during the summer holidays. He told me that he thought I was a very good shot. Of course, I've never fired anything like this before, but I'd like to try it out."

Debbie seemed reluctant to even handle the weapon. "Don't you have anything smaller? This FN, or whatever it's called, is too big and heavy."

"Yes, I do have an Uzi. It's a small submachine gun that fires nine-millimeter rounds and is made by the Israelis. It's light and has very little recoil. How about coming out into the bush with me tomorrow? I'll show you both how to use them."

They enthusiastically agreed; a time was set; and they moved on to another subject that had been at the forefront of Dick's mind ever since they had given him all that special attention when he was in the hospital.

Connie began by asking him why they had seen so little of him since he'd left the hospital. They'd made only one visit to his house when they came to his aid regarding poor Allison Freemantle.

Ignoring his disastrous period of domesticity with Valerie, he said, "Well, there's been so much going on but don't think I've forgotten about either of you. You've both been constantly on my mind. If that Freemantle woman hadn't been so pushy, I was hoping that it'd be only you two examining more than my bullet wound."

Debbie laughed before saying, "Well, we've been thinking a lot about you, too. Especially when you called to say that you were concerned about our safety and now offering to give us some gun practice. We both think that was very sweet of you, and we'd like to give you a treat."

Then, each taking one of his hands they walked into his bedroom where they began stripping off their clothes, told him to do the same, and treated him to his second opportunity of a ménage à trois.

The following day, Dick collected the two girls from their nurses' dormitory and drove them out to a deserted area of bush about three miles from town. He showed them how to load, aim and fire the FN, the Uzi, and the .38 Smith and Wesson revolver that he had also brought along, and they all took turns shooting down empty cans that Dick balanced on a convenient rock.

Sandy was remarkably good with the FN, pulling it firmly into her shoulder and gently squeezing the trigger with no obvious discomfort from the recoil. Debbie became more confident and relaxed with the Uzi as the morning wore on. By the time Dick introduced them to the revolver, they were both clearly enjoying the morning outing and when they were finished, they had proved to be quite adept at handling and firing his assortment of weapons.

He had completely forgotten about Taffy's envelopes.

Chapter Twenty Six

Chaos reigned for the following four weeks while the RIP and the WIP were vying for votes. Homes and villages were invaded, and headmen, tribal elders, and peace-loving Waranians were slaughtered. Wives and daughters were raped. Babies were swung by their ankles, their little heads dashed against trees or rocks, as both parties intimidated the general population in an effort to win votes. All done in the name of freedom.

The inmates in the 'containment camps' were released and the wounded agitator Solomon Chiweshi reinforced his efforts to become the leading candidate for the Waranian Independence Party, while a Chinese-supported candidate for the Rawania Independence Party, Joshua Ngoro, vied for leadership of the RIP.

Complaints came pouring in at police stations all over the country. Marigold Merriweather headed back to England three days after his conversation with Dick. Dick, still uncertain as to what he should do, was told that he was to assume temporary responsibility for the Zumba police area and received an immediate promotion to the rank of chief inspector.

Leaving Inspector Zibando in charge at Umbedzi, Dick drove to Zumba to find a totally overwhelmed African inspector, Robert Sibela, trying to cope with the same chaotic situation that Dick had left behind at Umbedzi.

"Patrolling your township is absolutely pointless," Dick told him. "Both the RIP and the WIP terrorists and their supporters are running rampant throughout all the villages and townships, killing and raping at will in an effort to force the poor people stuck in the middle to vote for their candidate. When innocent people are confronted and asked whom they are voting for, they try to make a lucky guess and have to live or die with the consequences."

To add to the problem, many of these intimidators, previously armed with sticks, stones, and Molotov cocktails, were now armed with automatic weapons thanks to their Chinese and Soviet sponsors. The rattle of automatic gunfire could be heard regularly in the townships, and there was absolutely nothing Dick or Sibela could do about it. They were essentially confined to their police stations and the small towns of Zumba and Umbedzi. Many of the businesses were closed and boarded up, their occupants having headed for Chimuka, where there was a greater degree of safety. Although all of the violence and intimidation was aimed at the black population, many Europeans had left the country, mostly heading for South Africa or the United Kingdom.

Many innocent civilians flocked to police stations throughout the country for refuge but had to be turned away simply due to a lack of food, accommodation, or sanitation.

Eventually, election day came, polling stations were opened and long lines of Africans awaited their chance to place an X in the appropriate box. Watching from a distance, Dick noted several individuals come out of the polling booth and rejoin the queue to vote again. Once the polling booths were closed, all the boxes containing the votes were shipped to Chimuka, where a manual count was expected to last at least three days. Several vehicles carrying ballot boxes were held up at gunpoint en route and the boxes were stolen and destroyed. Such was Universal Suffrage, Waranian style.

Eventually, the results were announced. Solomon Chiweshi was declared the winner with sixty percent of the votes, with his rival Joshua Ngoro receiving a paltry twenty-five percent. The remaining fifteen percent were declared to be spoiled votes.

Britain recognized Chiweshi as the duly elected leader of the country, whereupon they declared Warania to be totally independent and Chiweshi proudly presented himself as its first president. The Waranian flag, pale blue with a lion's head and with the Union Jack occupying the top left-hand corner, was ceremoniously lowered and replaced with a garish, multi-colored Waranian flag bearing the image of a warrior's shield and assegai with the silhouette of an AK-47 rifle, complete with its banana-shaped magazine and a bayonet crossed in front of it. Great rejoicing took place throughout the country although the RIP's embittered Joshua Ngoro from the southern part of the country continued to demand an entirely new election, claiming that fraud and all manner of skulduggery had deprived him of victory.

Dick, relieved that the election was over, was surprised to find that Zumba and Umbedzi had quietened down. He was able to patrol his entire area unmolested and decided that for the time being he would remain a member of the Warania Police force which, having dropped the word Royal, was now known as the WP, and see how things turned out.

His love life was very satisfactory, with regular visits from Debbie or Connie, and sometimes together if their nursing schedules permitted. They placed no demands on him, were inventive in the bedroom, and were almost insatiable in their sexual appetites.

With Dick's promotion to chief inspector came a considerable increase in salary, and he was able to purchase a rather sleek, three-year-old Peugeot 404, which handled the rough roads in his immediate neighborhood very well and at thirty miles to the gallon was surprisingly economical to run.

Being very proud of this new possession and the country appearing to have settled down, he invited Debbie and Connie on an outing, planning to travel northwest in the direction of the Belgian Congo, and perhaps call in on his old acquaintance Salty DuPlessis.

When the day came, the girls turned up loaded with cakes, sandwiches, and soft drinks. Dick's contribution was three bottles of cheap wine, some paper plates, and an assortment of drinking receptacles. Setting off just after eight in the morning, the weather was on the cool side but a glorious blue sky promised a perfect day ahead.

The Peugeot handled the dirt road well. All three sat on the front bench seat with Connie, who was seated in the middle, sitting with her right hand on Dick's left thigh, slowly creeping up the leg of his baggy shorts. Finding his boxer shorts a little impediment to her progress, she soon had Little Tommy in her grasp. With almost no traffic on the road, Dick was pretty lax with his steering, and once or twice almost veered into the storm drain that ran beside the right-hand side of the road.

After traveling for about an hour, Dick pulled over into a convenient layby, deciding that this would make an excellent mid-morning stopover. Out came the large blanket, flasks of tea, biscuits, and a delicious-looking chocolate sponge cake. The girls laid everything out and the three of them lounged on the blanket. Debbie was wearing a pair of very short hot pants and a white sleeveless blouse, and Connie wore a flared mini-skirt and a bright red top. It was quite apparent that neither girl was wearing a bra and from where Dick was sitting, it didn't appear that Connie wore any panties either. *This is going to be quite an outing,* thought Dick, *and so it was.*

Having enjoyed an hour of eating, drinking, and considerable foreplay, they decided to save the rest for later. The blanket and morning tea paraphernalia were packed away, and they continued their journey. Dick now had a clear view of the mountainous region ahead of them and with his last visit still vivid in his mind, he vowed that they would stay well inside Warania's territory. It had been several months since Dick had last visited Salty, but he easily recognized the approach to Salty's farmhouse. As he drove along the dirt road leading up to the house, he frowned. Whereas Salty kept his driveway well-graded and the grass on either side groomed, the road was now stony and pot-holed and the grass long and unkempt.

Pulling up in front of the house, he saw several African men, women, and children scattered everywhere, but no sign of Salty, his wives, or their children.

Telling the girls to wait in the car, he walked to Salty's front door and gave a couple of hard raps. The door opened and a young African man appeared, wearing a pair of camouflage pants, no shirt, and no shoes and carrying an AK-47 rifle loosely in his right hand.

"What you want?" he asked sullenly.

"Mr. DuPlessis," Dick replied. "No Mr. DuPlessis here," said Camouflage Pants. "Now, please go."

"What about his wives, his children? And what are all these strange people doing here? For that matter, who are you?"

"We are Waranians, and this is now our house and our land. You ask too many questions, and you are trespassing. Now go."

By this time, Dick was worried and decided that the sooner he left the better, but as he turned to go, he was confronted by three men, all carrying AK-47s and blocking his way. Glancing beyond them, he saw that the Peugeot was surrounded, all the doors were open and Debbie and Connie were being unceremoniously dragged out. "Hey, what are you doing? Leave those women alone, we're going," he shouted, but one of the three men confronting him, a big man wearing a T-shirt emblazoned with the words 'The Big Apple' and a silhouette of the New York City skyline, stepped forward, saying, "maybe you are and maybe you're not, white boy."

He then gave Dick a shove, which sent him stumbling backward and into the dirt.

Dick rose to his feet but had no option but to watch as Debbie and Connie were set upon by a swarm of women, eagerly tearing off their clothes until the two girls stood naked beside the Peugeot. The boot of the car had been opened and all their carefully prepared food, blankets, and wine were taken. One woman, at least fifty pounds heavier than Connie, was attempting to squeeze into her red top and flared skirt, while another somewhat slimmer young girl, was proudly parading around in Debbie's shorts and torn blouse.

Debbie and Connie, still huddled together beside the car, were tearfully attempting to cover their breasts and pudenda with their arms and hands. Then one of Camouflage Pants' cohorts laughingly jumped into the driver's seat of the Peugeot and started the engine. With obviously little or no experience of driving, and after much grinding and scraping of gears, he managed to find a gear, slammed his foot on the accelerator, and careened straight ahead, plowing through some sparse elephant grass and smashing headfirst into a tree.

The onlookers all cheered and danced around while their hero fell out of the driver's door with blood gushing from his forehead and collapsed on the ground. The Peugeot, with steam rising from beneath its bonnet, gave a quick shudder and fell silent.

Silently, Dick recalled Taffy Lloyd-Jones' somber warning about always taking a gun wherever he ventured. Stupid, stupid, stupid!

Within a short while, the girls were each given a small filthy blanket with which to cover themselves, and all three were taken inside Salty's house. The floor that once had meticulously patterned parquet flooring was now bare concrete, and in the large fireplace were charred remnants of the parquet, obviously burned to provide a fire on which to cook.

Dick was racking his brains, trying to think his way out of this mess. The two girls huddled together, not speaking and not crying, staring hollow-eyed at the chaos that surrounded them. Debbie noticed that their captors were very casual about the way they handled their weapons but considered that for the time being their best bet was to remain quiet and subdued.

Several men and women entered the house to survey their captives, but none spoke to them or came too close. Eventually, Camouflage Pants, who appeared to be in charge, asked Dick again, "Why you come here? What do you want and what am I to do with you?"

"We don't want anything. We merely came here to visit Mr. DuPlessis, and he obviously isn't here, so we wish to leave. With our car, if it's still working."

"Humph. DuPlessis and his family are not here. If you go, you make trouble. Best we kill you, but we wait until morning. We have some fun with you two ladies first. Never had white ladies before, but they look too skinny." He placed a large calabash full of water on the floor, told them that there were guards at all of the doors and windows, and left the three of them alone in Salty's living room.

Immediately after he left, Debbie whispered, "Dick, we have to get out of here, quickly. What can we do?" Connie's response was to comment that she didn't think they were skinny, just slim. Debbie sighed and rolled her eyes skyward.

Dick, like Debbie, had also noted that their captors were very casual with their guns and suggested that they wait until nightfall, try to lay their hands on some weapons, and make a break for it. "Otherwise," he told them, "we're as good as dead." He silently thought that their chances of getting out of this mess were zero. But given any chance at all, the fact that both Debbie and Connie had received some basic firearms training, particularly with handguns, might be useful. He was sure neither of them would be afraid to use them under the current circumstances if the opportunity presented itself.

Dick told them that it was obvious that Camouflage Pants and probably several of his companions were ex-RIP or WIP terrorists and that if they were to use their AK-47s, the chances were that they would fire them on fully automatic. "When they fire, they tend to lose control and most of their shots are high. So, if we get the chance to make a break, stay low, run like hell, and, if we're lucky enough to lay our hands on some firearms, use your shots sparingly. Now, let's start searching for some weapons."

They began crawling slowly around the living room but didn't find anything of use. The house seemed to be deserted, so they ventured into Salty's kitchen where surprisingly, a block of kitchen knives stood on the cluttered kitchen counter. They each selected the biggest and sharpest weapon they could find. Dick, still fully clad, was able to slip his knife into one of his long woolen socks. The girls, each barely covered by a small and filthy blanket, decided to tie them around their waists, leaving their breasts to swing free but giving them somewhere to slip their knives.

They had no sooner accomplished this small advantage when the back door burst open and Mr. Camouflage Pants cockily strolled in with three companions, one sporting a bruised and bloody forehead. "Well, hello," he said. "Look who's here to take turns with the ladies." He was casually carrying his AK-47 and Dick noted that one of his men was holding a Kalashnikov pistol, but neither were holding them in a threatening manner, letting them hang at their sides. The other two appeared to be unarmed.

Glancing at Debbie, Dick said, "I guess it's now or never." He lunged toward Camouflage Pants, embedding six inches of sharp stainless steel deep into his stomach and giving it a twist, at the same time snatching the AK-47 from his grasp.

Debbie, quick as lightning, slashed her knife across the throat of the man holding the Kalashnikov, grabbed his gun, and shot the third man in the eye. Connie was slower to react, and when she attempted to stab the fourth man, the incompetent driver with a bloody forehead, she tripped on her loosely tied blanket, losing it in the process, and fell before reaching him. He turned and fled.

The three of them immediately ran out the kitchen door and around to the front of the house. Although several people were milling about, none appeared to be armed. Dick ran to the Peugeot, closely followed by Debbie and Connie, in the hope that he could start it and escape. The keys were still in the ignition and miraculously it started. The girls clambered into the back, Dick slammed into reverse and reached the forecourt of the house before gunfire filled the air.

"Down," he shouted as bullets shattered the back window of the car. He clumsily engaged first gear and shot away down the pitted access road. Connie grabbed his AK-47 and was firing out of the now missing rear window into the pack of bodies standing outside Salty's house, using one single shot at a time, just like he'd taught her, and throwing their assailants into total disarray.

Dick gained access to the main road and sighed with relief as the Peugeot drew them further away from near catastrophe. Glancing at the dials on the dashboard, he was alarmed to see that the car had already overheated into the red zone. As he had suspected, the radiator was damaged, and there was no water to cool the engine. He decided to keep going, knowing that before long the engine block would seize, and they would be stuck.

While laboring with his rapidly dying Peugeot, Dick didn't notice that Connie was frantically scrabbling beneath the front passenger seat and was amazed when she withdrew her overstuffed handbag from beneath its depths. Within minutes, his worst fears were realized. The engine died, steam was pouring from beneath the bonnet, and they were left with no option but to walk. The girls had no shoes and Connie had no blanket. The car had been stripped of everything, so with a naked Connie with her handbag clenched in her fist, Debbie partially wrapped in her filthy blanket but somewhat comforted by her Kalashnikov, and Dick, fully clothed and carrying the AK-47, they set off along the long road back to Umbedzi.

After a few minutes, Debbie suggested that Dick give Connie his shorts and shirt and give her his undershirt or vest, and after due consideration, he obliged, now relegated to a pair of bright red underpants, shoes, and socks. He thanked God it was dark.

Chapter Twenty Seven

The long and painful walk along the dirt road soon resulted in both Debbie and Connie's bare feet becoming bloody and sore. To alleviate the problem, Dick tore off two strips from Debbie's small blanket and bound their feet. Debbie's blanket, which she had wrapped around her waist to form a primitive skirt, was now reduced to an exceedingly short mini-skirt. However, this may have been a blessing in disguise for shortly afterward, hearing a vehicle coming from behind, Dick suggested that Debbie step out in the road to wave it down.

Silas Ngokwe, seeing three scruffy people ahead of him in his headlights, one of them looking particularly alluring, slowed his rusty old Bedford truck and crept by despite their shouting and wailing. He did not like the look of the almost naked white man carrying a gun who began running after him, but being a Christian soul he eventually decided to stop. They did, indeed, appear to be in dire straits.

Dick caught up with him and gasped, "Please help us. We've been held hostage, robbed and threatened with rape and death by terrorists who've taken over the DuPlessis farm."

"Ugh. Boss DuPlessis. I know him well. A good man. What happened to him?"

"We don't know. We went there to visit him and found the farm overrun with men carrying guns and many women and children. There was no sign of Salty or his family. We need to get back to Umbedzi. Can you please take us there? To the police station, please."

"Definitely boss. These freedom fighters are running loose and causing all sorts of trouble. I will take you to Umbedzi, but I have only this small truck, with only enough room for two more people. The ladies can ride up front with me, but you will have to ride in the back."

By this time, the two girls had reached the truck and without further bidding climbed into the cab beside the driver. Dick reluctantly got in the back, accompanied by several bales of hay, a cage full of chickens, and a goat.

Silas, well pleased with the outcome, drove off with his scantily dressed passengers who, although dirty and bloody, made pleasant small talk with their driver.

As promised, Silas dropped all three off at the Umbedzi police station and the constable on duty at the security gate gaped in amazement as three disheveled individuals shambled into the charge office. Detective Inspector Elias Chibanda stood and stared at Chief Inspector Starling, standing before him wearing only shoes, socks, and a pair of gaudy red boxer shorts.

Dick explained what had happened to them after shepherding the two girls into the house where they could shower, bathe and bandage their bloody and blistered feet, and try to find something to wear. He then joined them, for once ignoring their nudity, and used what remaining hot water they had left him to shower. Once again clean, shaved, and dressed in uniform, he telephoned his old pal DCI Weeks in Chimuka.

"Hello, Starling old chap. You still with us? Thought you would have buggered off to Blighty by now. What's up?"

Once again Dick explained what had transpired, emphasizing that he feared the worst for Salty and his multitude of wives and offspring.

"I'm afraid that it's happening all over. There's total chaos throughout the whole country and Chiweshi seems both indifferent and powerless to do anything about it. There's nothing you can do for this DuPlessis fellow. He either got out or he's dead. My suggestion is to pack your bags and get out of Umbedzi. In fact, get out of Warania while you still can. Believe it or not, there are still flights leaving from the airport here although it's a devil of a job getting on one. I've been trying for three days now and no luck so far."

Dick returned to his sitting room to find Debbie and Connie seated on the couch, looking morose, tired and forlorn. Debbie had managed to find a pair of his trousers, and with the bottoms rolled up and a belt at her waist, she actually looked quite pert. His loose and far too large Hawaiian shirt added a colorful touch to her ensemble, but her heavily bandaged feet and her dark and tangled hair spoiled the overall effect. Connie, with her tousled blonde hair a completely soggy mess, wore a pair of his baggy khaki shorts, an even baggier police shirt still bearing the insignia of a chief inspector on its epaulets, and similarly bandaged feet. Somehow, Bentley had sensed that he was needed and sat beside her with his large head nestled in her lap.

Dick selected three bottles of cold Chimbuka from the fridge, passed one to each of the girls, and began to tell them of the situation he had just learned from the Special Branch. "What are we to do?" moaned Connie. "All our stuff is at the nurse's quarters. Is it safe to go there? Can we still work there? What about the patients?"

"I don't know, but we can drive down there in the Land Rover. I'll be armed, and we'll take a couple of the constables along too. Then you can check things out and collect what you need. If necessary, I'll bring you back here for the night."

With that, Dick removed a rifle and a pistol from the station armory, told Chibanda what they were doing, and set off for the hospital in the station's Land Rover with two armed constables and his two wards, Connie and Debbie, safely huddled in the back.

Although the hospital seemed quiet when they arrived, Dick sent one of his constables inside to check. A minute or two later, the constable returned, visibly shaken and beckoning Dick to come inside. "There is no one inside. No nurses, no patients, not even any furniture, sir. The place has been ransacked, and there are many dead bodies."

Upon entering, Dick was horrified to see seven or eight completely naked bodies, black and white, mostly women heaped in one corner of the hospital's reception area. They were covered in a mass of dried blood and the air was thick with great blue flies that were buzzing loudly as they feasted on the massacred remains of the hospital staff. One man, whom Dick recognized as Doctor Harold Salter, was sprawled on his back, naked and with a great mess of blood, flies, and gore spread across his upper thighs, groin, and stomach.

Much to his horror, he saw that the man had been emasculated. Dick felt his rage growing, and he began to shake violently, his brain unable to register what he had seen. He ran to the door and threw up until his throat was dry, unable to shake the awful image from his head. And then, leaning against the frame of the door, Dick began to weep.

When he was sufficiently recovered, he stepped outside where he saw, hanging on a stick driven into the ground, a white penis and pair of testicles, presumably those of the late Doctor Harold Salter. "Someone will pay for this," he muttered as he returned to the Land Rover.

Debbie watched Dick first vomit and then stumble toward them, his face a deathly pallor. She asked, "Whatever is the matter?" With tears in his eyes and still unable to speak, he shook his head, started the vehicle, and slowly drove toward the nurse's quarters.

More horror awaited him there, but telling the girls to remain in the vehicle, he took a deep breath, tried to steady himself, and entered through the front door. He thought that he had become hardened to the violent and primitive ways of Africa. He had dragged bloated and distorted bodies from the river, bodies whose skin slid off their flesh as they were pulled out of the water. He had recovered decomposed bodies from the bush, and partially eaten corpses that had been attacked and savaged by a variety of wildlife, but he had never encountered this mindless, senseless slaughter of kind, well-meaning doctors and nurses whose desire in life was to help the sick and dying.

He discovered three more dead bodies inside the nurse's dormitory, all young women stripped naked and obviously raped repeatedly before being bayonetted time and time again. Pools of blood lay on the floor and as he had seen in the hospital, the air was alive with swarms of huge blue flies. Blood was smeared all over the women's inner thighs, stomachs, and chests with great congealed pools of gore beneath their deathly white torsos.

Dick turned away in horror and stopped the girls from entering the building. "We must get away from here, now. You can't go inside, and you can forget about your possessions. There are none." And with that, he climbed into the Land Rover and drove them back to the station.

Telling Chibanda what he had found at the hospital, Dick explained that he was leaving for Chimuka with the two nurses. It was now Chibanda's police station to do with as he wished. He entered the armory, passing Connie his FN, Debbie the Uzi, and keeping a revolver and shotgun for himself. Filling a metal ammunition box with several fully loaded magazines for the FN and Uzi and plenty of rounds of .38 and 12-bore cartridges for the revolver and shotgun, he considered that they were ready to leave.

He rummaged through his desk drawers looking for his British passport and when, eventually finding it, he also came across the two envelopes that Marigold Merriweather had given him a few weeks earlier.

Stuffing his passport, Taffy's envelopes, and a few other bits and pieces of paperwork, and thoughtlessly including Taffy's sister's note with her address and telephone number into a small plastic document case, he shoved the lot into the back of his shorts and returned to the Land Rover only to find Bentley inside with the two girls. "We must take him," pleaded Connie, and with a sigh Dick departed in his fully fueled Land Rover.

The paved road into Chimuka was in good condition and Dick drove fast. Anxious to get to Chimuka as quickly as possible, they had only traveled about ten miles when up ahead he saw dark smoke rising and as Dick drew closer he saw a saloon car on fire, lying on its side and blocking the road. A dozen or so African men were running and jumping around the burning vehicle, all armed with rifles that they were brandishing and firing into the air in a frenzied dance of glee.

Dick couldn't see any sign of the car's occupants and had no way of helping them, so he told the girls, "Okay, it's a roadblock, and we're going through it. Open the hatch, load those guns, and fire at the bastards as soon as we're in range. Fire low and hold tight. I'm going to knock that car out of the way."

Recalling his earlier training on how to clear a vehicle from a roadblock, he put his foot down and aimed for the rear of the car. Traveling at about fifty miles per hour with the passenger side wheels of the Land Rover running on the dirt verge, he clipped the back end of the vehicle, surprising the terrorists who belatedly realized that he was not going to stop and began to fire wildly at them.

Connie and Debbie, with their heads and shoulders exposed through the Land Rover's hatch, took aim and fired consistently on single-shot, causing the terrorists to scatter, while Dick managed to send the obstructive vehicle swinging on its side sufficiently to scrape by and accelerate. "Well done, ladies. Thank God we had that firearms practice."

They encountered no further incidents as they approached Chimuka and once inside the city limits, Dick proceeded to police headquarters. The perimeter of the building was being patrolled by armed police officers, but when he identified himself to the gate guards, and they saw the state of his bullet-ridden and dented police vehicle, he was permitted entry.

He found DCI Weeks in his office and together with a bedraggled Connie, Debbie, and Bentley in tow, he described the devastation and horror that had occurred at Umbedzi's hospital and their narrow escape on the road to Chimuka.

Weeks shook his head at the awful state that the girls were in. Both of them still had their feet bandaged and wore no shoes. Their clothing was a total mess and once again, he repeated his earlier cautions and suggested they leave. "I've secured a flight back to Britain tomorrow morning and plan to stay put right here until it's time to leave for the airport. God knows if I'll ever actually get there for the place is packed with people trying to get out."

"What about driving south into Zambia? Would that work?"

"Same problem," replied Weeks. "The border post is flooded with people and the Zambian authorities have called in the army to maintain control. I hear that they've actually shot two people, white people, who tried to force their way in."

"Okay, so if flying out and driving out aren't an option, what's left? How about by boat on the Umfurudzi?"

Weeks hesitated before answering, his head at a questioning angle. "I never gave that a thought, but of course, it would never work. The Umfurudzi is quite shallow in places and full of rapids, but it does eventually feed into Lake Mweru on the Zambian border. In any case, where could you find a boat? No, forget it. It's fly out or stay here; they are your only realistic options."

Connie and Debbie had remained silent throughout this conversation but now Connie chipped in. "We're not staying here. We were contracted by the British government to work here as nurses for three years. Surely, it's their responsibility to get us home safely. We're going to the British embassy right now," and they hobbled out of Weeks' office.

"That won't do them any good," stated Weeks. "The embassy's closed. Those buggers were on one of the first planes out."

Dick turned and chased after the two girls. Catching up with them, he reported what Weeks had told him. Connie said, "Well, what the hell are we supposed to do? Sit here and wait to be murdered?"

"No," replied Dick. "We'll do what very few, if any, are doing. We'll go by boat."

"By boat? Haven't you forgotten something? Warania is landlocked and the Umfurudzi is impossible. We either have to drive or fly," Debbie said.

"Not necessarily. I've an idea. Are you coming with me or taking your chances here?"

Debbie and Connie looked at each other, shrugged and Debbie said, "I suppose we'll have to come with you, but first we need to find some shoes and get out of these ridiculous clothes."

Climbing back into the Land Rover, they first headed to a nearby grocery store where Dick told the girls to help him load up with enough food and drink to last the three of them and Bentley for a week. "Unfortunately," he said, "I have no money, but I'm sure you can find some in that enormous handbag that you've been carting around, Connie." She snorted as she rummaged through her handbag, clearly miffed, and paid the clerk after they selected their week's provisions.

They then searched for somewhere where the women could buy some clothes and were in luck, for on one of Chimuka's streets was a row of shops owned by East Indian merchants, sarcastically referred to as Bombay Alley. They found a clothing store where they purchased long pants, shirts, underwear, and some large and ugly shoes that would fit over their heavily bandaged feet. Connie continued to grumble as she ferreted in her huge handbag, complaining that it wasn't fair that she had to pay for all this stuff since she was the only one with any money. Now fully provisioned, Dick headed to a petrol station where he withdrew his wallet and smiled at Connie, who had been spending her money thinking that he had none. Ignoring her petulance, he purchased two five-gallon containers, and some two-stroke oil and filled the two containers with petrol. Finally, climbing back into the Land Rover, they set off not to Umbedzi but toward Zumba on the northeast side of the Umfurudzi.

Having driven for almost two hours, Dick turned west onto a dirt track leading down to the Umfurudzi and, using his uncanny sense of direction, he soon located the section of river where, more than two years earlier, he and Constable Machaka were pushing the corpse of Little Fatty back and forth across the river.

To his relief, a few hundred yards downstream was the same derelict wooden dock with the little aluminum flat-bottomed boat with its tiny Seagull engine, rocking slowly on the gently flowing Umfurudzi River.

Smiling, he said to the girls, "This is how we'll get home. This little boat will take us all the way down to Lake Mweru on the Zambian border. Once across the lake, we'll head to the British embassy in Lusaka and home."

Dick knew that it wasn't going to be quite as easy as that but thought it best to keep any negative thoughts to himself. They would encounter strong currents, rock-strewn rapids, a variety of dangerous wildlife, and possibly more trigger-happy members of the new and enlightened citizens of Warania.

They first loaded their provisions and fuel into the boat, which would be more accurately described as a dingy for it was barely ten feet in length, along with their guns and the ammunition box. Bentley climbed aboard, apparently more than content with his tail wagging nineteen to the dozen as he settled down for a nap while Dick tackled the Seagull outboard. These amazing little engines have stood the test of time and Dick enthusiastically filled the empty fuel tank, fully expecting it to start with the first pull but was sadly disappointed.

Try as he might, the Seagull wouldn't start and Debbie, anxious to get away, had cast off the mooring ropes and the slow current was drifting them gently downstream.

Dick discovered that the thoughtful owner had drained the fuel completely out of the engine and had placed a small toolbox beneath the center seat. Searching inside, he discovered a spark plug spanner and a feeler gauge, but he needed something with which to clean the magneto and coil contacts. Connie came to the rescue once again. After delving into her bag, she produced a toothbrush.

While Dick was busy with the outboard, Debbie, finding a short plank of wood in the bottom of the boat and using it as a primitive paddle, succeeded in keeping the boat in the center of the river as they continued drifting east.

With the spark plug cleaned and re-gapped, the magneto and coil contacts cleaned, and with a fresh supply of fuel mixture, Dick grinned with joy when their Seagull fired and began to run as smooth as silk. They were off at last. Connie opened a large bag of dry dog food for Bentley, a tin of corned beef for the three of them and Debbie amazingly tossed a green salad in Dick's sweaty bush hat. With plenty of water, they each quenched their thirst and began to relax, for salvation was hopefully just around the bend.

Chapter Twenty Eight

Dick estimated their journey along the Umfurudzi River to Lake Mweru would take between nine and twelve hours. He wasn't sure of the distance but knew that the river would meander as it wended its way eastwards and expected to encounter some difficulties along the way. The first obstacle was the abundance of wildlife, for after only traveling about four miles they encountered a small herd of elephants on the shoreline, splashing around in the shallows and squirting fountains of water left and right from their huge and amazingly flexible trunks. They were able to give them a wide berth and, in any case, the elephants showed little interest in their small boat as it glided past.

Later, Dick saw several hippos wading in the shallow river just ahead of them, almost blocking their way. When Dick stupidly attempted to steer between them, a huge male opened its great jaws and chomped down mere inches from their small boat's stern. Unfortunately, the animal's head struck their small engine which began to stutter and then died.

The enraged hippo, standing in about three feet of water, charged after them, and this time, its huge teeth clamped down over the stern, pulling the transom below the waterline and allowing a flood of river water to pour into the boat. Connie began screaming with fright while Bentley was barking and baring his teeth. Debbie, always a lot calmer than Connie, merely stared in horror as Dick grabbed his shotgun and fired directly into the animal's face. Their boat was released as the hippo thrashed wildly in the murky water that was slowly turning pink and Dick quickly grabbed the piece of plank that Debbie had used earlier to keep their boat mid-stream, using it to paddle frantically away from the bloat of hippos.

Once they were over one hundred feet away, due more to the slow easterly current than to Dick's paddling prowess, he rested and surveyed the damage. The stern of the boat was twisted, turning the outboard engine at an awkward angle, and there was a hole just below the waterline, probably caused, Dick guessed, by one of the hippo's huge incisors. He plugged the hole with his balled-up tee shirt as a temporary measure while Debbie and Connie began frantically bailing their slowly submerging craft, one with Dick's hat, the other with an empty corned beef tin.

Satisfied that they were well clear of the hippos, Dick slowly paddled their boat to the shore where he was fortunate to find a small, muddy beach. All three climbed out, unloaded their provisions, and dragged the boat up onto dry land.

"Wow, that was a close one," he muttered as he sat in the mud and began shaking and trembling as the full extent of their narrow escape dawned on him. "Just sit quietly and take it easy," said Debbie. "You're in shock. Breathe deeply, in through your nose, and out through your mouth." And she put a comforting arm around his bare shoulders, a nurse to the core.

Connie sat sobbing on a fallen tree and Debbie went over to comfort her as well. They must have sat like that for fifteen minutes before Dick roused himself and walked over to study the boat more closely. He was relieved to discover that the Seagull outboard was undamaged and appeared to have stopped due to the fuel line being pulled away. He thought the aluminum stern, although twisted, could be hammered more or less back into shape with a rock, and he should be able to plug the almost cylindrical hole with a piece of wood and recover his sodden tee shirt.

He immediately set to work and within the hour he was satisfied that they could reload and launch the boat and continue their journey downstream.

Afloat once more, and with the Seagull running as smoothly as ever, they began to relax, with the girls taking turns to sit in the bow of the boat to help keep the damaged stern a little higher out of the water.

Dusk was falling and, as is typical in Central Africa, in minutes they were surrounded by complete darkness. Unable to see where he was going, Dick ran their boat into the riverbank twice and had consequently been forced to throttle back until they were barely traveling any faster than the current of the slow-flowing Umfurudzi. As his eyes became accustomed to the gloom, he was able to discern the tall trees that grew alongside the river bank, and for hour after hour, they headed east at a snail's pace.

Without the heat of the sun, the night became quite cold and the three of them began shivering but had no choice but to keep going. *Around them, they could see the red, almost luminous eyes of crocodiles just waiting,* Dick thought, *for the opportunity to grab a midnight snack should the opportunity present itself.* Then, as if reading his thoughts, the Seagull stopped, and they continued to drift south in total silence as many pairs of red eyes began to slowly move closer.

"We'll have to paddle until we can get clear of these crocs," Dick told the girls. "I'll try to break our plank in two and if you can both sit up front and paddle, one on each side, I'll see what I can do with the engine. I think it may only have run out of fuel."

With that said, he picked up the six-foot plank, which appeared to measure six inches wide and one inch thick, and had clearly seen better days and attempted to break it across his knee but with no success. He needed to weaken it somehow, but the only sharp tool of any description was his Swiss Army pocket knife.

He succeeded in scoring a deep line across the plank which, after about five minutes of frantic cutting, became a groove perhaps a quarter of an inch deep. Another crack across his knee resulted in an audible crunch and after five more attempts, it broke in two. Handing Debbie and Connie each a section of wood, the boat picked up a little speed as they paddled furiously downstream.

He then clumsily attempted to fill the Seagull's small fuel tank with petrol, added what he estimated was an appropriate amount of two-stroke oil, gave it a shake, and attempted to start the engine. It coughed and spluttered a few times before starting, but eventually, they were underway again. Thankfully, those pairs of red luminous eyes were becoming less frequent, and they were chugging along once more on the calm waters of the Umfurudzi.

"Time for some food," declared Dick, still shivering from the cold but determined to add a positive note to their harrowing journey. "We must be well over halfway to Lake Mweru by now. When the sun comes up, we'll have to keep our eyes peeled in case the river opens into an estuary with the Umfurudzi diverting into several smaller streams as it flows into the lake. Then we'll have to choose a large one deep enough to get through or we may hit bottom."

While they were munching on some cheese and crackers, Connie suddenly tilted her head and asked, "What's that noise?" They listened carefully, but over the noise of the engine, neither Dick nor Debbie could hear anything. "Turn the engine off and listen," she said and when he did, they could distinctly hear the faint roar of water ahead and at the same time they noticed that the slow river current was picking up speed. Dick knew what it was, for hadn't Weeks warned of rapids being one of the hazards of boating on the Umfurudzi?

"Okay, we're probably going to enter some rapids up ahead. That's what the noise is. There will be large rocks and shallow water, and we're going to get knocked about a bit. I'll take one of the planks and try to fend us off as best I can. Debbie, you take the other one, get on the other side of the boat, and try to do the same. Connie, you hold on tight." With that said, he unscrewed the outboard engine from the stern of the boat and lifted it inside. Then they waited.

The flow of the river had notably increased as it narrowed and rounded a shallow bend, and through the gloom, they could make out white water splashing and cavorting in all directions. The roar of the rapids could now be heard clearly.

"Stay low and hang on tight," shouted Dick although there was precious little to hang onto. Then they were swept in among the tumultuous water. Huge round rocks and spray made it hard to see or even breathe. Water poured over the bow of their craft, which was crashing into rocks as it swung rapidly from left to right and, on one occasion, spun completely around before charging forward yet again and nosing down into the water, miraculously lifting to face the next onslaught.

Dick and Debbie's efforts at fending off the rocks and steering the boat were hopeless and all three eventually resorted to curling up together on the floor of the dinghy and hoping they would still be afloat when they came through the rapids.

Bentley was flung from one side of the boat to the other and eventually went completely overboard and into the thrashing water. With their bodies curled up together and hands clamped tightly over their ears, they weren't even aware that he was gone until suddenly, after ten minutes of pure hell, all was calm. The three of them were lying in about nine inches of water, but they were thankfully through the rapids. Dick peered over the gunwales to see that the Umfurudzi had broadened out and resumed its slow progress, but he noticed that there were only about three inches of freeboard between the top of their gunwales and the surface of the river. They were on the verge of sinking. Of Bentley, there was no sign.

"Don't move, either of you. Stay perfectly still, and I'll try to maneuver the boat over to the side." Very delicately, he hung his left hand over the port side gunwale and into the water, causing the boat to swing slowly to port, and eventually, he felt the bottom scrape against the stony shoreline.

Stepping into about a foot of water, he assisted the girls, one at a time, out of the boat before attempting to bail the water out. His hat and the corned beef tins were gone, but some plastic grocery bags that Connie had thoughtfully balled up and placed inside the ammunition box before they entered the rapids were put to good use. After half an hour of constant bailing, he felt that the three of them would be able to tip most of the water out by lifting the bow.

Looking around the deserted stretch of shoreline, he was not surprised to see that there was no sign of Bentley.

Trying to determine how to empty their boat of gallons of water, he found some solid logs which, if they could lift the bow a few inches, he would be able to kick under the bow and tip some of the water back into the Umfurudzi. The three of them found this maneuver easier than expected, and they thankfully watched as water poured out over the stern and into the river. Then they were able to drag the boat further up the bank and repeat the process until eventually it was almost empty.

Upon closer examination, it appeared to be a lost cause. The already bent and twisted transom was in an even worse condition than before and the wooden bung he had plugged the hole with was missing. The sides and bow of the boat were twisted and bent almost beyond recognition. *In fact,* Dick thought, *the boat more resembled a coracle than anything else, yet it had somehow managed to stay afloat and didn't appear to have any more holes in the hull.*

Most of the provisions had been lost during their tumultuous journey through the rapids. The Seagull engine, fuel, guns, and ammunition, being heavier, were basically all that remained. No food, no water, and not a sign of the wooden plank that he had so laboriously broken in two. Incredibly, Connie still had her canvas handbag and Dick still felt his small plastic document case wedged deep down in the back of his shorts.

It was time to check themselves over. All their fingers and hands and much of the rest of their skin were shriveled from constant immersion in the water. They had many cuts and bruises, which would probably appear much worse when they had dried out, but miraculously there were no broken bones or severe lacerations.

The sun was setting, and they were hungry and exhausted, so they searched around for a suitable spot to sleep. Connie once again rummaged in her handbag and produced two chocolate Mars bars, which she carefully divided evenly between the three of them. As the sun disappeared below the horizon, the temperature dropped significantly, and for warmth, they huddled together in a small hollow. They tried to sleep but had little hope of succeeding.

When the long-awaited dawn arrived, Dick decided to clean the guns and then, taking his FN, did a little exploring. He left the girls to attend to their injuries, clean up the boat, and have a pee if they hadn't already done so. He knew he had, several times and quite involuntarily, while negotiating the rapids.

Having walked only a short distance, he realized that he was on some form of game trail. Scat and droppings were scattered along the way and checking that his rifle was cocked he released the safety catch and stood perfectly still. Turning his head both left and right he saw nothing but knew something was there. Then, on the trail fifty feet ahead of him, he saw a pair of klipspringers, frozen as they stared back at him. He slowly raised his rifle, took aim, and shot the larger of the two small antelopes dead without the slightest compunction. It was probably the finest exhibition of marksmanship he had ever accomplished.

Returning to the boat, he found the girls in much better spirits although alarmed by the sound of gunfire. He proudly showed them his kill to which Debbie, hands on her hips and head cocked to one side said, "And how are we supposed to cook it? We have no fire." Dick smiled and produced a Swiss Army Knife from his pocket. Neatly tucked into its red handle was a small magnifying glass. "Stand back and watch, ladies."

And with that, he went searching through the bush looking for dried grass, small dry twigs, and larger combustible pieces of wood. He piled the dry grass in a loose bundle on the ground and set to work, using the magnifying glass to deflect the sun's rays onto one tiny patch of grass. Soon, the grass began to smolder and then smoke, and eventually, a small flame appeared. Once the grass was burning, he placed the small dry twigs in a pyramid over the grass and when they began to burn, he added more substantial pieces of wood until he had a sizable fire.

The girls, having seen the success Dick was having with the fire, used his knife to skin and dissect the klipspringer. "Did you know, Dick, that klipspringers usually mate for life? You've just left his wife a widow," said Debbie.

"No, I didn't. All I know is that he was the bigger of the two, and I'm hungry."

With the skinning and dissection of the animal complete and the fire reduced to a bed of glowing embers, they placed pieces of meat on the hot coals, turning them carefully with a sharpened stick every few minutes until satisfied that they were well cooked. Dick took his first mouthful and declared it better than the best fillet mignon he had ever tasted. Both girls agreed and before long, the meat that they had cooked had been eaten, and they quenched their thirst at the water's edge.

"Okay, let's get moving," Dick said, but as he turned around he saw that a group of fifteen or so natives had arrived quietly on foot and were staring at them. They weren't carrying any weapons and didn't appear at all hostile, so Dick asked, "Do any of you speak English?" He realized that the smoke from their fire, together with his gunshot, must have alerted the villagers to their presence.

A tall individual, dressed in khaki shorts and a baggy shirt, no hat and no shoes, stepped forward. "Yes, Nkosi. I speak some English but where do you come from?" Incredibly, as the man spoke, a large Rhodesian ridgeback walked up beside him, wagging his tail. It appeared that Bentley survived the Umfurudzi rapids after all and had found a new home. Relieved that these people did not appear to be hostile, he decided to speak truthfully, explaining that they had traveled down the Umfurudzi to escape the trouble in Warania and were heading for Lake Mweru and the Zambian border. Once there, he explained, they must find a way to get to Lusaka.

Studying the sorry-looking trio for a few moments, the man nodded his head and spoke in his own language to the group that stood behind him, four men, eight women and several children of varying ages. He then said, "How you cross Mweru Lake? It very big and your boat very small."

"Yes, I know, but this is all we have. How far is the lake from here?"

The man shook his head and smiled. "Only a little way, but the river goes many ways. If I come with you, I show you, but you must take me to the other side with you. I have friends and family there, and they will help you reach Lusaka."

Dick gave this proposal some thought before reaching a decision. "Okay, you help us, and we'll help you. Once we reach the Zambian side of the lake, we'll have no further use for our boat, so we'll give it to you."

Again, the man spoke with his followers and saw them all smiling and nodding their heads. "Yes. That will be very good. We go now?"

Dick hastily grabbed their few belongings, and having once more plugged the hole in the transom and beat the aluminum hull back into a more recognizable shape, he launched the boat, attached the Seagull and, after working some of his now familiar magic on it, was relieved to find that it started at the first pull. Connie, Debbie, and their new friend, who introduced himself as Manfred, climbed aboard, and they waved farewell to the villagers and Bentley as they disappeared around a bend in the river.

Manfred's 'little way' Dick estimated to be about two miles, but the river diverged in several different directions and Manfred indicated to go left. About one mile further downstream, the river diverted again, this time in three directions. Manfred indicated that Dick should take the center of the three.

The current, which was already slow, became almost nonexistent, but their little Seagull kept chugging away until eventually a vast expanse of water lay before them; all four laughed; and the girls clapped their hands in glee. Lake Mweru at last. A gentle breeze was blowing from the south and with no compass, he had little idea of which direction he was headed. As they traveled further out onto the lake, the breeze began to pick up and the calm waters began to get choppy. They had been traveling for over an hour and Dick and the girls were continually bailing to keep their boat afloat when, off to his right, Dick saw a tiny speck which, as they drew closer he saw was a large triangular sail and the unique hull design of a fisherman's dhow.

Manfred, who had spoken very little, told Dick to head toward the fishing boat. "They will tell us where we are and how far to the other side, baas."

Dick slightly altered course but, wary of being high-jacked or worse, he told the girls to arm themselves, and he drew his shotgun a little closer. Manfred laughed, saying, "No need to worry, baas. These be good people."

They eventually drew alongside the dhow, which had dropped its sail, and Manfred began speaking with the crew of three men. The chatter went on for quite some time before Manfred turned to Dick, saying, "We over halfway, baas. Maybe one more hour." With a wave, Dick pulled away from the dhow, and they continued eastwards through the choppy waters.

Connie, with one hand in Debbie's, stood sheltering her eyes from the bright sunlight with her other hand, peering ahead. "I see land," she shouted and pointed over to the left. "Dick, go more to the left."

"No, no," shouted Manfred. "There is nothing there, keep going straight. It will be closer to my kraal and the road that will take you to Lusaka."

Dick took Manfred's advice and before long he could see a low, flat stretch of land on the horizon. Some small dhows were drawn up along the lakeshore, and it was obvious that they were entering a small fishing village. Twenty minutes later, Dick grounded the boat on a dry, sandy beach. They were all parched, sunburned, and exhausted as they dragged the small craft a little way up the beach. But Manfred seemed as fresh as a daisy as he ran over to a cluster of small huts, shouting God knows what until a group of twenty or more villagers were gathered around him.

"Baas," he shouted, "this my family. Come. We eat, drink, and sleep. Then we plan your journey to Lusaka."

Chapter Twenty Nine

Dick awoke to find bright sunlight filtering through a coarse and poorly thatched roof. He didn't know where he was or how he came to be there, but sitting up he found himself in a small round hut that appeared to be constructed of mud and straw.

As his memory slowly returned, he recalled arriving at the Zambian side of Lake Mweru with Connie, Debbie, and Manfred. He remembered the villagers greeting them, offering them water that tasted better than the best beer he had ever tasted, and providing them with *sadza* and chunks of fish, food that he wouldn't normally dream of eating, and gulping it down as if it were a gourmet meal. He couldn't remember anything else. Where were the girls? Where were their guns? Where was Manfred?

He threw off the thin blanket that someone had covered him with and stumbled to the opening in the hut, which was covered by another thin blanket. Then, squinting as his eyes adjusted to the sunlight, he saw Debbie and Connie seated demurely on a log while two young women braided their hair.

When they saw Dick emerge, Debbie commented, "Well, look who's come to join us. Do you know that you've slept for almost twenty-four hours? And look, he's dressed to kill."

Their young hairdressers began giggling and pointing and when he looked down, he saw that he was completely naked. Quickly covering himself with his hands, he dashed back inside the hut, grabbed the thin blanket, and wrapped it around his waist.

Reappearing, he asked the girls, "Where are my clothes, shoes, wallet, guns, and ammo, and my plastic pouch?"

Connie replied with a smile, waving the small pouch in front of her. "All taken care of. Your wallet's in here with your other stuff and Debbie's left the guns and ammo in our hut," pointing to the hut next to the one where

Dick had been sleeping. "Manfred's ladies have taken your clothes down to the river for a free laundry service, and they are the ones who undressed you."

Then with a laugh, she nudged Debbie and said, "And I don't think they were too impressed either. Manfred will be back soon, and he will tell you about all the other stuff. And don't forget, you promised to give him the boat."

Just then a group of women, led by Manfred, arrived with his torn and shabby clothing, well-scrubbed but still soaking wet. "Good morning, baas. These ladies have washed your clothes and will lay them out on those rocks to dry. Your shoes," indicating Dicks well-worn veldskoens, "are clean and dry."

Dick accepted his shoes gratefully and slipped them on. "Okay, Manfred. Thank you for looking after us so well." Retrieving his damp shorts from the rock where they had been placed to dry, he disappeared back into his hut, threw aside the blanket, and put his wet shorts back on. Then, partially dressed, he said to Manfred, "Now I'll show you your boat," and the pair of them headed down to the shore where the dinghy still lay in the sandy mud.

Dick spent half an hour explaining to Manfred how the Seagull engine worked and with the aid of the small toolbox, what to do if he had difficulty starting it. There were still a couple of gallons of petrol in one of the containers and Dick explained how the two-stroke oil had to be mixed with the petrol when refueling. They then launched the boat and Manfred successfully started the engine and motored around for fifteen minutes before Dick was satisfied that he had the hang of handling it.

After beaching the boat and drawing it up onto dry land, Manfred laughed and again clapped his hands together in the traditional African way of showing gratitude, and they returned to the village.

Dick found his shirt was now dry and put it on, retrieved his wallet from the pouch and stuffed it back into his shorts pocket, and pushed the plastic pouch into the back of his shorts. He then went to find the girls and discovered Connie's blonde hair and blue eyes to be the center of attraction.

There was, however, no sign of Debbie, but he heard the bark of automatic gunfire nearby and guessed that she was showing off her wonderful little Uzi submachine gun to the men of the village. Following the sound of gunfire, sure enough, he found her demonstrating the Uzi to a small crowd of onlookers. "Hi, Dick. I guess we won't be needing our guns anymore, so I thought I'd show these people how to use them."

"Sure. We'll be safer without them now, but I think it would be better if we hold off on giving the guns and ammo away. We need money to get to Lusaka, and we don't have any. Perhaps we can sell them our guns."

"Don't be ridiculous," she snapped. "Do these people look like they have any money?"

"Well, don't promise them anything yet. In any case, I'll have to do some work on the FN and Uzi, so they fire only one shot at a time. Otherwise, they'll be out of ammo by lunchtime. I'll do it now, it's pretty simple." He gathered up the three weapons, retrieved the toolbox from the boat, and set to work immediately.

For the next two days, they enjoyed the hospitality of Manfred's extended family before Dick explained to Manfred that they somehow had to get to the British embassy in the Zambian capital of Lusaka, which was over five hundred miles south of Lake Mweru.

Manfred nodded his head and began talking with the other men from the village. The discussion took some time but eventually, when Dick saw them nodding their heads, he could tell that they appeared to agree about something. Then Manfred turned to him.

"Baas. You must take the bus which comes by here twice a week, to a town called Chilonga. It is very far from here in the Muchinga Mountains. There you catch another bus to Chitambo, and there you find many buses that go to Lusaka."

"But how long will this take and how much will it cost?" asked the now thoroughly confused and worried Dick.

"It will cost ten shillings each to get to Chilonga, then perhaps another five shillings to Chitambo. From Chitambo to Lusaka, it is more expensive, probably one pound each, so you need at least six pounds for bus fares plus more money for food. The journey takes one or two days."

Dick nodded and walked over to where the girls were seated and explained the situation. To the amazement of both Dick and Debbie, Connie informed them that despite their extravagant spending in Chimuka, she still had about two hundred Waranian pounds in the voluminous bag that she had been dragging around for the past couple of weeks. "Surely that will be enough," she said, "but you must both pay me back when we get home," meaning England, obviously.

"Okay," he said, and then taking out his wallet, he was counting out a small batch of Waranian banknotes when Connie snatched them from him, saying, "this will go toward reimbursing me for all the food and stuff that you made me pay for."

Counting it out, she said, "Now we have two hundred and thirty-seven Waranian pounds," and stuffed the money deep into her handbag.

"Fair enough, but look after that bag of yours as though your life depends upon it because it probably does. And keep those guns handy, Debbie. Things could get nasty. Anyway, I doubt very much that the bus drivers will accept Waranian pounds for our bus fares. They will want Zambian pounds." He then returned to Manfred and his group of elders.

Picking up the shotgun, Dick said, "Manfred, you and your family have been very generous and hospitable to us, and we are very thankful. We have given you our boat, our engine, and our tools, plus the petrol and oil and our dog, but we cannot give you our guns and ammunition. For those, you must pay us. Not very much, but you must understand that they are very valuable, and we need Zambian money in order to reach Lusaka."

As Manfred translated this, Dick saw an immediate change in the attitude of the men around him. Their smiles and the hand clapping were gone, replaced with scowls and expressions of anger and disappointment. Even Manfred, who had been so friendly and jovial just a few minutes before, now snapped, "You must give us those guns. We have no money to buy them. You leave now, but not with the guns."

"Very well, we'll leave, but the guns go with us," and he had no sooner finished speaking than the two girls, Connie holding the FN and Debbie holding the Uzi with the revolver wedged in her waistband, appeared behind Dick.

They slowly backed off as the angry villagers began shouting and gesticulating at them, but none followed. They had already seen what these weapons could do.

Once obscured from view, Dick, with his plastic pouch once more stuffed down the back of his shorts, carried the heavy ammunition box, shotgun, and pistol while Connie, with her voluminous bag slung over her shoulder, carried the FN, and Debbie shouldered the Uzi. They picked up their pace and had walked about a mile when they heard a shout behind them. Manfred appeared, waving something at them and telling them to stop. When they did so, he approached slowly. "Baas. We will buy the guns. I have five pounds and some shillings and pennies. That is all we have."

Now Dick was even more worried. If he handed over the guns, Manfred could then shoot all three of them and retrieve the money. "No. You must walk with us to where the Chilonga bus stops. When we get on the bus, then we give you the guns, unloaded, and as the bus leaves, we will hand you the ammunition box. But you must give me the money now. No tricks."

"Augh. Very well baas. I will come with you." He handed Dick the money and with that, all four marched off to the main road some five miles distant.

When they reached the road, Manfred squatted down to wait. He had no idea when the bus would arrive, only that it would come eventually, and Dick was amazed at how patient and mindless Manfred became. Sometimes he slept and sometimes he simply sat and stared at nothing. Occasionally he wandered off, returning with a calabash of water but nothing to eat.

The day passed excruciatingly slowly and night was falling when Dick heard the sound of a diesel engine in the far distance, and then headlights came into view. As promised, the bus rolled to a stop and two women climbed down. Both women balanced large bundles delicately on their heads and each had a baby slung in a shawl on their backs in the African manner, both babies fast asleep.

The bus was painted a bright yellow with a broad band along the side bearing the words Zanaka Bus Company. On the large roof rack, they could see items of furniture and mattresses and could hear the bleating of goats and the clucking of chickens. Dick spoke to the bus driver to confirm that he was headed for Chilonga. He established that the bus fare for the three of them totaled one pound ten shillings and paid him the money before handing Manfred the weapons. Then, standing in the doorway as the driver was about to pull away, Dick handed Manfred the ammunition box and bade him farewell.

The bus pulled back onto the narrow dirt road and the three of them managed to find a wooden bench where they huddled together. Initially, they took short, shallow breaths, for the overpowering smell of sweaty and unwashed bodies, their own included, plus the collection of animals that had not been banished to the roof, permeated the warm air inside the bus. During the overnight journey to Chilonga, the bus made several stops until the three of them became oblivious to the embarkation and disembarkation of passengers. Their attempts at sleep met with various degrees of success, but when morning came they arrived at what must be their destination. Chilonga appeared to be a small town.

The bus terminal consisted of a large dirt patch with a dozen or so brightly colored buses, parked haphazardly, which seemed to be the main gathering point since there were crowds of people milling about. Desperate for some food and water, they saw many hawkers with items of fruit spread out on the ground before them and had only wandered a short distance when they saw what looked to be a small café or restaurant with a banner strung across the front, declaring in English in bold red letters "Aunt Mima's Fish and Chips—Sudza and Relish—Coca Cola."

Very conscious of apparently being the only white people in the entire town, Dick entered the restaurant and approached a glistening and rotund woman behind the counter, and asked for water and some fish and chips for three.

She burst into action, welcomed all three, and supplied each with a large, cool bottle of drinking water, saying, "Fish and chips will be a little while, baas," before scurrying off to begin cooking their meals.

They each took a large bag of potato crisps from the counter and found a reasonably clean table where they sat, drank, and devoured their bags of crisps. Dick surveyed the two girls, still dressed in the cheap clothing that they had purchased in Chimuka and looking totally bedraggled, bewildered, and forlorn. They were a far cry from the two pert, clean, and demure nurses, dressed in their starched and pressed uniforms that he had met only a few months ago.

Debbie was the first to break the silence. "Shouldn't we find a bank that will change Connie's Waranian pounds into Zambian money? Once we've done that, we have to find a bus that will take us to Chitambo."

Dick took the money left over from the five pounds and the change that he had obtained from Manfred out of his pocket. He had a total of almost four pounds, including the loose change, and hoped it was enough to pay for their meals.

The fish and chips arrived after about twenty minutes and surprisingly looked quite appetizing. Dick asked for three more large bottles of water and his bill and was surprised to be told that the total came to four pounds even. Explaining that they had to get money from the bank, he handed her the last of their Zambian currency and asked Aunt Mima for the whereabouts of a bank, promising her that they would return with a generous tip. She looked positively disgruntled as she gave him directions, but he again thanked her and promised that they would return.

The Standard Bank stood at the corner of two tarred roads. A cement sidewalk graced its entrance, and the building itself was quite an impressive two-story affair with two Gothic pillars on either side of the staircase and an imposing front door.

They entered the high-ceilinged foyer, and Dick motioned Connie to go ahead of him since it was her money that they were exchanging after all.

Connie fussed around in her large handbag, withdrew a wallet that was still soggy after being immersed in water a time or two, spread the sad-looking two hundred and thirty-seven Waranian pounds before the teller, and asked that they be exchanged for Zambian currency.

"Wait one moment please, madam. I have to speak with the manager." As the teller walked away, Dick was left with a nasty feeling that things were not going to be so easy after all. A full five minutes went by before the teller reappeared.

"I'm sorry, madam, but the manager says that due to the current state of the situation in Warania, their currency has been declared valueless. Therefore, your Waranian pounds are worthless." And with that bombshell, he pushed Connie's Waranian bank notes back across the counter.

"But we have no other money, and we have to get to Lusaka," she pleaded. "Please, may I speak with the manager?" Again, the teller disappeared, returning this time with a smartly dressed gentleman in tow who smiled before explaining once again why the bank could not help them.

Dick stepped forward. "Very well. We understand that with the mess that Warania is in, their currency is useless. However, we are British citizens and seek assistance from the British embassy in Lusaka to get us back to the United Kingdom. What do you suggest we do?"

"Ah, I see. Why don't you come through to my office? I think I have a solution to your problem." He led them into a small office and gave them each a chair before flicking through the Cardex on his desk. Picking up his telephone, he dialed a number, spoke briefly to whoever answered, and then handed the handset to Dick with a smile, "The British embassy."

Chapter Thirty

After explaining their predicament to the embassy official, Dick passed the telephone back to the bank manager. A long conversation followed before the manager hung up and smiled. "The embassy is wiring two hundred pounds here as we speak. As soon as it arrives, you will have sufficient funds to continue to Lusaka via Chitambo. Unfortunately, the local bus is the only means of travel to Chitambo, but from there, you have the option of another local bus or a car rental, though a car rental will be rather expensive."

While sitting patiently for the wire transfer, the girls agreed with Dick that they would rather take the bus to Lusaka than waste money on a car rental. No sooner had they made their decision than the teller called them over and handed them two hundred Zambian pounds in crisp new banknotes.

Returning to the bus station, they found that the next bus to Chitambo would not be leaving for three hours. Debbie reminded Dick that they still had to settle up with Aunt Mima, so they returned to the restaurant and handed two pounds to the now-delighted restaurateur.

To kill time before the bus arrived, they wandered along what appeared to be Chilonga's only street of shops and selected some additions to the garments they had purchased in Chimuka. The girls bought new shoes as their cut and swollen feet had healed sufficiently to remove the dressings. The shoes they bought in Bombay Alley were now far too large. Debbie bought a thin, long-sleeved cardigan, thinking of the chilly autumn weather they would face when they arrived back in England. Connie, far more interested in style rather than practical considerations, purchased a cheap necklace and earrings.

The girls spent less than twenty pounds in all, and Dick managed to find some shorts, a shirt, shoes, and long woolen socks that all fit perfectly. The new shorts were roomy enough that the plastic pouch containing his passport could now fit comfortably.

The bus to Chitambo was similar to the previous one, only much more crowded. Among the first to board, they quickly claimed a wooden bench for the two-hour journey, which would put them in Chitambo by mid-afternoon.

"I never really appreciated London Transport buses until traveling on these ones," complained Connie. "But thank God for the British embassy. They really saved our bacon."

Perhaps she spoke too soon for upon arrival at the much larger town of Chitambo, they discovered that they had missed the last bus to Lusaka and would have to remain overnight to catch the first one leaving the next morning at six o'clock.

They found a cheap hotel not far from the bus station and checked into a single room, which unfortunately only had two single beds, but to their delight, had a bathroom, shower, hot and cold running water, and a decent restaurant right next door.

Having purchased basic toiletries, they took turns luxuriating in the hot shower. The girls shampooed their hair, and Dick had his first shave in almost three weeks. With the girls almost restored to their former glory, they fell upon steaks, eggs, and chips at the restaurant next door, complete with a bottle of South African merlot, before retiring back to their hotel room for an early night.

Debbie and Connie agreed to squeeze into one of the single beds, while Dick had the other to himself. Although all three were dog-tired, each of the girls took turns in Dick's bed, trying to take pleasure in the activity that all three had missed for weeks. Dick serviced Debbie in double quick time before immediately falling asleep. And come her turn, despite her attempts to wake him, Connie could not arouse Dick sufficiently to garner a repeat performance. Little Tommy just wouldn't rise to the occasion, and after giving it her best effort she eventually gave up and fell asleep beside him.

The hotel's receptionist phoned to wake them in time to get dressed and board the bus to Lusaka, which thankfully had padded vinyl-covered seats. Although there were the usual chickens and goats aboard, which were dropped off along the three-hundred-mile route, and despite many stops, they arrived in the city of Lusaka by mid-afternoon and quickly located the British embassy.

The young woman at the front desk listened to their story and told them to take a seat. After a few minutes, they were ushered into a small office where she introduced them to Mr. Archibald Threadgrass.

Threadgrass, a small middle-aged Englishman with a bald pate fringed with ginger hair, shook their hands, saying, "Glad to see you made it. Jolly uncomfortable in those old native buses, what?"

"After what we've been through, they were a godsend," said Dick. "And thank you for wiring the money to us in Chilonga. Otherwise, we'd have been literally up the creek without a paddle."

"Yes, well about that. You do, of course, realize that it was a loan, not a gift. Do you have any assets here or overseas with which to reimburse the Crown?"

"No," said Dick. "We've all been working in Warania for the past three years. All the money we have is tied up in Warania, and it's apparently worthless."

Threadgrass cleared his throat and, failing to look Dick in the eye, said, "Well, that is all well and good, but I take it you expect the embassy to fund your airfares back to the United Kingdom. Is that correct?"

"Well, yes. We came out to Warania as British citizens, me to join the Royal Waranian Police as that country was a self-governing colony of the United Kingdom. Now anarchy has broken loose, and we've barely managed to escape with our lives."

"Yes," added Debbie, "we're in the same position. Connie and I are both registered nurses and were sent out there by the British government on a three-year contract. We would have fulfilled that contract had the country not collapsed into chaos."

"Well, let's get the ball rolling then. Let me have your passports."

"Passports?" The girls gasped simultaneously as Dick withdrew the plastic pouch from the back of his shorts, took out his British passport, and smugly handed it to Threadgrass. Dick added, "They don't have passports. The hospital and nurse's quarters that they were living in were attacked and looted. They were lucky to escape with their lives."

"Well, how did you get into Zambia then?" he asked the two girls. "Don't tell me you entered this country illegally."

This sent a cold shiver down Dick's back. *Oh, Christ,* he thought, *this is going to turn into a bureaucratic nightmare.* Taking a deep breath, he reminded Threadgrass of the conversation he had with the embassy when phoning from Chilonga.

"Oh yes, that was with Mulroney, a total incompetent. He's been sent back home. Thoroughly unreliable chap. Now, where were we? Oh yes, passports."

"We crossed into Zambia in a tin boat, up north across Lake Mweru," said Debbie. "We have nothing. No clothes except what we're wearing. No luggage, nothing. Of course, we don't have passports." She wanted to add 'you bloody fool', but restrained herself.

"So, you entered this country illegally, which incidentally is a crime, and you expect us to bail you out?"

"Yes," Dick answered defiantly, staring directly into the man's eyes.

"Well, you can't stay here, and the minute you leave, you're liable to be arrested. Wait here, and I'll see what I can do." And with that, he shuffled out of the door.

"What do you think he'll do?" asked Connie, who had gone wide-eyed and pale. "Surely, he won't hand us over to the police."

"No, of course not," Dick replied. "He's obviously a low-ranking civvy and has gone to ask someone else what to do."

Fifteen minutes later, Threadgrass returned, this time with a tall young man who shook hands with each of them in turn and introduced himself as Thomas Fairbanks, an embassy official responsible for British expatriates in Zambia.

"Well, it sounds as though the three of you have had a harrowing experience. I understand that we have many British nationals still stuck in Warania and trying to get out. None have shown the fortitude that you three have, however. We're in the process of sending the Royal Air Force into Chimuka to evacuate them. Perhaps you should have just waited."

"Yes, perhaps we should have," said Dick, "but we're here now. Can you please help us?"

"Well, yes, we can and will, but it will require the three of you to stay in the embassy while we check with the passport office to ensure that you young ladies are actually valid passport holders and are who you say you are. We'll then issue temporary travel documents, clear it with the Zambian immigration authorities, and put you on a commercial flight to London Airport, which has now been renamed Heathrow, by the way. We have temporary living quarters here at the embassy; not very comfortable, I'm afraid. But it will probably only be for one night, and you'll be fed." Turning to Threadgrass, he told him to escort them to their quarters before bidding them a curt farewell and leaving the room.

Following Threadgrass up two flights of stairs, they were shown two bedrooms, two beds in each, and told to wait there for further instructions.

The two rooms were identical, and each had an en suite bathroom, a small coffee table and two chairs, a small bookcase, and two beds but no windows. The three of them sat in one of the rooms, pondering their next move. Debbie asked, "How much Zambian money is left from the two hundred pounds that they loaned us?"

Pulling notes out of his pocket, he counted them slowly before replying, "One hundred and twenty pounds. Why?"

"Well, we've each got to go somewhere once we land in London. Do you think they'll let us use their telephone? If so, I'll phone my mom and dad, and they will probably pick me up. But if not, I'll need some money to get to Southampton. What about you two? Do you have somewhere to go?"

Connie said, "My aunt Marion will pick me up. She has a car and lives in Chiswick. What about you, Dick?"

He sighed deeply before replying. "I'll be okay. I have a brother living in Notting Hill who I can probably stay with, but he doesn't have a car. If we change our Zambian money into sterling, that will give us about thirty pounds each. I'll get the tube or a bus from the airport. I hope he hasn't moved. He's a bit of a loner."

Fairbanks, the embassy official who had been most helpful, willingly allowed the two girls to telephone England, but Dick had no one to call for the brother in Notting Hill was a spur-of-the-moment fabrication. He had no one.

The following day, they were taken to Kenneth Kaunda Airport and put on a BOAC passenger jet to Heathrow. Upon landing, the three felt rather ridiculous, the two girls in their cheap and flimsy African print frocks although Debbie did have her newly purchased cardigan. Dick looked even more out of place in a pair of shorts and a thin shirt, especially since it was the beginning of December and freezing cold.

After clearing customs and immigration, Dick hugged and kissed the two girls, who gave him their phone numbers and addresses and said their goodbyes. With slightly over thirty pounds in his pocket, he stepped out of the Number Two terminal into a cold and blustery autumn day. With no relatives or friends at all other than the aunt he used to board with and who was probably dead, he was at a loss as to what to do. He decided to hail a taxi and told the driver to take him to the nearest pub.

Sitting inside the warm and cozy pub before a roaring open fireplace, and with a pint of Watney's Red Barrel before him, he contemplated his future. His only possession, save for the clothes he was wearing, was his almost empty wallet and the flimsy but fortunately waterproof, plastic pouch that contained his passport and a few odds and ends.

Placing it on the table before him, he opened it and sorted through its meager contents, staring at the two envelopes that Marigold had given to him what seemed like months ago. They were still unopened, but both had his name and Taffy's conditions printed on the front in Taffy's handwriting. "Well, Taffy's certainly dead," he thought, and he examined the contents.

The first one he opened amazed him, for it was the last will and testament of Hywel Lloyd-Jones, his old pal Taffy, and he had left all his possessions, his collection of firearms, his numerous stuffed animal heads, and his entire life savings to Richard Percival Starling.

This caused Dick to swallow hard. He knew Taffy was a remittance man with family in Wales, but he supposed they would have no use for Taffy's mounted hunting trophies or his collection of firearms. His life savings, all probably in worthless Waranian currency, were unlikely to amount to much. Dick was nevertheless deeply touched that although they had become good friends, Taffy would have picked him rather than anyone else to be his sole beneficiary.

Opening the second envelope, Dick found it contained a detailed bank statement from National and Grindlays Bank in St. Peter Port, Guernsey in the Channel Islands. The statement, addressed to Mr. H. Lloyd-Jones and dated three months previously, showed that his current account stood at one hundred and seventy-two thousand pounds, five shillings, and sixpence. Dropping the statement to the table, Dick realized that Taffy must have left every last penny of his family's remittance in this account and was not a kept man after all. He was an expatriate by choice, not by disgrace.

It took Dick a little time to realize that he was now a relatively wealthy man. Everything had changed in a matter of minutes. It was approaching the end of 1965; he was twenty-one years of age and had some serious thinking to do. What should he do with this windfall, and for that matter, what should he do with the rest of his life?

Milton Keynes UK
Ingram Content Group UK Ltd.
UKHW022328051024
449173UK00003B/77